# *Diabolis*
## *of*
# *Dublin*

Michael
Mulvihill

# Diabolis
of
# Dublin

**Diabolis of Dublin**
Copyright © 2014 by Michael Mulvihill
All rights reserved

ISBN-13: 978-1-4993-0786-3

First Printing, 2014
Printed in the United States of America
A Michael Mulvihill publication
Edited by Mytzyg Ryuzka
Cover Design: Tomi Kerminen, Macabre Media
Interior Formatting: Tomi Kerminen, Macabre Media

# 1 Filthy Blood

## Prologue: R.I.P., Dublin

October visited the Irish capital city of Dublin, heralding nervous preparations for the *Bram Stoker Festival*. The City Council wanted to put on the best show possible, at least by their island nation standards (and promoted by the usual propaganda machines—a kind of eternal inflation of the country's ego). The *Bram Stoker* was boasted to be a festive production meeting international and global parameters, comparable to the best festivals of mainland Europe and the Americas. With the ever overreaching, megalomaniacal desire to show the rest of the world how proud the Council was of the country's literary heritage, they went online, on TV, and on the airwaves to remind the populace of how important this month was.

Within the narrow, conditioned, lifetime-institutionalised minds which comprised the upper echelons of such organising bodies (who ruled, or thought they did, the city of Dublin), the hierarchical squadrons imagined, because they had plenty of spare time for visual hallucination, that they would spare no effort to show that this festival was of the highest standard, and that it was indeed possible to create a superb myth. Their recession-mutilated citizens could still feed themselves lies that things can be normal in abnormally, globally depressive times and that such festivals are not just a waste of time and resources (lo, thou squandering herds!).

Only a stone's throw from a poster declaring the Bram Stoker Festival's arrival, dates, and planned activities crouched Byrnes Lane, a gathering place for souls bent on mutually-assured self-destruction. It was 3 pm for the end products of the activities involving the walking dead. Sleeping blankets lay beside an eleven-foot-high, massive steel fence. Discards—syringes, beer cans, excrement, soiled clothes, human urine, cider cans, coke cans filled with spirits, and empty Red Bull cans—gave evidence of what happened here. Blood did out, life did derail, and the self aborted, as personality, mind, and soul were drained.

What coloured the path to slow death? Love, the vitality of human life, had been choked out of those lost souls of Dublin who pilgrimaged toward self destruction. They were beings the city's public judged, not only to be lost, but as degraded, less than human, and, thus, forgettable.

Being less than human, the Vampire Lucis Diabolis of Dublin discerned, was radically different than being dehumanized. On *earth* the dehumanized lost rights and became estranged through ostracism. In this antechamber of *hell* (most often witnessed and experienced from the ground), roof tops, which housed either apartments or the tops of office blocks, dismissed the misery. From their physical position, in their inorganic state, the slates on roofs and the panels of windows could afford to be aloof from and immune to the destruction below. Surely the blocks of these buildings would never make contact with the ground horror, unless, that is, they fell! Distance symbolized a kind of collective laughter spawned from indifference.

The sun in the autumn sky above reflected on the front walls of surrounding houses. The sun lacked the sense to know it should not shine down on other peoples' misery, even that perceived as self-induced by those whose empathy does not stretch to a deeper understanding of the tragedies that befall an individual in this life.

The lost souls gathered here because local businesses, restaurants, and hotels, simply banned them. Only public transport stop points and public spaces allowed them to loiter. They were even barred from toilets and public restaurants. Only to the city's open public common areas could they go without being removed.

In Byrnes Lane one's humanity exited via a twelve-millilitre syringe sucking the living blood of the body into a plastic tube and replacing it with heroin—slow morbidity pumped through the veins of slaves mastered by toxic drugs and the quest for euphoria. This recycling consisted of used syringes discarded on the ground or thrown into a junkyard where anyone could reuse them, followed by HIV and hepatitis being transmitted from one person to another, yet never quelling the desire to use.

Meanwhile, Ireland's president declared his humanist leanings. An intelligent man of words, empathy, and knowledge, he resided in the *Aras an Uachtarain*, just a few miles (which may as well have been light years away) from the lane where humanism's principles yielded to the powers of dehumanization. The laneway's bleeding humanity provided a bleak contrast to their high-minded leader's aspirations.

Intravenous consumption de-humanized citizens; human indifference, neglect, social marginalization, and degradation continued their death spiral. In the landscape where this horror proliferated, whole communities were lost. Dublin's untouched masses walked right past those whose humanity was bled out of them—the walking dead, defined by their morbid dependency. Could their story here resurrect them from mere pitying description to absorbing narrative life?

# I

## Dublin Night Life

As did the living undead, the vampire Lucis Diabolis set the night world alight. He, however, had demonic helpers to draw more to their ultimate destruction. Like evil germs, hell's minions lurked in Dublin's own guts with their enormous power accumulated over centuries, having learned to manipulate perception. Strange how hours passed here! Natural time was distorted by the demonic patrols that dragged in lost souls to be chastised, their victims unaware how much time passed.

The demons overseeing Byrnes Lane could envision the complications of time travel and master it with such superiority that they fast-forwarded the hands of time. By day the thriving city was populated by cars and preoccupied pedestrians. Once night overtook the town, demonic hordes emerged, and Lucis Diabolis exited his suburban dwelling and travelled into the city centre...

On that first night the vampire, Lucis Diabolis, driven through the city in his limousine, ordered his driver, Anton, to pull over. "Collect me on the left corner of Lower Mount Street at half-past three."

His trusted driver closed the door behind him and waved as Diabolis exited, knowing that what the master liked most about

Anton was his unquestioning obedience, his policy of noninterference, and how he always knew his place—distant and nearly invisible.

Diabolis looked directly through the closed iron gates of the Irish Parliament. The exterior appeared grey, unimpressive, even drab, all its windows closed like sleepy eyes oblivious to the proximity of the National Museum and the National Library.

Lucis exited the black limousine and strode onto Kildare Street, vigilant and excited. A select few, who partook in relating to their sixth sense, could actually see this strong and fit figure. Blood as a life force kept him well-preserved. His tuxedo suited his six-four frame exquisitely. Lately successfully blooded, he did not look a day over thirty. His appearance, however, could change easily, according to his mood and shape-shifting habits—a multitude of bodily expressions exclusive to those 'born of blood'. To this end he sensed what type and dosage of blood would allow him to continue his youthful semblance.

As he strolled through Dublin's streets, Lucis noted how much it had changed since his youth. He first knew Dublin as a dirty village populated by whores and merchants. That village had little in common with the place that became one of the central administrative cities for the British Empire, and later developed into a mass of urban sprawl, post-independence.

Thanks to his supernatural ability, Lucis Diabolis could sense all the drug users altering their minds in Dublin that night. He was not the simple supernatural creature depicted as merely able to infiltrate human skin with steel-hard fangs. There was more to his kind than the lupine savagery of the werewolf which takes on only a simple, bestial design. His kind could capture hearts and bend minds to its will and leave in its wake an entire city of the dead.

Toxic Byrnes Lane, its denizens enmeshed in their personal vulnerability and chemical dependency, was but a written invitation for Lucis Diabolis to dine. These foolish souls were incapable of letting "the right one in" every time they partook of their 'sacrament' by syringe.

He smiled as if the keys of the city had been handed to him with generous gratitude by the Lord Mayor of Dublin, asking, "Is there anything else I can do for you?" *And there was!* One could always help to make this city more violent, homicidal, maniacal, drug-infested, if one truly cared to be an ally to Lucis Diabolis.

He walked through the grounds of Trinity College, but nothing there could whet his appetite. Tonight he wished for a blood type he had never consumed before, to help him discern whether it was noble blood he needed, or blood from a totally different class. He decided to begin his experiment with the blood of the heroin-using underclass of Dublin. Could he enjoy the feral abandon that goes with drinking debased blood?

On leaving Trinity College Green, Lucis walked along waiting to find the right place and opportunity to advance upon his prey. After awhile he came across the perfect area where he could wait within his dark, blinding fog. The place would, with his supernatural gifts, prevent even the sharpest eye from witnessing his habits, since privacy was needed. Although he could kill invisibly if he wished, the terror in the eyes of his prey was an addictive seasoning for him.

Dame Street Archway joined two establishments together, leaving within their parting area space for people to walk through to the back streets. The archway had been created to conjoin the streets from behind with the streets in front of these establishments. The archway did not have enough room for the homeless man who always slept there to stretch out across it. He considerately slept along the left side so as to give passers-by the space they required to avoid him.

When Lucis Diabolis walked inside the archway, visibility to those walking past was nil, for it was obscured by his preternaturally dense fog. The homeless person shifted in his sleep, aware even in slumber of a supernatural presence. Lucis Diabolis saw below him a weather-beaten face, black with grime above a scruffy beard.

The vampire's eyes took on a crimson glow. For the first time in awhile he was actually excited to drink from a person. The overpowering curiosity to taste the blood of the self-condemned was a delicious gift waiting to be unwrapped.

The first sight of this hovering creature with the face of a biblical demon was like the worst delirium of alcohol abuse and drug withdrawal to the homeless man. He thought he was dieing from the poisons he had been drinking, the drugs he had been injecting, the cocaine he had been snorting, the crack he had been smoking, and the tablets that he had been swallowing for the majority of his adult life. He sprang up.

"Don't think you'll get away lightly, *Jack*," Lucis Diabolis warned, angry at the sight of his prey trying to escape. "Tell your friends that what they've been chasing after all along has come for them."

*How does he know my name?* Jack did not wait an answer. He went from standing to running. But when he attempted to exit through the archway, Lucis Diabolis loomed before him—upside-down, under the archway! To look up at Diabolis would surely have made a less intoxicated individual faint. The dark, gothic archway and Diabolis' position within reminded Jack of a fang in a mouth that opened to the foulest regions of demon-haunted hell.

"Now you know this isn't where your friends hang out. Turn yourself right around and get going. Run to Merchants' Quay, the Luas Line on Middle Abbey Street, and visit all the boardwalks—erected and reserved so conveniently by the City Council for your kind as a public, shooting-up gallery—and announce my arrival."

"Who ar' ya, ya' bleedin' eejit?"

"The very master you've been seeking."

Jack drew himself up like a man who'd just grown a set of balls, swaying a little. "Ur not me master dealer, ya mad thing. What type of eejit do ya bleedin' take me for? Yer not bleedin' *real*, just somethin' in me fuckin' head. Get out, ya fuckin' monster. Yer not fuckin' invited!" Jack tried to laugh, but his throat was dry.

Lucis Diabolis examined the man before him, taking in the addict's unwashed face, the filth under his nails, and the reek of bodily odour, ignorant defiance written all over the man. Then he replied stiffly, "No one calls Lucis Diabolis, who has become refined through centuries, 'a mad thing'. Your foul inner-city Dublinese is wasted on me. Whatever estimation you have of me, put it in your pocket with your small change. Keep your unwashed face that houses your mouth—which vomits out the nonsense your illiterate brain wires to that stupid hole—shut. *You* are a thing, *not I*, a nobleman who was transformed into what the ancient Greeks called *Vrykolokas*. I am vastly superior to the slime that is you. You, Jack as you are called by your equals—*Jackass*, as you are called by me—are a cancerous growth in the belly of society. Your worthless kind society vomits onto the street."

To emphasize his point, Diabolis punched Jack's nose and matched this with an undercut to his jaw, deploying a mere fraction of his supernatural strength.

At this, Jack reeled and folded, groaning. In the course of his life there had been many punches. With all the opiates in his body, he rarely felt them. But this punch really savaged him.

When Lucis Diabolis saw the blood flowing out of Jack's nose, he dropped from the arch and stood above the fallen man, growling, "I'll tell them myself, you fool. I was giving you a chance your kind doesn't deserve."

Lucis Diabolis grasped Jack's neck and, with cruel, incredibly overgrown nails, gouged out his two blue eyes, and gorged on them as if they were gourmet treats. Before Jack could scream, Diabolis' fangs tore into his victim's neck, allowing the vile blood to flow from that polluted body into his own. After Diabolis drank the junkie as dry as desert sand, he dragged the limp remains to the top of the archway and hung them there by tying the man's jacket sleeve to the black drainage pipe attached to the exterior walls and noosing the other around his savaged neck.

Pausing in thought, the vampire smiled to himself and flew bat-like to the drain, opened the lid, and, delighted by the presence of the rodents underneath, declared: "Tonight I offer you a feast, which you must eat whole…or I'll ensure your kind's eternal exile from Dublin."

The rats stopped what they were doing, moved in droves to the sewer opening, and watched Lucis grab the addict's corpse from the top of the archway and strip his body naked. He threw the corpse into the sewer, where the rats dug their sharp incisors into the body as if their lives depended on it. The rats avidly devoured the body until not even a single piece remained. Having just imbibed the junkie's blood, Lucis could feel every part of the victim's body being consumed, until, when he looked into the sewer to ask the rats, "Are we finished?" they squeaked a very definite yes. Lucis then blew a fiery breath onto the clothes of his victim. The middle of the pile started burning, and spread to the rest. When the clothes were burnt to ash, he threw the ashes into the sewer.

"I'll get my message across somehow. It's still early," he muttered.

The vampire glided away from Dame Street Archway and watched the pedestrians, especially the young girls in their short dresses and skimpy tops, who spent hours beautifying themselves for the young men in packs looking for whatever might come their way.

He kept walking until he reached O'Connell Street, which visually announced its arrival, not by statues, but by the illuminated needle facing the River Liffey like a giant hypodermic interrupting the ground in the middle of this street. Planted thus, the modern architectural rendering seemed designed to excite heroin addicts and mock the smaller statues to great Irishmen like Daniel O'Connell and Jim Larkin.

Lucis Diabolis looked at the spire in front of him, at the illuminated bottom and top of the sculpture Dublin called "The Monument of Light." This was an insult to what he remembered as "Nelson's Pillar," a large granite column topped by a statue of Horatio Nelson. A thing of beauty, the monument had overlooked the General Post Office until its destruction in 1966 by Irish Republican Army bombings.

His reflections were distracted by a couple verbally abusing a beautiful blonde girl of roughly five-foot-seven, who was exiting McDonald's. The girl, juggling fries and a large coke, did not want a fight. But her path was blocked by Antho—hair shaved, freckled face dominated by menacing grey-green eyes, and wearing a pointed white Puma hat and white Nike sneakers. He was with Jacinta—five-foot-four, with carroty dreadlocks and red dragon tattoo on the right side of the neck, who egged on her hero.

"Antho, who da' hell does that brasser think she is, sticking her elbow into me back and not even bleedin' apologisin' like she's queen of the fastfoo-id joint? Lookin' li-eke all miss important. The gee bag is t-uu important to say d'word 'sorry'. I swayer on me granny I'll bang the jaw off her face, so I will, and rip da' tongue bleedin' out her hole, and shite down her throat so's she won't be getting up in anyone's face again. A cunt li-eke ya' is not goin' out li-eke dat, no bleedin' way."

*Charming*, thought Diabolis, who truly belonged to a century where women were expected to be just a little bit less expressive, let alone downright uncouth.

The blonde girl begged innocence. "I apologised and I said I did not put my elbow into your back, but I am sorry if you think I did that."

"Look at tha-? Look at it? Antho, she's tryin' to make a bleedin' thick outta ya'. Do somethin', horsebox, or I'll shove this bottle up yer arse. Show me who's d'boss of tow-in and the number one homes and yunk fella of this city."

If Antho wasn't going to get off his fat hole like his mot told him and slap the girl a few and dig her to the ground, Jacinta sure as hell was going to show her who the *real* queen of O'Connell Street was. She raised her hands to her face, clenched her right hand into a fist, and gave the girl a strong right punch in the nose. The force of the punch knocked the girl to the ground so hard that it could easily have split her head open, knocked her unconscious, and maybe even killed her. This was an offence Jacinta would have been proud to do time for, a badge of street honour.

Luckily, the girl, though stunned, remained whole and aware. After a punch that could have knocked out Katie Taylor, the Irish Olympic Female Boxing Champion of the London Games, blonde Linda could hardly move from the shock of her head hitting concrete. (Lucis discovered the beauty was Linda when her boyfriend Shane shouted out her name and she repeated his.)

When Antho saw that Shane was considerably bigger, the creepy little coward, who had not ever fought fair, did something that surprised even Jacinta. He took out his carpet cutter and sliced Shane in the chest and arms. When Shane fell to the ground, bleeding, Antho, feeling now like a true man, kicked him in the head with his right shoe a few times, hard and without mercy.

The fracas had started because Jacinta could see Linda was more attractive than she was. Her fella' Antho had said so thirty minutes ago, when noticing Linda going into McDonald's: "She's a bleedin' ri-id. What I'd do to hur in an alleyway after I shoot up me gear! I'd ride the hole off her and wouldn't care who's watchin'."

Jacinta had looked at Antho as if she wanted to smack the face off him. So Antho, being the good boyfriend, consoled her, telling her, don't be getting all angry because he'd ride the hole off her also like a threesome that ya' see in the ride movies. They could do it together, share the sex like they did with the local girls in the community. But the thing was, Linda would be a posh one for him instead of the usual slappers Jacinta got him. Jacinta was having none of it; no way was she sharing her yunk fell with a good-looking posh one, no way, Jose.

Jacinta didn't mind doing threesomes. But it had to be with someone local she could trust to leave once her boyfriend was finished riding the two of them together. And if they dared text him? Antho was *her* fella and she was good at leaving scars, cuts, bruises, black eyes, and knife blade tracks on anyone she thought was messing with that special thing she had with him.

The problem with Linda was simple. Linda was a real ride, a proper beauty, and not one of the local mingers with faces destroyed because such girls went around abusing their bodies, turning them into emaciated, bony, and debased versions of what they originally set out to be if nature was allowed to do its work.

Linda, who was into education, proper diet, clean clothes, and *never* used, was into looking after herself. How could Jacinta compete with that in a month of Sundays, for goodness sake? A proper female street thug, though, Jacinta could tear the skin from her rival's face and rip enough hairs off her scalp to have her hair ending up looking like a chronic case of alopecia. Then Jacinta could take a picture of her on the mobile and have a right laugh showing it to her friends, saying how she stood on the stealing cow's face and that this was what all the girls should do when their man tried to play the field.

Jacinta did not want to admit that Antho was into playing the field with a posh one. So the best thing she could do was sort pretty puss out once and for all. "Yer goin' to look li-eke a disgustin' pussy from now on; not even the bleedin' lizards dow-in yu'ur si-ad of tow-in will want to go near ya'," she said, chuckling away like a disordered dying hen, that before they die fly their wings all over the place, going nowhere. You don't try to steal my Antho' from me with your figure and all, and think you'll get away with it."

As Jacinta ranted, the girl could not help but look at her as if all the brains in her head were missing.

"He's my ride and you can't share him. Yer not from he-ur. Ye'er not one of us, ya bleedin' eejit. People li-eke yews are not truly from Dublin like wees a-er."

Jacinta went over to the fallen Linda, sat astride her, and bit her in the left cheek. She picked up the blade that was lying on the ground. Antho did not need the blade anymore because he was busy doing a job of kicks and punches on Shane. *This Linda bitch won't be trying to take any man of mine ever again.* Jacinta placed the blade on Linda's eyebrow and the veins beside her eye and cut them through. Fluid gushed out of Linda's face. It was gross but excruciatingly funny for Jacinta; this was justice right in front of her doing a lap dance for her and her fella.

*No cunt that was not from inner city Dublin can shite around the city thinkin' they can ride my fella or turn him on. Jacinta was elated to see the posh one getting her due. Goin' out tryin' to look like the sexiest woman in the city, like who does she think she is, just because she's wealthy, livin' in a big house and all, and loaded with money and posh designer clothes? I swayer such fuckin' bitches need to be shown a real lesson with a right hidin' from a proper bitch like me, reared on the stree' and real proper urban, rap an' all.*

"PIGS!" Johnno, a friend of Antho's, alerted the crew.

"The pigs are comin'. Let's go ta the Italian quarters. I got all the gear. Let's get ta hell out of he'ur. I don't like it when those thick, dirty, country, sleeveen culchies come round and

19

start actin' like they're from Dublin and thinkin' they can ask us questions...li-eke we don't know Dublin and they do. I'd love to show them blue shirt cunts a thing or two with their stupid fuckin' caps on them."

Antho was delighted with himself. He thought he looked like a real thug in front of Jacinta and she would give him a good threesome tonight just for that—after a feast of drugs—which was basically as good as life could get for a street thug like him. That pretty geebag was sorted out and it was like all the worries in Antho's life were sorted because he knew his bitch was beggin' for blood to be spewed on the street.

Running to Byrnes Lane, surrounded by a number of restaurants, but regularly used off Middle Abbey Street for shooting up, Antho felt real hot, like the second coming of the Notorious B.I.G., street style, all big up for it, and he was the face of super thug, Tupac Shakur, a true legendary gangster from a different mother.

"Your bleedin *amazin*'," he told himself. "You're cool like the IRA's Quarter Master; the babes will love ya'; the thugs will respect ya', Brando-style. Jacinta will have to arrange all kinds of things in the bed when the neighbourhood hears how I stuck up for me mot. I'll be doing all kind of birds in me flat—anal, oral, fetish, the whole of fuckin' fifty shades of greys. The springs in me bed will be wrecked, so they will."

"Yer so slick!" said Johnno.

"I am?" Antho replied in mock modesty.

"The General and the Monk step aside. Antho is in da' house tonight—fuckin' yeah, yeah, yeah. Be prepared for da storm he has to give da city," said Johnno.

"But first let's get high. I'm dyin' for a bleedin' high," Jacinta added.

"Then you and that bird next door is joinin' me. After that, a thug needs an all-nighter."

"Oh," said Jacinta, "I got the right bird ready to spread her

20

wings with us tonight, just for you. What you did tonight shows me that you can be the daddy thug of my yung-uns."

"Oh, I'm gettin' jiggy with me mot tonight."

*Interesting,* thought Lucis Diabolis, *how violent and mad this posse is!* He followed the herd because he was certain they would find in him their remedy (after swallowing chemicals, snorting coke, smoking crack, touring all the legal and illegal drugs possible).

As a group, although by no means all violent like Jacinta and Antho, left to cope on the streets they were drawn to, they were simply misunderstood. Streets showed these destroyed characters little forgiveness and even less mercy.

In order to follow these crazies, who were running at a mile a minute through Dublin's inner city, Lucis Diabolis transformed into a bat. He loved flying in the Dublin sky above the streetlights as they reflected and gave much needed light to the Boardwalk, and above bridges, like the Ha'Penny, connecting the north side of the city to the south side. The city was a shadow-shifting mass of concrete buildings that never went too high, and in their midst was a shining mass of flowing water. He even imagined what it would be like if, instead of catching all the water from the mountain streams, the River Liffey could catch all the blood from the people of Dublin. It was a fantasy tantalizing as an adolescent's wet dream.

He could see how strongly and viciously the River Liffey he once called *An Liphe Agus An Rhuirthech As Gaeilige* (the first name meaning *life*, the latter meaning *fast and strong*), flew like the furious temper of Jacinta. He loved watching the water that regularly took the unwary and destroyed them with its intense cold or strong currents. There was no swimming in the Liffey unless you knew what you were getting up to.

The lost souls he was following reached the Luas Line on Middle Abbey Street.

"Jacinta, can we just go ho-im and shoot up?" Johnno asked.

"I'm dyin' for a hit, so you go off home, but I'm shootin' up."

"Let's bleedin' shoot up he'ur?"

"Here? Ya' askin' me? Ask me li-eke an eejit, why don't ya? Where do we shoot up all da' ti-em? Like you pretendin' to be da thickest in da posse? And I thought da teachers when we was goin' to school thought you could be a bleedin' brain box—yer brain dead—brain box, me arse, more li-ekes horse box."

"Get out a da garden, ya' bleedin' tramp. I'm nearly eating me sweat here, wantin' to get high. So where da' hell can we shoot up?"

"Behind the Spar Shop, there's a laneway; it's where I left me syringes and gear. We's goin' there now. "

Antho' started singing the song from Cypress Hill, "I WANNA GET HIGH."

Behind the spar shop on Middle Abbey Street was the side entrance to Byrnes Lane. Adjacent the nice restaurants and a hotel for tourists was a sight that also attracted attention, due to its reputation as an open-air shooting gallery for iv-heroin addicts. Rarely was a member of the police seen here. The addicts simply would go to the end of the lane where there were steel gates erected beside an empty, open-air car park. There they would do what they had to do. Sometimes they'd have a smoke with a few cheap beers or cider or tablets; otherwise, they just prepared their tool kits and junk for injection.

The charm of this laneway, a remnant of the deceased Celtic Tiger, included its function as an open air toilet. Junkies were refused entry into most of the toilets in the city pubs and restaurants. Since all the public toilets were closed and/or non-functioning, either outdoor venues, one's own gaff (provided the gaffer of the home did not mind), derelict houses, exits of car parks, bushes in public parks, and shopping malls were the typical places to "go" in Dublin City.

This laneway was also convenient for the disposal of used syringes, faeces, and garbage. Here a few cans of piss-poor cider was an unofficial welcome to Dublin for the numerous tourists that usually, totally unwittingly, walked by such areas and witnessed this. It would certainly leave an indelible memory of Ireland.

From the rooftop, Lucis Diabolis watched the posse prepare their gear. Lucis knew what the next step in the ritual was. He summoned helpers—time for the rats of inner-city Dublin to answer a call to duty! When the rats heard their master calling, their eyes turned a dark red, their bodies sweated buckets from the adrenalin rush, bloody saliva dripped from their mouths, and their teeth became razor sharp. Instead of going directly to the laneway, they climbed the tall red bricks of the surrounding buildings.

He only required four hundred rats. When five hundred came, he disappointed one hundred rats by telling them that their presence was not required now. With the remaining four hundred vermin awaiting his instructions, he told them to sit still beside him and be patient, whereupon those four hundred rats settled beside him like obedient dogs.

Antho waited like a lord being served his dinner. Jacinta and Johnno busied themselves in a hurried way as if this was their last ever hit. She did not cook the heroin, for she knew cooking it wastes it. She got a water bottle, removed the cap, and drew some water on the set. Then she ripped off a small piece of cotton and rolled it into a ball and placed it in a cap, put water into the cap with the heroin, and mixed it, but not too much. She drew the heroin into the syringe, tapped it, and squeezed it to get rid of air bubbles. And, like the excellent chef she was, she told the lads their heroin was ready for injecting.

"Deadly," Antho accorded, showing that his blood certainly approved.

Lucis Diabolis transformed into a giant rat with wings. The rats were elated at the sight of this display by the great Vrykolokas Diabolis. The creatures were overjoyed that he indeed became one of them, a rat with wings, the full size of a man, with sharp teeth like theirs. Was there anything this un-dead man could not do to show that he was master, and, for the rats, the superhero of all superheroes?

At his, "Come to me, my pretties," the rats grabbed onto the vampire's giant-rat body and wings with the passion of true followers. They swooped.

The junkies heard a WHOOSH! so loud and beheld a vision so terrible that the veins in the parts of the body where the syringes were inserted almost froze in the night air. This was a bad trip—the worst Antho, Johnno, and Jacinta were ever on. Jacinta decided she must be hallucinating and just lay back on the concrete and proceeded to laugh hysterically.

"I'm going to beat the head off that prick that gave you that bag," Antho warned. "But first I'm going to beat the head off this thing in the sky."

The rats were one in mind and body with Lucis Diabolis. In front of the three junkies, prone on the laneway, strung out, was the sight of hundreds of eyes blazing a red the colour of a furnace from amidst a vermin gray that succeeded in disgusting them enough to be putting them off the drugs.

"I'm never going to take another drug!" sobbed Johnno raggedly, peeing his britches.

"That's what you say—and do—every time you have a bad trip, but, sure as hell, you'll be back on the gear the next day," scoffed Antho.

The three junkies tried to rise. But, before they could say 'heroin', their faces were covered by rats biting into their eyes, noses, scalps, and skulls.

Lucis Diabolis turned from being one big flying rodent into several, and covered their legs, buttocks and backs, devouring not only the blood of their bodies, but also the flesh. Sharp knife teeth devoured their hips, knees, elbows, and, finally, their brains. Blood splattered the ground of the laneway, but the rats swarmed around every drop and licked it up with avid tongues. Not a single piece of their bodies was left on the surface of the laneway. In fact, by the time the rats finished licking, the lane looked like a fastidious council person had personally used a special, high-tech machine to clean every portion to immaculate spotlessness.

Come two o'clock the clean-up was completed. Even the stench was gone.

# II

## Dublin's Dark Fraternity

Once Byrnes Lane was clean, Lucis Diabolis returned to his human form. Something within the tainted blood did not satisfy him, however. No, this was not the blood he was looking for. Knowing this blood was not right for his system, the vampire felt confused and compelled to stay here to see what might better suit his needs better. Unlike ordinary folk, bi-location and his supernatural nature made him privy to otherwise unseen things. Desiring a panoramic view of the darker dwellers of Dublin, he looked down from the sky at lost deceased souls who could not receive light because they were too disturbed.

A beheaded soul, in his twenties, kept staring at the ground where his human head had been crushed by an articulated truck. He had been forced from the corner into the middle of the street by a horde of thugs who did not like the way he spoke. He'd spoken politely when spoken to and protested to them that he did not want any trouble. Since all *they'd* wanted was trouble, he hadn't given them the fight they craved. Too bad, so sad!

Away from the main arterial streets, the vampire flew to the little streams Irish call laneways, which connected to a bigger network of roads. There he saw a body in Rutland Lane, near Barry's Hotel, where people from the country congregated on a Saturday before a big game in Croke Park, to gossip and drink some pints.

Apart from the warm shelter of Barry's, Diabolis noticed a body frozen over because the night's cold was too intense. A soul had frozen two years earlier in a part of the lane where its penniless drifter owner believed he could find enough shelter to survive the night. Although the body was carted off by ambulance, the soul froze in place. The shade's corpse appeared fully clothed. The body underneath carried self-inflicted scars from razor blades, bread knives, knives heated to burn, pen knives, Swiss army knives, and even a machete. Though his body bore witness to the mental state he was in before he froze to death, it was not 'death by a thousand cuts' which killed him, but despair.

There was no shortage of ghosts to see. Another man, a half mile from Rutland Lane, cleanly shaven but with the reek of the unwashed, wandered by the Quays, heeding the call, as he had for the last two years, to "Jump in. Go in, right now!" The shade jumped into the river at the exact time of his watery demise every night to re-experience drowning and his remains being devoured by the life in the river. If asked, the same soul would not know why this act was repeated, unaware of the years passing while he never tired of this nocturnal activity.

Turning to the main street, O'Connell, Diabolis witnessed, though not in real time, assault after assault from the past. A man was repeatedly stabbed in the neck. People violently dispatched miraculously stood up and walked away. Hordes followed upon hordes of walking dead souls, withered and restless because their deaths revolved around the heroin scourge eliminating life all over Dublin's inner city.

Lucis Diabolis returned to Byrnes Lane, but decided to leave it for a nearby restaurant whose patrons were totally oblivious to the laneway's activities. He seated himself in a secluded part of The Lemon Jelly. Islands of people were seated, deep in discussion of the minutia of their lives. In hyper-sensory arousal, Lucis Diabolis could tune into a thousand conversations at once. But, unlike the hyper-schizophrenic, whose psychological state renders them so fragile that their mind shatters when it is overwhelmed by input, the vampire was able to participate in the sensations around him.

A waiter dressed in black took orders. Two men discussed dj-ing and tuning difficulties in their music. Three office workers spoke about their Christmas preparations, which felt completely inappropriate for October. Three other women, who, dressed to the nines, looked and spoke more intelligently, were relating their difficulties and experiences in managerial roles.

To Lucis Diabolis, amidst these table islands—some intended to fit couples and others that could seat eight—the patrons were no more than lowing cattle in a shed, waiting for slaughter and butchering. Had everything not been so public, the restaurant could have been farmed for its human blood and meat.

Just like Lucis Diabolis did, the people needed to dine. He saw how the majority of human souls around him liked to be seen in groups talking casually about the most trivial aspects of their lives. But some beamed the distress signals of a life that was crucifying them slowly. Others had banality written all over their faces; life had left puncture holes in those personalities. Still others looked as if their own point of view was burnt out of them in childhood and never came back (or, if it did, it terrified them).

A youngish woman waited anxiously for her date to arrive. She checked her phone, drank, and checked it again; when he could see her eyes, he was sure he saw tears waiting to spill. Within moments, though, her face was illuminated, as if the man who'd just arrived was a hero come to save her from her worst nightmare, the horror of being alone in a crowded place.

The spiritual energy of these quarters was low, the decay from the laneway seeming to drain the life force. The laneway, planned to allow the crossing of four pathways, had imposed a claustrophobia that only allowed souls to partake more freely with fellow lost souls. Diabolis was not sure if this really was the right place to go after drinking, but he remained, immersed in a sordidness that had found itself a vacation spot.

Among those around Lucis Diabolis obsessed with the miniscule, he closely observed the girl who had so anxiously awaited her date. She dressed her best and did her best to look her best, but her make-up did not stop the signs of aging as she'd hoped. She did try to court a more youthful appearance, especially with the use of hair dye—trying to look just a few years younger. The dye did an unforgivable job of amplifying whatever good looks she should have had, but had lost through age, alcohol, or stress. The overall effect of the colour in her hair was a haggard golden-grey; it's sparkle unintentionally highlighted her skin's powdery-talc hue, which so many women attempted to combat by purchasing fake tan cream or spray, or using tanning beds in an attempt to make up for the lack of sunlight typical of Ireland.

"These Quarters," her drink-flushed date declared out of the blue, "are a metaphor for the Irish economic boom that exploded into the bust." He was a long-winded soul and needed to be heard by her—by talking abstractly, pompously, weirdly, and nonsensically.

"Really?" she said, leaning toward him, overly keen to appear interested.

"Well…I mean…it depends on what you read from various sources; they say some strange things."

They both laughed at the word *strange*, as if nothing in their Dublin surroundings could be labelled as such, and as if anyone who admitted that strangeness existed here must be an eccentric weirdo.

"And so," she said, her face flushing as if mesmerized by his wisdom.

"Well, this very laneway is meant to be a symbol of Ireland's economic boom that went bust." His peculiar statement notwithstanding, she knew it was necessary for her to encourage him to continue.

"Right?" she said, her smile trying to hide that she considered what was being said about as delightful as watching human hearts being yanked out and offered to invoke the Aztecs' sun god.

"Yes, it most certainly is," he said, leaning forward in his chair in anticipation that she could be fascinated with his every utterance.

"The planners who designed these paths shaped them like a cross turned upside down. This area was nothing. During the boom it became a symbol of rejuvenation. But a cross turned upside down is never supposed to be anything but a mark of deception. And now, as we look around us, we realize that the place we are in is a symbol of our country's decay. Ireland is now in a morass of a debt the usurers who are currently running the show want back with extortionist rates of interest."

"Wow," she said, although in truth she followed none of this (to her) weirdo talk.

She did not believe him. All she could do was relate to the story like she was one of the observers in the rhyme, *Hey-Diddle-Diddle*. Just like the little dog, she laughed at a cat playing the fiddle, a cow jumping over the moon, and a dish was running away with the spoon. She was laughing at his absurd notion of an Ireland at the mercy of pathological gamblers and grotesque usurers allowed to play openly with the nation's assets on the world's markets. He was *always* singing that tune.

The truth was that the invisible demon, Apostasy, prowled the streets of Dublin to prod people away from God. Shillelagh in hand, he suddenly stood beside Lucis Diabolis and motioned for him to follow him to the laneway. So Lucis Diabolis left the couple to it and followed the demon out…without any prodding.

Diabolis, who could discern that Apostasy had in mind a specific objective, said, "I've seen you and your big stick on occasion around and about the city. Tell me, what is your *true* name?"

Apostasy, flipping long, straight red hair out of his soot-black eyes, replied: "My names are numerous, but my motto hasn't changed through all the generations of living upon the earth—'You think *I'm* bad? Wait till you see what's comin' after me.' This motto promises that the earth will be constantly under attack and the humans who inhabit it constantly under pressure."

Lucis Diabolis laughed to hear this (over the sound of a heavy Dublin rain pelting the laneway). The close, tightly packed buildings looked like they could choke to death the people who walked through here daily. But the rain had no trouble reaching every nook and cranny of the place, soaking citizens and making them feel depressed, as well as claustrophobic. So the almost constant drizzle did not bother the vampire in the least.

"Yes," accorded Diabolis, "I've lived my immortality by that very motto, feeding on the misfortunes of those I encounter as I search for blood compatible with my noble type. I prefer true blood, but good blood is getting harder and harder to find."

"I agree that the search for blood is a fit ambition for demonic forces," Apostasy chuckled slyly, "but there's more to it…such as being more horrific and terrible than anything that has come before. Look to my appearance when you ask the demon who turns people away from God, his name; consider my appearance. Amongst my numerous names are: Appolinarius, Arian, Mani, Priscillian, and Valentinus. I can assume the aspect of a hairy giant who goes around invisibly kicking people away from God, but for every generation I take on a totally different appearance, and that's how I stay strong."

This meeting of demon and vampire was unusual. Most of the time demons did their own thing—hurting others, not socialising. Is it possible, thought Lucis Diabolis, *that I'm speaking to myself?*

But Apostasy uttered his usual trademark farewell to Diabolis, who watched him jovially greet one of his demons busy supplying heroin to a soul starting their voyage of destruction.

The demon drug dealer, 'Mr. Rich', was impeccably attired and gleamed with health. He was obviously pleased with his mission to lost souls. He appeared dressed as if just passing through on a trip to Monte Carlo. Rich handed his stuff over for a large amount of blood money in return (so he could afford to send his patrons straight to the bottom level of hell, where the lowest, most degraded demons and condemned souls dwelt).

The demon's mobile phone tingled with a message from a girl who wanted to exchange sex for a fix. Mr. Rich grinned smugly. Thanks to all the heavy lifting he'd been doing, all the vitamins he'd been consuming, and the refined diet he insisted upon, he'd be able to give her *exactly* what she needed (even without Viagra). The successful look of the drug dealer—well dressed and coifed, expensively perfumed, and dripping with diamond and gold jewelry—reassured Apostasy that the devilish enterprise was up to professional standards.

The vampire next spotted one of the emaciated locals abusing a pigeon, kicking it from one side of Middle Abbey Street to the other because the bird's wings had been clipped, rendering it flightless. This sordid sight, even more than that of the drug dealer, appealed to the morose and macabre elements lodged within Lucis Diabolis' personality from the moment of his inception into vampirism.

# III

## Bad Blood's Side Effects

Lucis Diabolis returned to his tomb in Mount Jerome Cemetery after demanding to be driven around various locations in Dublin. At six am he closed the steel doors firmly behind his tomb so that not a speck of unwelcome daylight could possibly enter.

His brain started to fully register the tainted blood he'd just consumed. And this registration was certainly not a pleasant one. The vampire was almost in total shock.

Lucis had never gone 'ghetto' in terms of blood consumption, akin to that dreaded consumption of a bygone era from a population considered taboo. In contemporary Dublin *they* kept to areas like Parnell Street, Mountjoy Square, the Quays, and O'Connell Street—emaciated, walking skeletons, devoid of any purpose save knocking down what got in their way. To drink their blood was the vampire equivalent of drinking straight from the polluted river off O'Connell Street, or, more realistically, from the slimiest, blocked sewer in Dublin.

How could he tolerate the blood he'd just consumed? It irritated the living hell out of his stomach. He swore he'd never taste its like again—solemnly, like a child, having transgressed greatly, confesses, promising devoutly to their guardian that they will not bring this level of wrongdoing on themselves again.

The maliciously unwanted affects of the blood violated the vampire's body. On the way home the lights on the streets looked like those the Gestapo or the KGB might use to interrogate people. His head felt like the smoke from a revolver after it fires, a thousand unwanted chemicals gushing out of a hole in his skull and onto the wooden base of the coffin supporting his head.

He was able to supernaturally perceive that this blood within him was like a black filth running through his body, petrol-thick with disease organisms. This was a cancer to his system. He wanted to cut his wrists and bleed out the bad blood. He was even tempted to walk out into the daylight for cleansing. But burning to death once he opened the coffin was not an option, so he stayed where he was.

Lucis was fearful of what lodged within this blood. Would it disease him? Would it malnourish him? Would it turn his frame into sawdust? Would it cause him to lose the ability to look young, since he had heretofore religiously consumed healthy blood in order to maintain a youthful shell? The sanguine gourmand had often fantasized that he'd someday be able to consume noble blood and look (and feel) even better.

*What about contagion?* His hair rose at the thought, recalling the horrors he'd inflicted on his victims down through the ages. All the anxieties that had visited others from his actions were hellishly coming to his door and creating within him utter terror. *What might HIV and other blood-related diseases do to an immortal vampire?*

He was too petrified to purge after his binge. Vomiting, especially during daylight hours, could cause him more problems, more irritation. In any case, if his blood was diseased, all the forced vomiting in the world would not eliminate whatever he might have contracted.

Questions and doubts kept gnawing at Lucis. They were devouring him the way a cannibal must devour the skin and bones of a body. While cannibals devour what is outside them, the vampire wished to devour what was within him so utterly that it would disappear.

His head kept spinning and drilling dread straight through to the core of his very being. Eventually, the waves of pain he felt, those ebbs and flows of repulsion and discomfort, would subside. But he realised pain amnesia only insured that the same behaviour that caused the pain was doomed to be repeated. Although he was driven to acquire a better blood source, right now he was paying the price of failure. His insides felt like they'd been sliced and diced and shoved grossly back inside of him.

Lucis Diabolis wanted and needed a remedy—noble blood—a personal fantasy dear to him. The more refined the blood, the sooner he could return to the way he was when alive, brimming with hopeful enthusiasm.

What was ideal for Diabolis was not realistic in an Ireland less and less visibly noble. He was sure, however, that a compromise could work. It might suffice to feed on the blood of a well-bred, contemporary person who'd achieved some status in life using their intelligence. Consuming their blood meant taking on their life's essence and energy. This rich blood would warm, enliven, and maintain him, revitalising his whole body.

*What* was *last night?*

Having always consumed 'safe' blood, Lucis Diabolis had been toying with the mad desire to taste those living on the dark side and experience what their blood would arouse in him. This compelling ambition, first aroused in the 1970's, with each succeeding decade grew more unbearable. The more he saw of the fallen underclass walking the streets, defying the laws and shameless in their reckless abandon, the more obsessed he became. It was so bloody a horde—spewing tears as they gouged the eyes out of each other, while uttering vile insults—that if anal eliminations could have spoken they'd have been more eloquent. But fantasizing what it would be like to consume weird, debased blood assured that the usual fare bored him. Because he'd been looking too long for noble blood, this alternative temptation distracted him from the frustration of his fruitless quest. He finally decided that maybe it wasn't such a crazy idea to find and taste something different, just like a lover of food likes to try different and exotic dishes.

Now, in his tomb, Diabolis stayed restless and overwrought. His body moved from side to side, unable to succumb to the natural, rejuvenating gift of sleep. He considered grabbing a quick snack—animal blood. That blood was okay, but human blood, being a relative to the eternal, provided true sustenance. Animal blood, not a direct source of eternity, merely kept one alive, and was the poorest meal he could take (other than tainted 'street' blood). And dawn was almost upon him.

To purge during daylight within his tomb would be unwise. Surely this violent vomiting would arouse unwanted attention. It was absolutely prohibitive to leave his tomb during daylight hours without serious skin damage. A second objection erupted when his mind informed him that he could use its power to purge with less noise. He concluded that this reasoning was flawed. In his own time he would eliminate the bad blood. Should he attempt to disgorge what was within his system, it would be impossible to clean up. The mess would stay in his tomb and he would have to abandon the resting place made in nobler times especially for him.

Outside was dangerous daylight, but inside the tomb was hellfire and hallucination. He could feel the addicts he'd killed kicking him, sticking syringes in every orifice, including his genitals. He saw the ugliest junkie he could imagine, the flesh of her face almost eaten off.

This gangrenous female brayed at another, "Yous fuckoff! *I'm* fuckin' me master."

"So am I!" bellowed her hideously decaying female companion, whose grey hair looked as if it was filled with insects and whose wobbling breasts were massive syringes with plunger nipples.

Then both females did a naked dance, and Lucis felt his whole body rapidly age one hundred years.

Their genitals bled what the vampire recognised as the same filth he'd consumed. But this time its colour was faecal brown. Their breath reeked. The clothes they discarded were fit to walk on their own.

"The rats told me all about ya' when they turned me body into sludge and put me down the sewer," the first said. "You're da one iye shud be havin' threesomes wi' and no' that thick cunt, Antho. Now fuck the two of us li-eke we's Queens of the Damned."

Every part of the speaker's face became micro tablets. Thousands of capsules formed her features. Lucis pictured the top of her head opening and a torrent of tablets exiting the breach. The rest of her body was pierced with holes—syringe holes—out of which flowed a vile scum of drug-toxic blood.

"Yes, master, I seen you in me dreams dow-in lanes whilst gettin' high."

The two junkies' foul maws gaped; they seized and unzipped their master's britches, and, while one sat on his mouth, the other mouthed his phallus.

Diabolis realised he was being assaulted by the worst possible blood delirium. But he had his own methods of defence against it. His maker had taught him how to use the power of his imagination to get the shell of his outer body to disappear, and then re-emerge when appropriate. Diabolis knew that what was before him was not the dead souls of junkies filled with exalted admiration of his prowess, but merely badblood-induced figments.

To avoid being driven from his tomb into further trauma, he entered a deep trance. The more he meditated, the more his body disappeared. He imagined the bones in every part of his skeleton fading away, his whole being flowing like pieces of ash in the wind. Within five minutes, this came to pass (for what the mind perceives it can achieve). Lucis Diabolis took full control in a different form of experiencing and existing, smugly thinking, *Assuredly, once night comes, this shell will re-emerge restored to youth!*

# IV

## Lucis Diabolis in Tomb and Town

When night arrived Diabolis arose from his tomb and opened the doors. He strode slowly and thoughtfully through the graveyard of Mount Jerome. He admired the skilled hands that had created such fine stone masonry. Work going back to the 18$^{th}$ century in Ireland had been carried out with professional heart, in contrast to the make-do houses and bland architecture of the present age.

The Masonic regalia exposed here thrilled him. He thought of those golden lives of centuries gone when Ireland was under British Imperial control, wishing he could resurrect the wealthy Victorians who'd had these monuments built.

He'd adore such fragile folk, treat them like porcelain. Diabolis pictured himself the size of a giant. Yes, he would cherish those people like a child would a doll or a teddy bear. He would maintain them in order to feed on their precious, privileged blood.

He understood well the type of wealth required in creating these monuments, and the psychology behind them. An elegant tombstone enables one's relatives to flaunt their family wealth. Even unto the present age, this theatre of ego-maniacal sensibility bore witness to past glory.

To fully appreciate this theatre, one would need the help of a visitor—some pathetic creature struggling to make ends meet. A soul of low circumstances, barely able to rub one shilling against another, would provide a fitting contrast. Here, he would behave like an enamoured soul, easily seduced by the display of wealth. Epitomised by misery, misfortune, and struggles, such a creature would be utterly distracted and overwhelmed by envy. This passer-by would be condemned to several moments of mental arithmetic to figure out how much money had been wasted in making one of these stone marvels, and would leave the graveyard discouraged by his personal failure. Unable to afford a home of his own, he could only dream about a burial as wonderful, splendid, luxurious, upper class, and wantonly wealthy as this.

*In the attainment of great wealth priorities prostrate a person to Mammon. Only an enormous will enables these noble things to become a living reality.*

Lucis Diabolis' fangs were crawling out of his mouth like fingers as he considered this. He longed to be engorged with the type of blood which had once suffused the veins of the rotting old corpses that lived under this earth the City Council was speaking of removing. Yes, should one shovel go too near a noble gravesite, he'd descend upon the diggers with all the hunger of hell for grace (although theirs was not the most exquisite blood a vampiric gourmand might desire).

From unconsecrated ground immortal Lucis Diabolis observed these monuments to the mortal, and the irony of the situation was not lost on him. *Look at the efforts they made to have such an extravagant burial, and yet all they achieved at the end of their days was to have their skeletal remains boxed and covered in mud. These dead, remembered so briefly in stone, what great days under the sun they must have lived! Some of the monuments are rotting, depicting in stone the dark comedy that is death. The once high and mighty must also submit and rot away—the sandstone tombs, especially, mimicking the bodies underneath. And for what special purpose did it serve their lives to be noted? Everyone who lives dies, this being the poignant essence of life. Was the grand purpose of having such extravagant graves an attempt to fulfil one final fanciful flight…so that the masses would appreciate their fame?*

Walking among the graves he took note of a very special feature on one monument. It depicted a dog, and he wondered: *Would this wailing mutt crying over his master transform himself if he could from his stone status, dig into the dirt of his master's grave, and emancipate him from the earth? And what kind of loyalty was this when the dog was made of stone and therefore had no other choice but to remain static in this graveyard?*

Interesting as this was, there were no live pulsing veins available for Lucis Diabolis here. What use could this place be to him other than for rest? His immortal life was guided by the need to feed, not to ponder.

"One must always think of the sunny side," went a common mortal aphorism. As an old time vampire, Diabolis desperately needed to rephrase that statement to suit the nature of his kind.

He felt more inspired by the sight of the sky as he approached the gates and the long road out of Mount Jerome Cemetery. It was a calm October night, sensually autumnal. He gazed upward, adoring everything he saw. The night sky still held visible white clouds, living in oblivion to the encroachment of the dark. Scientists might describe this phenomenon in their terms, but never *who* put them there in all their cosmic splendour.

What made *him* live? BLOOD. He craved and relied on it to live. Without it all that was left was death. He negotiated with himself about what he should do in this quest tonight. Would he find a body to appease his sanguine hunger, or simply dine on food and alcohol like the rest of Dublin society and observe. To find special, rich, and truly delicious blood was an indescribable rarity.

*Anthony's services will not be required tonight. I wish to do a solo discovering.*

42

Diabolis set out towards the town of Rathgar intending to end up at The Old 108, order a pint of stout, and watch the locals drink and murmur together as if compelled to blather tediously until closing time, when they'd depart the pub, depressed at the thought of abandoning booze for home.

To enjoy a meal here he'd have to rid himself of the diseased dregs of yesterday; he was not sure if he wished to do this now, which induced a huge fantasy. Still outside the pub, he fingered the scarf in his pocket. Soon, this was covering his mouth's hyper arousal as he entered the vision.

*People driving by stopped, and, rigid as statues in their cars, just watched the vampire mutate into monstrous demonic form, eyes blazing red, leathery wings unfurled. Then Diabolis summoned all the vermin of Dublin to converge on Harold's Cross Road. They swarmed the streets, shops, bars, and restaurants. When anyone's hand emerged holding a mobile phone camera, he simply willed their arm lopped off at the elbow, and the blood and meat therefrom devoured by his four-legged minions.*

*People congregated, all their concentration upon this spot. They were easy targets when he let loose an extraordinary wave of supernatural power. He was able to seize bodies and open veins. A river of blood drenched walls and mixed with paint. Those previously staring into space became lifeless statues sitting in their cars, trucks, and buses, rapidly going nowhere.*

*"Rats, your time has come, my pretties!"*

*Obedient rats scurried towards the dead to devour them, piece by piece, little finger by long finger, by thumb, by eyebrow…one fleshy morsel at a time.*

*Lucis assumed his giant bat form. He crawled over every wall and gorged on blood every bit as fine as the blood of the now-deceased nobility had been in life—pure, rich, and chaste as ice.*

What was so special *in this moment* to drive Diabolis into such a feeding frenzy, even though he did not want to be enslaved by his lusts? (Not everyone deserved to be bled dry; most deserved mercy.) He'd striven to be more discriminating in order to survive in the populous metropolis, her throngs infused daily with people from all walks of life and all five continents. Until now, he'd dared not be overwhelmed by his appetite.

As an older vampire he'd developed an increasing need and, therefore, a stronger drive for blood. This more impulsive, irrational drive made him less and less able to endure abstinence. He wanted to preserve his youth by blood, just like the humans around him did by means of cosmetic surgery, tans, and hiding the grey.

Diabolis considered noble necessity an anti-aging activity. He detested decay. To him years were locusts, stripping fields bare and laying waste previous pasture, turning it into dust bowls.

He compensated somewhat, with a bad habit: <u>smoking</u>, valuing what humans considered the worst evil in cigarettes—the carcinogenic toxins that blacken the lungs and close the valves of the heart. His bodily frame oscillated from immaterial to material when he smoked, as if tarring his insides restored his flesh and bones and all his organs were fully and naturally lodged within.

His mind told him he should feel guilty that his personal code to never give in to blood lust had been broken. He even thought he saw an admonition flash across the sky as he left Rosie O Grady's for The Old108.

On his way to the next pub, Diabolis strolled through the South Dublin suburb. He saw people in houses smoking. He inferred that they too were hoping their insides would re-emerge, and thoughts lighten up. Darkness within the vampire was the kind that comes from ostracism. It did not cause him to feel totally apart from those who lived within their own spiritual void. He was glad to be reminded that in this part of Dublin, plenty of spiritual pestilence resided. Many chronically depressed souls were, like him, hiding their unhappiness behind dreary stone façades.

For Lucis Diabolis this land's climate excellently suited his delicate skin. It also helped incubate the darkness in people: neighbour turning on neighbour and individuals on themselves. Introverted faces were glued to the grey pavements; souls scourged each other with formality and erected boundaries between one another. Centuries like this, and, just like the island, a man could be an island unto himself and separate from whoever (or whatever) dwelt here. The vampire recognized alienation in many of the souls born to this land.

Humans arriving from warm countries had a much different outlook. Foreigners did not share the sad, negative Irish attitude. Not estranged from the sun all their lives, newcomers were least seduced by the degenerative depression and heathen discourse that choked the nation's spirituality.

Natives, by contrast, in growing numbers, were hanging themselves, drowning themselves, cutting themselves, or at least courting suicide. Every town, village, and by-road in Ireland was touched by unemployment, brutal violence, and addiction. Divorce was rising with the smoke of the chimneys. Loneliness was flying higher than an eagle under perpetually grey skies. Suicide was becoming the only option for escape. Corpses were the end result of violence caused by hidden underlying emotions; self-neglect, self-hatred, self-pity, and self-reproach were supplying fodder for cemetery plots or crematoriums. Guilt, the hammer of unwieldy emotion, penetrated the collective psyche and killed like *phytophora infestans* had in the 1840's and 50's, when the Irish potato crop was devastated by blight.

Diabolis, being a vampire, knew neither pity nor guilt. He merely observed society.

The more unfortunate victims of negative feelings who died through self-destruction, having passed through the hands of state pathologists, if not buried, were turned to ash and in-urned, just as in Ancient Rome or during The Black Death. The 'burial game,' like so many businesses in modern Ireland, extorted huge sums. (A vulture knows the best food lies where the corpses are.) Simply putting a deposit on one's plot was a mere down-payment on a whole array of funeral arrangements.

Ireland certainly did a booming commerce in death, generated from foolish degenerates whose thinking had infiltrated Western Theology to devise the profitable plan and benefit a capitalist world. To "make a living" from the dead, the dying, and the consciences of the living, made morbidly good business sense. Besides, replenish charities' pockets with gold and currency, and all wrongdoings were forgiven! The deceased Irish believer's family might impress those who attend funerals with a rich display of coffin and hearse. Nice words might be said about the deceased at the altar, which the person could only have appreciated while living.

The comedy of the living, the dying, and the dead was exquisite entertainment to a vampire. At the very least, the estranged, emerald-grey inhabitants of this morose isle, lived in profound spiritual crisis. The dutiful Diabolis could easily afford to feel less alienated from this mass of nonsensical detritus. Darkness was at home within him; removed from all mortality, he was a clear and present danger to it.

Yet…intimate darkness felt more confusing to him than the distant mortal darkness he owned. House after house he passed impressed him with the truth: their gardens held more life and emotion than the houses' residents. Normally, these large containers built of bricks hid the flesh within. But to him all became transparent via supernatural gifts. He could see and hear and smell the lonely islands of desperate lives caged within these dwellings where, between the ears, raged infernos of stress.

He paused to observe one dishevelled man, deformed by self-induced hardship. He could see him clearly, face filled with bearded hair incapable of forming a smile and frowns as good as any demon's. He looked at the man's wife, who boldly scolded, not only the man, but all outside her gate.

46

The man's emaciated body was seldom nourished by good food or thoughts; his blood was undrinkable, as was that of his mate. The pair's blood was soured by the self-inflicted oppression of their lives. Her blood was rancid because she despised so many people and was extraordinarily self-righteous. The two were simply designed for each other. They acknowledged this by building extra tall borders around their property so that no one from the outside could see them. They kept and fed a large dog, who was also permitted to defecate liberally in their back garden. If the dog's teeth did not deter people, the possibility of slipping on the products of its bowels might.

Lucis Diabolis held his hands to his mouth—not from hunger for their blood, or from chagrin. These souls were in love with mammon, which he heard in the buzzes from their brains. The man sat there, eyes glued to his television. Any of the vampire's acts of aggression in feeding would release him from the hell of feeling. In an invisible form, his mouth outstretched, Lucis was about to sever the twisted man from his misery, but stopped. *No, not in a million years will I take his mortality from him, let alone allow such an uninspired soul, a slave to the wage and avarice, to become one of my kind. He's hardly one of his own kind, and thus would not understand what it takes to be un-dead, constantly living in uncertainty. Even though this person has the certainty of his own home, he feels contrary towards his own humanity.*

He walked past house after house of Suburban Dublin, with exteriors that resembled fortified jails, as if their bricks were saying *'stay out'* and their high walls declaring that the world outside was to be feared. The more he walked, the only things he saw that seemed unashamed to be alive were the tall old trees that grew in these parts. The place felt to Lucis like an extension of the Catholic Purgatory. No one spoke his or her mind, or the truth, as if around here that would be a grave offence.

When Lucis Diabolis finally did arrive at The Old 108 of Rathgar he was gravely disappointed. In the more than ten years since he'd last been here it had changed dramatically. Renamed The Rathgar, the business was not nearly as rustic and thriving as it used to be. What before had resembled a pub for builders now had a restaurant look, a change Lucis did not appreciate. Like a cat, he could not take to once-familiar things being revised, even though, as a higher life form, he knew revision must be accepted for life to progress.

He could not stay caged within the establishment. The people around him seemed unconscious, robotic; alcohol, cigarettes, and small talk were pulling them under more profoundly than the corpses in his cemetery. They were fumbling, negative ruminators about a dead past, full of bitter regret or loves lost through incorrigible folly; codgers disparaged younger men—"millionaires!"—while boasting of their various antics on the field of sport. All of it felt insanely idiotic. To Diabolis, the auditory odiousness was akin to being poured a draught of one's own urine and, at gunpoint, being forced to drink it. The living did not really belong here in these suburban pubs; he—a representative of the living dead—did not feel at all right here either.

Lucis Diabolis knew that all public ale houses on this side of the city were alike. Amid the alcohol-permeated pseudodead, oddly, a lively updraft blew through the door of Lucis' mind, and teased him. He extinguished his smoke and waited for a mood, an emotion, a particular feeling to open the door wider, until, all at once, he realized he was far more enlightened than the souls around him!

*Dublin, Baile Atha Cliath, is special. She helps me feel almost alive again.*

On admitting this, the vampire felt the wildness of youth emerge, as if he'd not aged a day beyond his first awakening. Boldness bloomed within Lucis Diabolis. The dance of youth was playing within him. The chains of expectation as to what a vampire should be were broken!

*I am not some sedate pseudo-person sentenced to be austere, anxious, shy, deadly dull, and blend into this grey world. I AM IMMORTAL.*

He scanned his body. None of the blood he'd consumed the previous night could stay in him. He placed a scarf over his mouth so that people could not see it had changed as he left The Rathgar. No one need know what he truly was. Over the years he'd lived in these suburbs among these strangers unto themselves and each other, who, just like him, made no effort to allow anybody to really know them.

Diabolis walked down Rathgar Avenue, feeling as alive as the proud trees standing in such contrast to the many-storeyed houses amongst them. Between Rathgar Avenue and Wesley Road he found himself the perfect laneway. Lucis Diabolis eyed his long nails, perfectly made for this. His stomach had not yet done its job of vomiting out the filth of drug users. Their blood was unfit for the consumption of a vampire in a thriving mood, who was re-emerging with the sentiments of youth. He was falling in love with the life he knew in his youth. For a life of adventure, his body was telling him, he needed to be reinvigorated, awakened from dormancy, and enabled to operate on full power.

Lucis Diabolis bent over, knowing that the sight of a person vomiting in Dublin at night would be nothing new. Since what came out of him, however, were litres and litres of blood, he stayed well hidden. No one could see him. The dogs in the neighbourhood were too paralyzed with fear to bark. When he reached the end of all the blood within his organs, he did not feel empty and hungry because he felt he was giving himself life again. The next blood he would take would be truly nourishing—the very type he yearned for to live completely.

Straightening up to return to his tomb, the vampire longed to feel intimately a part of this new surge of energy within him. It promised to provide him the bounty of young life, not the dead life in which he'd been submerged from being around it too long.

*Yet, this might be the voice of madness speaking. I am dead and living in Dublin as the only living-dead vampire here! I need to sleep on these thoughts. Surely I cannot go around Dublin with the same vitality that I experienced before death? Surely I've aged through my undead experiences and can never fully return to the way I was on the day my life was taken? Perhaps I'm suffering from a kind of Peter Pan Syndrome...*

If Lucis Diabolis was fooling himself like old people do, fantasizing and unable to separate what is real from what is unreal in order to feel much younger, he would soon feel the pain, the stupidity, and the folly of this. He abandoned the bloody vomit in the laneway, reminding himself that if he wanted to return to the way he once was, he needed to be fastidious about what he consumed in future.

# 2 Dublin's Own 'Vrykolakas'

# I

## Home Base

Those who ran the cemetery knew full well how to keep Diabolis their secret, for he held sway over their minds in more ways than one. They sensed his temper, power, and capabilities, and, therefore, dared not wrong him. If gates needed to be opened, if supplies needed to be ordered, if a driver was needed, all of these demands were always met without question. They admired as much as feared him, for he was one of the city's hidden treasures, more unique and more of a potential Dublin landmark (if it ever came down to that) than the Spire, the Floozy in the Jacuzzi, the Jim Larkin statue, and the Daniel O'Connell monument put together. His *person* was more interesting than the *places*, like the Glasnevin Cemetery, folk frequented because his aura was hypnotic.

The dark came early this night. A hive of thoughts buzzed in Diabolis' head. He could not stay in his tomb. He needed to go to Harold's Cross Park, where he knew his mind could dwell on how he, though born of blood, had begun as an ordinary human wanting a normal life…and how immortality had robbed him of that.

Lucis hopped over the pointed gates that surrounded Harold's Cross Park, a beautiful, nicely maintained sanctuary—a rectangle of peace amidst busy roads with, on its south side, a tall Celtic cross hewn from stone. On the north side he sat down to mull the many memories the place brought back, especially those of when he first became a vampire. He vividly recalled the attraction he'd always had to this spot as he sat on a bench that overlooked tall trees on the far side of the rain-sodden lawn. Despite the wet day, not a drop fell from the evening sky, and light from the street held back the shadows.

The lawn in front of him had not always been a green and tranquil place. He thought of the executions carried out for centuries here since the 1500's, where heads had been hacked off with sharp blades. Or, if head cutting was not called for, choking upon the gallows would do the job—by strong ropes used for hangings. This violence passed for state-approved justice, despite the sixth commandment injunction: "Thou shalt not kill."

Even before Lucis became a vampire he'd visited the gallows as a spectator interested in the peculiarities of this event, and been duly entertained by it. Red spurting from necks freshly cut by blades made him almost as joyous as a prospector watching an oil gusher. Yet, before he was a vampire, how could he have imagined the deeper implications?

After he was made, Lucis followed his desire for others' blood and visited the gallows to draw life from the well of death discreetly. He did not discriminate between sucking the blood of his own victims and draining that which the state executed. Any prey that came his way was either a living kill, or dying. To a few he gave a simple choice: be initiated or be dispatched.

When he thought of the gallows, Lucis' mind returned to a place that was real, not imaginary, one he recalled very fondly. Immersed in this world, his favourite reminiscence came back to him from the period of his own mortality, prior to his vampiric induction. He was swept up like a body into a sea beset by gale-force winds and monstrous waves. Thrown from shore into the beast of the ocean, there to be devoured and destroyed, he was drawn to the temporary safety of remembering one special mortal.

# II

## Diabolis' Pre-Vampire History

Once, love and human company had mattered to Diabolis. To him the most important person had been Mona Westard. She worked in The Old Flour Mill near Mount Jerome, beside the River Poddle. The mill was a place of hard labour. Mona resented her work place and the husband who forced her to go there.

He, Shane Westard, at home most hours because he half ran his business, showed Mona nothing in return for her hours of toil. He managed his tavern through exploitation. Exploitation was his bottom line.

"I'll make you pay for this someday, Shane," she'd promise as she prepared his meals. But, just like her work, her words were empty. Being a woman of her day, with no rights, she had no power to better her lot.

Shane was a filthy pig in her eyes, and she was not the only one who thought so. Others thought him either a pig or a rat or a dog. To some, he was lower than a rat, whilst those he truly embittered called him "lower than dog waste." He'd always looked and acted swinish, so she'd resolutely refused to marry him. At first, her dad agreed, for Shane had nothing to offer in terms of the advancement of her sire's status and means.

But Shane got wealthy. The next step was simple. Her father forced Mona into an arranged marriage with Shane, a man twenty-five years her senior. Fitzsimons' daughter was expendable once the right amount of money was offered to claim her. She was told, fearing and knowing she'd be tempted to do this, not to return to her birth home and *never* to complain about her husband to her father.

Shane was of forty and six years to Mona's youthful eighteen when they married. He had money, but was not interested in giving her any. He liked holding onto money, grasping those pennies and shillings made from being owner of a pub situated in the north part of the park (where Lucis now sat ruminating).

This tavern, "The Scab's Brew," ran itself, more or less, for the proprietor had help to whom he paid a pittance, and plenty of bullying tactics he offensively called "by order of the proprietor," transforming the meaning of the words into *Great Satan.* And this is what he embodied.

He thought he was being most practical when she came to his house by sending her straight to the mill. He forbade her from entering the tavern, where he drank whenever the need occurred to him. His marriage and his pub were run to suit his whims. He detested opinions and suggestions contrary to his notions of how a place, a house, and so on, should be run. No way was he going to employ his wife in his tavern and give her an easier life. Doing so might make her soft; she needed to suffer and be hardened. He did not want a soft thing around him. By the time he was through, she'd be well-tempered metal, a useful tool in his hands.

Mona knew Shane was but a typical example of why females needed protection from the inequality laid down by menfolk. Come hail, rain, or snow, she was only going one way and that was off to her work. He wasn't interested in a child bearer bringing screaming rascals into the home. Any woman interested in that type of thing and using the excuse of carrying on the family name, well, he'd sooner murder her brats than put up with them, since children, like females, were lower than men, and thus disposable.

As long as she was breathing she had to be working. And she knew full well what he thought of a little lassie or gossan coming to the door. Shane told her graphically how he'd drown a baby like a stray kitten or pup. There'd be nothing anyone could say or do to stop him. The law would not catch him because he'd destroy the evidence. He assured her he knew of good places for that type of thing. The man did nothing to produce a child; to say he disliked sex was to understate his dislike. He hated intercourse as much as any normal man craved it. So why was he talking about destroying his young when he had no inclination towards siring? To torment her with threats should she stray! He despised sex so much that he insisted upon their sleeping in separate beds. Maybe such a marriage would have been considered illegal by Church Standards and Irish Law, but Mona, shy about such matters, never dared bring them up, even in the secrecy of the Confessional.

He only visited Mona's bed to wake her up for work or a beating. He was regarded by hard men and soft alike as the cruellest, most twisted bastard any woman must put up with. But, to be sure, he wasn't unique in the history of Dublin, Ireland, Europe, the world, or of men in general.

What of her point of view? He would not spare the rod for fear her opinions might wander too far from his or the accusation be made that he spoiled her. Children and women were to *be seen not heard*, their minds being equally dim.

Shane adored sharing his philosophy with a certain calibre of fellow that he entertained at The Scab's Brew, who he thought did not see him as hypocritical in his beliefs. If asked about inconsistencies in his logic, he silenced the conversation with a crude remark, a dismissive gesture, or a menacing statement that squelched the entrance of logic or further discussion. After all, solid drinking men went out to drink to get some peace and let in some merriment. They didn't aim for their drinking time to be molested by a moron upstart who just wants or needs *his* views, and not Shane Westard's, to be heard.

At home, Shane wanted to be true to his word as a man who helped support anti-female policies because such creatures, especially his charming spouse, were subhuman and un-evolved. If he thought he heard the slightest objection or any potential for asserting her own individuality, or if anything started not going his way, he had various rituals of physical abuse to perform to put her back in gear. He knew her wage down to the schilling and the penny, and insisted she bring it home and put it straight in his hand every Friday.

On pay day Shane would do what his cruel, selfish heart felt appropriate. Not an ounce of consideration was given by Shane that Mona had earned that money. It was his by right as head of the house, any statement to the contrary notwithstanding.

He was content doing the selfish thing. His mind had long ago liquidated the decent and the ethical. His reason for entitling himself to abuse her was simply on the grounds that her father had sold her to him. His agreement was to put a roof over her head and nourish her. He was not told to spare the rod, fist, hand, or cane, or to treat her like a lady. And it was not in this property description to adequately look after her, especially if it meant he could save the money instead. As for fancy clothes, or getting anything that could liberate Mona into thinking that she was more than a mortal in the grip of a dominant, all-powerful man, well, you could forget about all that nonsense.

Shane was not there to make his wife feel good about her self. For him she was only a notch above a vagrant or a tramp, and often, pending the mood, she was even beneath that. Why? Shane was 'new money,' and new money always has a complex about their status that tells them they must do their uttermost to prove that there is worth for them in this life. He'd run into his money by way of a wager he'd placed and gotten lucky on. Since then, he'd used bullying to get everything he wanted. To think that a plate would have to be lifted was offensive to his privileged gender and position in life. To think that a lower status person deserved to hear a kind word from him was impossible.

When Lucis Diabolis met Mona he was bathing naked in the River Poddle. She saw his muscles, his long brown hair, his bold eyes, and liked what she saw.

Wild at the world for all the injustices dealt her, the laws of what was the norm for her smothering her, she'd begun to nurture the seeds of rebellion. So she'd gone walking by the river, alone.

Lucis' gaze met Mona's, and his feelings matched her fire. He suspected theirs would be nothing more than a casual encounter, but hoped it wasn't just that.

Mona's heart beat faster. After all, she was fed up with the status quo and the quality of life rendered her as she fulfilled the duties befitting a housewife of this age. She saw that the stranger had laid out his commoner clothes beside black shoes that looked in desperate need of repair. She lowered her eyes, aware that her shabby black dress was bereft of the jewellery normal for a woman of her quality.

To Lucis, Mona was highly attractive. On this summer's day, at this time, this district being a semi-rural part of Dublin, the two were on their own and, if they needed privacy, had it.

Mona had every reason to be here and none to be at home. If she went home her husband would only accuse her of not having gone to work and slap her face. She would deny his charges. So, as usual, he'd have gotten out the leather strap and used it on her. Mona was neither a masochist, nor the mis-attributed receiver (according to the Marquis De Sade's version of sadism), for there was no precondition of sexual gratification being delivered in this equation—just sadistic cruelty and downright abuse.

Her husband was not interested in her sexually. Mona had never had sex with Shane, but had discovered certain facts in a pamphlet from London, which a female co-worker gave her with the intention that she might at least learn. The inner contents contained explicit hand drawings intimating that the sex act could be pleasurable.

Her husband, however, was not equipped to please a woman, having sublimated his sexuality into power over others, violence, and abuse. By cruelty, he was primitively letting her know that he existed. This was his outlet for who he really was—pure, unadulterated, and uncontaminated—complete in his rawness and depravity.

Mona was not blind. Despite the beatings and ragged clothing, she was still an alluring woman. She knew how men looked at her, and was not ignorant of what these looks actually meant.

The young man remained in the water, not wishing to expose himself to the pretty young lady before him. He loved looking at her eyes, the hair that fell to her waist, and the perfection of her curves. Instead of walking past or away from him, she'd walked closer to the river's edge.

"Sorry," Lucis said to her. But this girl, instead of pretending to be shy of a stranger, smiled directly at him. How could he emerge from the water if she was here? And, as he clearly saw, she was not going away.

"Sorry," he said again, eyeing her rich brown hair and voluptuous form, "but I *must* put on my clothes."

With those words, Mona awoke to reality. She turned her back and was about to walk away.

"You do not have to leave. I will not be long dressing."

No matter what Mona felt for this man, she had to hide it,

even though she wanted to stay near him to have someone to talk to. So she waited. As he emerged from the water, she resisted any urge to watch him dress. What no one could take from her except by her own free will, the honour her uncouth brute of a husband would love to hear was taken from her, remained intact. (No one had explained why honour of this kind was to be coveted.) Already acquainted with misery and oppression, she feared disgrace less as the minutes passed.

Her desire to tell some living person the sufferings she had to endure almost overwhelmed her. But she could not tell this stranger. She did not know him. It would make more sense to say nothing, and just take him…inside…very far inside…as deep as he could go, and let Shane Westard be damned!

Yes, Mona wanted him in her, for her 'owner' was not interested and this had kept her intact. To allow herself to submit to those energies within her, for which her husband provided no outlet, was her fondest wish. This stranger surely would know what a woman's energies were for. She would think with her body and ignore her mind. She'd let her body follow its natural desires and run with the fire that consumes and overcomes an adult when they reach maturity. By doing this, she would not have to live in the miserable desert of thoughts.

"What are you doing for the rest of the day?" he asked.

"Nothing," she replied.

"Would you like to spend time in my company on this beautiful day?"

Mona walked with him. What was she supposed to do— talk about the weather? It always rained a lot, yet today it did not. They were already finished discussing the peculiarities of Irish weather and how they should be most grateful to be living in Baile Atha Cliath, the part of Dublin that tended to get milder weather than other parts. She asked him if he had family. He said *no*, but left it at that. He did not talk much, but held her hand, something no man ever did. The more she nervously asked questions, the more monosyllabic he remained and the more firmly he held her hand. Once they approached a small cottage in a remote area known as Rathgar, far from gossip and prying eyes, the dynamic between them grew even more apparent.

Just as she was about to say another word, he gently touched the side of her left cheek with his palm. A hand from a man that neared her face usually meant the onset of a beating. With his right hand, in which hers rested, he pressed the small of her back and looked down upon her, smiling.

Was this how she was supposed to feel? Was this how a man was supposed to match the desire within her? Because they were totally alien from any of the feelings that her husband permitted in their relationship, when he pressed against her, she naturally decided this was what the drawings attempted to capture. He wanted her to kiss him. She had never been kissed. She wanted to be kissed now. But he drove her crazy. He held her so strongly that it felt like an ox was holding her and that she was as light as a feather in the hands of a strength she could not, but wonderfully did not want to, overcome.

For once, being held by a man did not repulse her, nor did it mean desperately wanting to escape. She wanted to stay. She looked intently at him, so much so that her nerves were shaken and her breath warmly exhaled into his face. Being very shy, she could not articulate what she wanted, having never been presented with what a woman should want. She had an idea of what that could be like, and was burning for his response. Experience did not say that it was proper for her to feel such things. Right now, if she could be taken where this arousal was going, or where she thought it should go, she was sure it would satisfy her.

He maddened her with anxiety. Instead of following through, he let go of her, abandoning her while she was still in his arms; his eyes looked away from her and towards the door. Her whole body, especially the place where it all must start and finish, was afire. And her bosom, which he gazed at so boldly, was swelling. If he was to ignore her now and just let her go, she knew it would torment her. And she would be left with a gnawing curiosity about what this thing her body wanted to complete really felt like.

How good it must make a person feel, how welcomed, how desired, how needed, how aroused, how attracted, body to body, closely together, even if it meant that one's clothes had to intervene! She could not know where this was going or initiate and complete it, for she felt she was the passive participant.

He did not hold her or say a word to her. The cottage looked nice, the surrounding woodlands beautiful, as if a soul could get lost in them and never come out, unless one were to run with the wolves travelling here from the Dublin and Wicklow Mountains. No, the wilderness was not a recommended area.

"Where are you going?" she asked him, for it seemed like he was walking away from her. He turned and started towards her. Mona felt something she never had, as if this yearning he had for her made her ready to fulfill it. Though too ashamed to admit it, she longed to fondle him. She would, desperately she would, if she could, if he wanted to, if he wanted her to give in to him, do so completely. But maybe she was repulsive to men, contrary to what the mirror told her, or others had said who knew her and pitied her for being unlucky in her marriage. *Maybe it's all lies. I'm unworthy of love. Da was a martyr paying someone to house and feed me, and Shane knows my true place in life is nowhere but the mill.*

She was untouchable. Her virginity, which now sat like a weight upon her hopes, would have to stay locked, never opened for what was waiting inside to be released. She would stay untouched, her being harmed from such neglect. For some people chastity is a gift, a state of abstinence they can easily endure. For others, like Mona, chastity can be a curse.

Since her ill-fated marriage, Mona had found that, no matter how hard she worked, at night she could not sleep. It became so bad that often she thought of what she was not doing that stopped her from sleeping. The problem became obvious, and the solution too. Normal sexual intercourse is what she wanted, and regularly. She wanted to have what she overheard the other women, who seemed less inhibited, talked about openly in the factory (but not with her, since she was considered clueless and innocent).

The wanting, she thought, would go away, so long as she stopped listening to those conversations. Such talk was not for her kind. But, then again, what *was* her kind? She was human and must be allowed to feel that way and not just be brutalised.

Mona thought she had finally conquered sexual desire by simply thinking of it as a trivial thing. By calling it a thing she could depersonalize sexuality, making it less of a problem for her. By ignoring it, it would not be there.

Then a lady started to visit the factory every Friday for flour. She had the finest figure a woman could have and the most joyful exuberance—a round face, large eyes, and lips that could cover your face, golden hair neatly tied at the back, and a body perfect for childbearing. She was not like the rest of the ladies of Rathgar and Harold's Cross. She exuded warmth that Mona never knew could exist. When Lady Beverly Hattersby saw Mona, she knew who she was, knew of her husband and her suffering. These past twelve months, she had started to spoil her, feed her, make her feel good about herself, and encourage her to leave Shane.

"But how," Mona had objected, "am I to ever do that?"

Two days ago, the answer was whispered into Mona's ears,

"Come, girl, and stay with us. After nagging my husband like a dripping tap, I got nowhere. But then I got him to change his mind decisively."

"How?"

"How, you ask? The details are not so important. If you live with me, I'll raise you like my own."

"But seriously," Mona had said, "although this is a wonderful proposition, I want to know how you changed your husband's mind?"

"By simply following the rule: *if you want to keep a man, you must spread your legs; if you want a man to leave you, cross your legs.* I opened them, much longer and more often than what was considered normal, and did the things I learned from visiting certain female specialists in India."

Mona's eyes dilated with elation, and excitement streamed from the tips of her toes to the top of her head. India sounded light years away to the unworldly and innocent girl.

"And the results of this were as if it was the first time we two ever touched."

Mona felt her body stiffen. If this man could touch her like Lady Beverly was touched and she were to touch him in return, she'd know what it was like to feel womanly. She was sure that if she was to be touched on this maiden voyage of discovery it would alleviate all the negatives she was holding onto about herself, and, by the end of the day, she'd feel strong enough to leave that brute, Shane. But the young man had walked away!

*What is he doing? Is he going into the cottage on his own?*

His head nodded for her to go inside as well. Mona entered slowly, calmly, with her eyes on the ground. Her body felt warm, and not because it was a nice day. She was breathless and lethargic, quivering like a cello's strings that, with gradual subtleness increase from the vibrations of a bow drawn across them. The places which she had not the words for were anticipating the advent of a change that would spark an emancipation. She was swimming in a sweet odour channelled into a liquid which came from her body. Would he like this scent or run from it in disgust?

There was a silence that defined an uncertainty. Mona did not know what came next, could not possibly know. Though her imagination helped her the best that it could to know, it was unclear.

"Please feel like a guest in my home," he said.

"A guest," she said softly, wanting but not wanting, To express hidden hopes was not so good when it exposed one, so was best kept private. Her heart beat at a rate she'd never experienced before with a man.

He could see she was breathing so deeply that it accentuated her figure and made her eyes dilate, as if his presence lit up the world within her. The distance between them was six feet, for she stayed behind him at all times, just in case she had to flee. Men were a species her husband made her feel she had to be careful of. His right foot moved towards her. She saw his right foot step towards her; her left eye on the ground, her right eye looked upon him. Although she stayed still, her body trembled as if it would shake the ground.

He moved forward again, to reassure her, for he sensed her fear. She feared that he would withdraw from her, reject her, and leave her in unparalleled pain. He inhaled the scents which she knew too well were coming from her body. As his chest moved to inhale, without even one touch, she anticipated she would, indeed, be touched.

He closed his eyes and thought how natural, pure, elegant, feminine, lovely, and agreeable she was to all his senses. His heart was pumping a mile a minute. He feared that she would reject him in favour of values that scarcely anyone could live by, anyone human, anyone normally made.

Looking at her, he couldn't help but imagine what it would be like to be within her completely. He longed to realize the moment that her legs wrapped around him, his left hand holding her lower back, his right hand in her hair, and she, nakedly manifesting that there was simply nowhere better to go than to surrender finally and sweetly.

"Please," he begged.

"Yes," she whispered.

"Yes!" he replied, and his eyes looked directly into hers. He then lost every word his tongue wished to say and his mind refused to recall.

She smiled a nervous smile that said it could not be possible or correct or within her power to finish what he was trying to say.

Next, he stood beside her, his face close to hers, and, when she looked at Lucis, he said in a soft whisper, "Do not be afraid."

Mona moved into his strong arms. What passed between the two was seemingly lust, but he realized that there was trust there too, and was confused by this. Lucis the man did take her unto himself. He helped her learn she was a woman. And, after they made love, she did not want to leave.

Mona kept visiting him. She started to stay with him during the day. She grew fond of him, became totally independent of, and then abandoned Shane. Lucis, in turn, declared his undying love for Mona.

And life was set to go very well...until...something very, very dark happened.

Thus, the story of Lucis Diabolis unfolded, not only from narratives of his present life, but from those left behind long ago.

# III

## Quest for the Noble Blood of Lost Youth

Lucis Diabolis left the park bench, distracted by more questions than he could possibly answer. But he felt a revolution emerging within his psyche. His virility had been strong, and he'd loved kissing women tenderly, dancing, falling in love, even puppy love, and making love. He'd swum and run and gone dancing on a regular basis. Rest had involved enjoyment of life's variety—classical composition, literature, drinking, and appreciation of the erotic and the exotic. He'd loved life and was full of life's energy.

Particularly drawn to philosophical literature and discussing it with friends, his present philosophy was sobered by the knowledge that he'd been killed while still a youth—becoming neither fully dead nor fully alive.

He'd loved eating, but absolutely nothing bloody. He'd preferred his meat well cooked, along with bread, potatoes, cheeses, chocolates, ice cream, fruit, and dairy products. He missed that now. He missed eating fish he'd just caught in the river. He missed drinking whole pots of tea or coffee.

Being athletic and highly sexual had never meant displeasure or pain for others. Nothing in his life on earth had prepared him for the violent consumption of blood. His sexuality had not been at all abnormal. He was just a regular guy looking for mutual attraction—the more voluptuous the woman, the more feminine and juicy, the better. He loved watching women for the usual signs of arousal—easy smiles, bold eye-to-eye contact, dilated pupils, intoxicating laughter.

He was given by his maker at the time of his supernatural transmission to that darker, unfamiliar side, an introduction to the duties his nature entailed. Now he realised this list was lacking because it had no room for loving or being loved, and it forgot that he was still a young man, who had not really died. Worst of all, he was given a new name, not of his choosing, to go with the new way of thinking about who he was in the world.

When he first made love to Mona, it was the first time he felt what it was to fall in love with a woman, genuinely and completely. It was the first time he knew how strange and powerful intimate love could be.

He wanted to experience that amazing sensation again, to feel like he needed someone and that someone could need him—helplessly, completely, adoringly, and absolutely. But there were problems before him, huge barriers to overcome. What he'd been told was his constitution was made for roles he must fulfil, insane as this seemed. He'd been living centuries in the shadow of laws made by a man he had not seen in as long. That long departed man was very different from a night creature herding rats, executing junkies, and drinking animal blood during periods when human blood was scarce. Although this man once had no interest in the macabre or morose, he came to embody it. That mortal was light years' apart from this dark beast of a vampire.

Diabolis had been physically fit—lean and tall, a man of strong frame and broad shoulders. He used to love doing pushups, going for long runs, staying strong, and watching what he ate. He'd loved physical work because he knew it developed his body and channelled his energy.

Lucis Diabolis kept thinking and rethinking his position in

life. Within the vampire's psyche a revolution of experiencing and understanding was underway. He did not accept himself as just a dark and deadly duplicate of his live self. He felt like a plate smashed on the floor and shattered into several pieces. The mood he was in led him to believe he could reunite his shards and re-emerge whole to be who he truly was. The rules by which he was abiding, what the mythic essential vampire should be, felt like a false version of what he was. The rebel inside him wanted to overturn every rule and discover what the true rules were.

Yes, like Icarus, who disobeyed his father, courage felt good and he had no illusions about exploring any possible limitations and finally seeing them clearly. His ideas constructed this framework of conjecture in relation to his nature. Mulling these ideas, he entered his tomb and wrote down what had invaded his mind. This is how his internal monologue of thought transpired.

*Did I dream myself into this strange immortality that lives on flesh and gives breath, year by year, through the mystery called sanguinity? Everything feels like a dream stacking upon a dream...waking to feed and fighting the light. Weary of the eerie, I stalk the grave where I should lie lifeless. The mystery presents itself of how I know this life like nothing I knew before I became. This strangeness evades me. Given a label not of my own design should present a mystery to me.*

*In this present Dublin, which persists in the grey of its nature, and using my own blood as ink, I set down the origin of Lucis Diabolis on this paper before me. I'm lost in the myth of having to create a sequential series as if life has a sensible linearity to it. How can what lives within me be described? My origins present a mystery as perplexing as the weirdness of how I became me. I place these words upon this page, attempting to create a thesis of what I am now and who I was then.*

*Here is what I know of those days: my court-assigned executioner, Alex Leman, believed in me. He said I was a true professional killer, and looked into my eyes as he asked, "So why did you kill her?"*

69

"Her?" I replied angrily, as if he was sticking me with red-hot pokers.

"Yes…Mona, why did you kill Mona? Her husband is begging for your blood."

"I loved Mona from the day I met her. I could not lay a hand upon her unless it was to kiss her hair."

"This is what people say."

"What do they say?" I asked nervously, outraged that there might be a counter thesis to me loving Mona.

"They say that her husband abused her, but you loved her."

When my assigned executioner said this I thought of how deeply I loved her. Then, though, I diverted my thoughts to hate. I hated being interrogated for a crime I'd never commit against the one I loved so deeply. From the day I pressed her bosom against my cheek I knew she'd been unloved and sought to make up for this great deficit to the best of my powers.

She confessed her fantasies, which came of her fascination with literature from medieval times. So I had made for Mona the best clothes of that era my purse could afford, and adorned her and the house we shared with flowers I picked myself. I dressed in the full uniform of a knight and spent hours just chastely holding her.

Thus I loved her truly, and knew her murderer was the husband who sneered at me in triumph as I awaited execution.

My would-be executioner saw, in my eyes and soul, a darkness that had overwhelmed it, which had caused me to venomously thirst for revenge. The venom he saw in me grew daily, until he found me ripe for recruitment to the world of the vampire. My condition was all he needed to ensure that a bloody appetite was matched with a sense of total injustice, blind hatred for, and contempt for a world that could let this happen.

I'd had my fill of the way things were in society and was baying for blood. My maker knew that my blood was hot. I was willing to make an alliance with the dark side of eternity. Alex, willing and able to continue an ordinary life of being around people and to have his true identity unknown, told me that there was a way for me to survive this tragedy and to outlive the forces that had condemned me to death. This most unusual way *would cause me to become like him.*

*I did not care what this implied. Like one who listens to the radio and, upon listening too much, turns the radio off, I tuned out the details. I just went along with his suggestions. There was nothing more to decide on or to know further. I knew that I had life still left in me and was being executed prematurely, for I'd expected to live way beyond this date and time. So I consented to a worse abomination than execution.*

*More than a hundred years after my vampire initiation, I feel the same desire to kill as I did when I struck down Mona's husband, Shane Westard. I drowned in his own blood the man who had cruelly drowned his wife. Yet, I did not think being born of blood, a condition of which I knew little, meant I'd need to kill random people, or, occasionally, leave them for dead. Killing that leech must have made killing others easier. A bite on the neck and a letting of enough blood, and the job is done.*

*The blood I imbibe lets me assume all sorts of shapes and configurations, but does not help me to figure out the nature of my being. I relate to time in a strange way. Days seem dead, useless…unless I centre on what I should do next. Sometimes, between kills and blood-lettings, I wonder about myself. I worry about my nature and my origins and purpose. But I have no answers as to what power forces me to spend immortality simply craving the life-blood of others.*

*I used to share my tomb with Alex the Executioner, who proudly boasted he'd never lack for work and never tire of it either. The work never got to him. Criminal reform acts did. So, he moved on to less green locations, where state-sanctioned murder was accepted and he could enjoy the fruits of his labours.*

With all of his musings placed on paper, if Lucis Diabolis was bent on setting out to spend a life defined by his own rules and without preconceptions, it would have to wait. He was exhausted. His blood was thin, but he knew if he slept he would recover. He was much too tired to make another killing, and tomorrow night must come before he could again step outside and feed.

## 3 *Better Blood*

# I

## On the Way to The Bruxelles

Lucis Diabolis awoke a different vampire. *Goodness, where is there a drab of blood when a vamp needs it to cool the embers of his nerves?* This energy low was akin to what a diabetic feels when they need to inject their insulin because blood levels of it are insufficient.

*What the hell was last night all about? I didn't even top up on supplies or feed.*

He had a reaction to the thought processes he'd allowed his mind to entertain the previous night, and this reaction was hellish. How dared he be so foolish as to think 'outside the box' (in his case, the coffin)? He'd strutted around like he was not a vampire but a young mortal able to live without the blood of some other living organism coursing through his system.

*What the hell was wrong with me?*

Lucis Diabolis questioned the absurdity of wanting to think and be something he was not. His youth had passed him. He'd died years ago. That young romantic hero was from a different age, and no one in this land of the living recognised that person. He was a vampire, and, most of the time in this strange city of Dublin, he'd kept a low profile, invisibly safe and totally private.

He believed he was no more than the riddle of the Sphinx (at that stage just before we are extinguished). He was old, haggard, and dependent on blood to maintain his supernatural energy. He always made sure to eat because he didn't want to know what happened if he did not.

*I'm called a vampire because I feed off others' blood and transfer myself to the land of the living to do so. Why can't I just be the way I always was, content being a vampire and doing vampire things? Stalling only reduces the life blood I have within me.*

*I might just be what the humans would call a ghost. But there's no deep exact knowledge of my nature. Years fall away to dust like old books. Sometimes I feel like two or more people live in me. The vampire who feeds off blood and is called Lucis Diabolis requires blood and daytime rest. There is the man I used to be. There is the one I am now—supernatural, but still clueless because no one is telling me there is more to this.*

Upset by this inner turmoil, there was only one way to go, and that was into a feeding frenzy. But Lucis Diabolis had hardly enough energy to exit his tomb. He knew he had to stop thinking and to feed more often. This promised to be a hellishly cold winter. The cold had always made him to want to eat more. The fact that people's blood (especially going into November and December) was much warmer and tastier than at any other season meant it was only proper that he fortify himself for the winter ahead.

What was with today? Last night had been weird, given all the dead of Dublin mingling with the living, helping them to say and do wild and nasty things with each other.

He started the evening by strolling along the grey paths of Dublin and admiring the way millions of lights lit the place up. Such a view was afforded by simply travelling via the Luas line to Sandyford, and then walking for a while around the Dublin Mountains overlooking the Irish Sea and the glow from domestic and commercial premises that allowed city dwellers to function when darkness descended. Lucis Diabolis was overly familiar with that view. Having seen enough, he returned to the Luas and headed off to the city centre.

In the city centre, the vampire was intrigued by the sight of a dead, headless ghost who sat on Dawson Street watching passers-by. Although mortals could not see this ghost, Lucis saw him clearly. The man was dressed in the clothes he'd died in. From his upper body, where he wore his white v-neck jumper and white shirt, gushed blood. His decapitated head in his hands, the head's eyes followed the restless throngs.

A double-decker bus passed the corner. The ghost raised his right hand. With his index finger he pointed at the bus. Instantly, his demise flashed before the vampire's eyes. Two youths, who'd towered over the man at around six o'clock two winters ago, started to attack him over something trivial. The man had been smoking at the bus stop and refused to give them a cigarette. He was side-kicked ferociously in the chest. The kick's impact meant that the sharply angled heel made optimum contact with the mid-stomach area. The only option was to fall or slide back without falling down. A victim hit by such a kick might easily slide quite a distance before collapsing. The bus driver had no way of perceiving or controlling what happened next. The man's head was torn right off him by the bus as it pulled to a stop. The bus driver was in total shock. Nothing could possibly have been done to prevent this sorrowful tragedy. The man's head rolled to lie below the bus door, where a homeless man walked up to and slapped it as if he expected a sign of life in it.

"What are you doing that for?" a pedestrian asked, knowing this site should be treated like a crime scene.

"I swore he was looking at me and his eyes moved. He was asking me for help, so he was. And I love to help people, for I think it is a noble thing to do."

"Leave the head there!" the pedestrian advised.

Returning to the present—two years later—the ghost sat with his head in his hands, severed from life by the force of the bus wheels, thanks to the action of two thugs willing to kill for nothing but smoke.

This ghost was useless to Diabolis, for his fountaining blood, though enticing, was only a visual hallucination. The vampire decided he needed to go to the top of some tall building for an overview of the life blood this city had to offer. He found such a building near Dublin's O'Connell Street. Like a great bird of prey, Diabolis spread bat wings and flew to the top of his chosen perch.

Once atop the Heineken Building overlooking O'Connell Street, he threw away his cigarette. He walked down the Heineken Building via a more scenic route, one decidedly less travelled. The stairs and lift were for mortals; Lucis simply walked off the roof, gravity not being a concern for him. He walked straight down, thinking, *Vertigo is for sissies. Looking at everything upside-down makes more sense.* On the way down he played in his head a song he often heard in one of the numerous bars of Dublin, *Your Pretty Face Is Goin' to Hell* by Iggy Pop. It was Lucis Diabolis' favourite song.

The Vampire Lucis Diabolis dreamed he could dance right then and there, although his black spirit did not accommodate him. If he could have danced, Dublin was the city for it. This was the place where anyone could be high up in the air and still be living under the ground. According to the media, a new party drug was concocted every week in an Irish lab and on the streets in no time. Diabolis envied all these consumers how soon they'd be moving to the beat and embracing the mad dream that they could live forever.

Walking across the Heineken sign, at the front exterior of the building, he overheard one of the cleaning ladies working inside the big building, its face toward the statue of Daniel O'Connell.

A young redhead walking past her did her best to make conversation, "Did you have a good weekend?"

"It was alright. Did you?"

"I watched 'Coronation Street' last night. I find a bit of television relaxes me. Do you watch television?"

"No," the cleaning lady responded.

"What do ya' do, read?"

"No."

"What do you do to relax?"

"I sit around and have a few cans. I love alcohol," she admitted.

Yes, you do, thought Lucis Diabolis, *love alcohol, because it relieves something inside of you. It gets the tension and it pulls it down so you can feel that you're running on automatic again.*

Lucis Diabolis, who was standing on the outside of the building, admired how this worker also had a dependency on something liquid, although totally unaware how turned on he got by his libation of choice. How greatly blood pleased him!

Alcohol was something Diabolis had been neglecting. He might go out tonight and, having enough money in his pocket for the beers of Dublin pubs, see how a passion for alcohol could make him feel. Possibly, it would compensate for his desire for blood, serving as a substitute which would offer him some sensation of satiation.

Strangely, the vampire's mouth began to salivate, not to fang. His mouth watered, he wanted it so badly.

All vices begin in the body, starting with an insatiable desire for some degree of satiety, but ending when the body learns that there is no end, full stop, or remission from that outrageous desire. Lucis Diabolis wanted to discover the mystery behind the patrons flooding Temple Bar, O' Connell Street, and Grafton Street, searching for that pint. What ease, what relief were they looking to achieve?

It started to rain. Lucis Diabolis started to dance—at first, only in his head. He'd not trained his body to dance, and his dark soul could not fully grasp the joy of music that led to dance and song. He could hear in his head the song, *Singing in the Rain*. Feeling like Gene Kelly, he imagined that he sang and danced all over the Heineken sign, leaving bloody footprints to contrast by day with the grey print facing O'Connell Street.

Tonight he was going to down some Heineken, Stella Artois, Carlsberg, and top off with a pint of Beck's and a few glasses of Smirnoff Vodka, followed, perhaps, by enough ecstasy (or whatever chemical he needed to get high). He figured these would ensure he was sufficiently chemically altered.

*Maybe,* the vampire hypothesized, *the Irish are right to adore alcohol. Maybe there's something powerful and mythical in it.* He conjectured that he was yet to see what alcohol could do, since human blood was far more powerful than anything else he'd experienced. He'd never gotten into the grog, nor did it get into him.

It was time to go into any of the number of bars of Dublin created for the young, where their brand of hyperactive music was played, to help the chemicals to achieve good adequate soakage in his undead brain and to allow the brain to be opened up to alteration.

First, he wished to take in the night life of O'Connell Street, the beating heart of Dublin, whose other streets were just its arteries. Although O'Connell was quiet, Lucis Diabolis could still see at the far end of it (where Parnell Street began), near the Garden of Remembrance, ten burly ambulance attendants attempting to sedate a teen off her head from a head-shop high purchased near the Quays—a 'legal Dublin-sold' high.

Lucis Diabolis could see the demon of her intoxication attacking her as a vampire might his prey and crushing her sanity like a crocodile would the bones of a human skull. The demon could have stepped out of Edvard Munch's painting, *Vampyren* (1893-1894). Crimson hair covered his body and his frame was thrice the size of the druggie he was shaking like a rag doll. He was infusing her with superhuman strength, which resembled electric bolts shooting into her body, for he had seized her completely.

The demon's eyes were white orbs with small dots of ruby red centred in each. The entity was as soulless as he looked, grinning hideously at the ambulance attendants, who kept trying to inject the girl with sedatives, while attempting to cuff her hands together. It was no use. She slipped their clutches, ran out into the road, and started to jump on a taxi. The morbidly obese cabbie, five-six, with a rounded head and bushy black eyebrows overshadowing his triple-chinned, sweaty face, fancied his chances of sorting the situation. He stopped the cab and got out.

"Off the road!" he ordered her, motioning to her as if to say, *I'll sort this mess out.*

She punched him with enough force to knock his block off. The man hit the ground like a sack of potatoes. He lay there unconscious as the ambulance men rushed over in concern. The girl got into the cab and sped away, but the ten burly men, now busy with the obese cabbie, hardly noticed.

*Interesting,* thought Lucis Diabolis, *most interesting indeed.*

Diabolis decided he had no business on O'Connell Street tonight, and turned right around, heading for Grafton Street, where he'd go to *Bruxelles* on Harry Street, just off Grafton. He expected choice music in his favourite genre, making him feel exactly like he belonged in this place and time.

Walking through Grafton Street, the vampire noticed pools of blood on the ground. He was unsure if this was real, or just wishful thinking. But the blood was real, for its aroma teased his nose. He knew by its smell what it would taste like. He'd consumed blood like this before. The blood came from two men, one of whom who was nursing his cheek and neck with a white cloth.

The other man had been stabbed by a bottle in the neck and a knife to the stomach. Oceans of blood were pouring from his wounds. Silent observers stood like statues, while others walked by as if gushing blood was the norm in Dublin, and even viewed as a tourist attraction (possibly titled, *The Flowing Vampire Paradise of Eastern Erin?*).

Ordinarily, Lucis Diabolis was turned on by the sight of so much blood. But, as tourists and shoppers looked on in shock, Lucis was not expressing his usual arousal. Broken glass lay on the wet surface in the middle of pedestrian-oriented Grafton. The violent row had been fuelled by the best fuel for these things—alcohol, mixed with an ally, cocaine, some of which had fallen out of the stabbed victim's pocket and powdered the pavement between the broken bottles of beer.

A totally wasted vagrant, clutching a two-litre bottle of cider three quarters empty in his right hand, started inappropriately singing, "99 bottles of beer on the wall! You take one down, pass it around, and 98 bottles of beer on the wall…"

The other bloody man, one side of his face slashed by a rusty Stanley knife, shouted, "Shuddup, ya' bleedin' eejit, or ye'll be singing through your blood when I get out of this."

Within a few minutes Gardai on horseback and in cars arrived at the scene and were placing samples of the splattered blood into bags. Unbelievably, Lucis Diabolis had no desire to interfere with this evidence. The police did not look at all shocked. It was as though they were just strolling through the nearby Saint Stephen's Green Park and about to take out those plastic bags, pull bread out of them, and throw bread crumbs to the pond ducks.

The Dublin Police were completely accustomed to gruesome violence, especially after experiencing a summer blighted by numerous city centre assaults. Though this scene was dreadful, one Garda told another it was small potatoes in comparison to what he saw awhile back on O'Connell Street that summer. There 15 men and women assaulted each other with Hurley sticks they'd grabbed from the passing Bally Og Under-14 Team.

"There was pools' o' blood all over the place," the Garda said. "And there were bloody discarded clothes there too, like something that you would see in an abattoir. The attackers were from the inner city...a rough group to find y'self in the middle of—unconscionable curs, so they were, with no rearing in them whatsoever, all dragged up on the streets. Pity no one ever grabbed them by the pin of their collar and gave them the fiercest clattering that you could imagine. A clout of a stick on their legs and back would make them think twice of inflicting that type of pain on somebody else."

"Sounds rough."

"Rough isn't the word for it. There was an innocent boy who was sticking his hands out trying to shield himself from this vicious attack and he got some almighty hits. There was nothing he could do against that."

"What kind of an image of Dublin does that tell the world?"

"Ah sure, I don't know. But who-that-matters gives a flyin' feck about crime in Ireland anyway? The whole place is goin' to wrack and ruin. There's not a thing to be done about it...just laugh, whilst people are left on the street, prepared like dead cattle, ribbed apart, almost like they were sent to the slaughterhouse. Sure, ye'd see more humanity between a butcher's knife and the livestock put before him."

"Ah! You would surely."

Did overhearing these things make the Dublin city centre more appealing to Lucis Diabolis? It did not. This was *not* the type of blood he was after—low and deprived of class. The blood flowing here was befouled with disorders and diseases one should not consume. Most of the living blood in the city centre was far from ideal for consumption. The blood wasted on the streets through violence was usually the most revolting blood one could possibly consume.

Walking through the blood-infested streets, the vampire enjoyed a smoke. The splendid cigarette chemicals made his insides feel less hollow. He felt as if he could actually have the heart, the soul, and the spirit he knew he'd once had. If the Devil, whom he saw glorified in the works of so many of his fellow citizens, was around, Lucis expected to meet him, or at least one of the dark minions who followed him.

He'd thought of that once. When they'd lived together, Alex Leman had talked about the Devil. Leman had said: "There is in our state of un-dead immortality no need to *follow* the Devil. There's plenty of Devil in the world already. All you have to do is look inside and let the Devil within you out. In Dublin today, the living go Salsa and Tango dancing with demons. Carte blanche is given for the Devil to do whatever he wants."

No, one did not have to be a 'lost soul,' eternally un-dead. Those hyperaware of their sixth sense, common and intellectual alike, could feel the darkness of the city, especially when the quilt of night covered her. There were no gun shops (luckily) in a capital renowned for its knifings alone.

Tragically, this abundant bloodletting was not releasing the type Lucis Diabolis craved the most. His older, part demonic, self never knew the meaning of mortal expiration. This side of him harboured the deep desire to gorge on blood and bleed victims dry. He resented being born of blood in the wrong time and place—*You can't beat the good old days when primitive civilizations had altars soaked in the blood of human sacrifices...like the Aztecs of South America.* There he'd have been an out-of-the-coffin vampire, free to roam the world and elated by how those civilizations allowed, in their thinking of the afterlife, room for carefully prepared libations fit for a vampire's palate. *One could live free, out of the coffin, and roam the earth unrestricted by the culture and western morals that forced my kind to go underground.*

*Alex Leman told me that the Devil inside guarantees that I don't have to worry about the Devil outside; for, within vampire nature, the Devil takes up residence once you bleed, kill, consume, and thus partake in the destruction of innocence. You carry out your malevolent duty, amassing sin upon sin, and are never apart from all-embracing darkness.*

The lost mortals of Dublin cultivated their Devil inside. Alex Leman had promised Lucis that the Devil would grow even more visible here, but to watch for his kind on the streets. *Proof?* The utter violence of Dublin was proof. This mania was 'limbic' because of the way certain drug highs acted on the brain, causing derangement of the neural system responsible for both appetite and impulse control. Such toxic activation commonly triggered war atrocities and homicides, and was also responsible for most of the violence in an amoral city awash with drugs.

# II

## Seduction

At last he reached the Bruxelles off Grafton. Diabolis materialized enough so that he could enter the establishment (where he would become the fullest possible version of himself), expecting this to be one of the best nights of his life.

To his dismay, the owners of the Bruxelles, having obviously no appreciation for those born of blood, were playing the most inappropriate song for his tastes. It was as if the proprietors, who catered to what *they* loved—everything rock and roll—did not know enough to welcome someone as refined as Diabolis. Nick Kershaw's "Don't let the sun go down on me…" assaulted the vampire's ears.

The sun was a bitch and a bane for Diabolis' kind, worse than any unfaithful lover. Thus, he could stomach Ireland where the sun was so fickle, and even befriend the island's doleful brand of humour. But to him artists in love with that incinerator in the sky were the equivalent of guardsmen for vampire death camps.

Alex Leman had warned him that the price of immortality was ironic. For vampires, mortal enemies of natural light, could never court it. A song glorifying the sun gave Lucis a rash, made his heart feel close to bursting, and threatened to turn his entire façade to slag. He could hardly breathe.

The situation reminded him of his reaction to the film, *Countess Dracula*. He could definitely relate to some of its direst content. The more Diabolis heard of that 'sol' music, the more he feared that, just like the Elizabeth Bathory character, his skin would age like old parchment and shrivel. The power of auto-suggestive words, especially when repeated in song, drove him to a frenzied state of terror. If he dared look, would he see a with-ered shell of a man inside the mirror above the bar? He sensed a conflagration from the outside in, brought on by those lyrics. Why, his skin and bones might evaporate at any second! He was sure his hair was already standing up and about to singe.

Alex's admonition about humanity had been blunt: "Feel only one emotion, hatred. Hating them makes it easier to feed on them. Suck them dry. Take everything they have, leaving them nothing but to live on *in you*." Taking his own advice to heart, Diabolis' maker had chosen to live in parts of the world where the death penalty had not yet been abolished, so that he could still execute people. Lucis had not seen him in years. Unwelcome visions haunted him, emerging on the screen of Diabolis' mind, of the Alex Leman he'd once thought witty and powerful. The more he studied his own face in his worst moments, the more it seemed to resemble Alex's own arrogant aspect.

Alex had admonished his protégé that those meant to be a special breed of vampire were fair of skin and hair. These Chosen must be preserved from their initiation for eternity. They are the true inheritors of the earth, who, before being made vampires, induced progress in the world for which they were responsible.

The ideal vampire was bred to hate, spewing it forth, in-different to anything or anyone. Indifference led to emotional independence, self-reliance, and ultimate survival. (Hadn't 'mak-ing a killing' become synonymous with acquiring wealth?) Once the right ones were killed, a healthy sum of money from what they left behind became accessible, and not a power in the world could stop a vampire from making it their own.

When Lucis Diabolis walked down into the basement, he could see red lights along the grimy walls and flickering in candle holders on tables. There were quiet corners for drinking and a lone satanic symbol, which he did not mind. A tall, thin man beside him, wearing a cap, told his friend what the symbol was and to include it in his research files for his forthcoming project. That mid-twenties gent nodded sagely in agreement.

Alex Leman had been interested in egotism, selfishness, and other hallmarks of spiritual darkness. But he did not ascribe this darkness to Satan alone, although it was in his domain. Alex did not care to "go too deeply into things," merely to acknowledge that darkness could live inside of you and "be all yours if you just let it".

Lucis Diabolis walked through the crowded, red-lit darkness. Heavy metal blared from televisions. Among patrons dressed like denizens of the innermost halls of Hell, he should have felt right at home. He leaned on a bar counter and ordered a pint of Stella Artois; having paid, he cradled the cool pint in his hands and stroked it, observing the three sections in the wonderfully curious establishment. Each catered to a different musical taste—whatever ear candy a client preferred to consume along with his or her liver poison.

Diabolis glimpsed himself in the bar mirror. He felt both grateful and unashamed when he saw that his face had changed. He'd grown more handsome, as if in his youthful prime of twenty or so. Long brown hair to his shoulders was held back in a neat pony tail, complementing keen blue eyes and a nice white shirt tucked into black trousers topped by an elegant black jacket—not at all how he'd looked before entering the pub. From the mirror's depths, the penetrating stare that he knew resembled Alex Leman's gazed out at him. This abnormality of his maker he immediately recognized as being responsible for the man's charismatic magnetism. They had seemed the eyes of a person who could help someone escape a desperate situation.

At the time of his own initiation into vampirism, Diabolis had thought that compliance with Alex's demands would let him emerge unscathed from his troubles. It was akin to the wave of hope washing over a crowd that idolises a leader who promises them a glorious future (in return for a generous payment). This peculiar sense of providence overcomes ordinary caution. Starved for security, they will sell their souls.

Sitting here taking his first sip of Stella Artois, Lucis Diabolis knew his new look was a total con. Alex Leman's *ideal* vampire was not how Alex Leman himself looked. His mortal eyes had been brown, his body puny, and his face lined and tan. How had Lucis Diabolis not discerned his hypocrisy?

It was great to feel the cool alcoholic beverage enter his body, but he could stop recalling his unpleasant origins and focus on just being here. And it did not take him long to realize that it was just him and his glass. Nobody else could relate to him. Dublin knew how to be a lonely place, especially if you were strange and trying not to be, and really struggling at the task. The alcohol started to relax him, though. He could understand fully why drinking was considered a relaxing and recreational activity. With each sip, Lucis Diabolis took in more of the weirdness around him. He reflected that this would certainly be the place to experience Halloween adequately.

Although the alcohol served was most agreeable, could he ever fit into the modern Irish pub life of people congregating in small numbers around tables to watch each other get drunk? They required no food to help absorb the alcohol, just pure, unadulterated poison, and—unlike their British counterparts—not a toast, let alone two, to the dead, the living, love, family, country or anything else, nothing that expressive or intimate. Sitting near them was like keeping company with dead souls interested only in the smallest grains of life. All they were doing in the name of passing time with one another was sifting to see if one of those grains could be different.

A lady sat near Diabolis. He took a good look at her. She looked promising. He even thought for a second, *Could she be like me?*

*No, she could not.* Enshrined in the constitution of his thought processes was the dogmatic belief that, since Leman had departed these shores, he was the only one of his kind in Ireland. Surviving in this isolationist way had forced him (using all the constituencies of his mind) to overcome what he considered the most painful emotion of them all: loneliness.

The splendid woman near him, of five-feet and seven inches, was a visual delight. Her cloud of hair was as black as night, her skin white as powder. Her eyes were a deep, mysterious blue. His infatuation for her grew. Yet, he also discerned the depression most could not, another faculty granted him as a vampire. He knew hers to be like an endless winter. Nothing grows in winter; everything ages and dies off. Life's joy cannot enter this melancholy domain. He knew this instinctively, and hated seeing the shadow that hung over this girl.

The negativity she was spewing to her male friend made Diabolis queasy. This girl of twenty five had tired of life. She thought the whole thing a misery. Her friends who joined her for a beer seemed to love the jars of depression they were drinking from.

Diabolis wanted more than her blood. At first, he'd only wanted to seduce her, with one goal in mind: Could he achieve intercourse once he succeeded in seducing her? The raw side of his mind told him that, if he could adequately romp her, all the depressive energy within her would evaporate and shake off her fixation on the dark nonsense around her.

"Deborah," began her friend Christopher, an acne-infested twenty-something of five-five or so, who looked like he was there to agree with everything she said and remind her that she was not alone in the world. "So you're starting to go to Dublin Business School on Aungeir Street? How's that working out for you?"

Christopher, whose face might any second erupt (its natural pallor due to an almost vampiric aversion to sun) asked this question in a way that insisted he was half asleep and hoping that the person listening would be too. Despite his scholar's spectacles, he was a boring runt who pretended to have more than sex on his mind.

"Yes," she replied to his mundane question as if she'd woken from her coffin but was still groggy.

"And what do you study?" Christopher asked, trying to hide that he had no interest in her answer.

"Psychoanalysis," she said, adding pretentiously, "...psychoanalytical anthropology with an evolutionary neuropsychoanalytical emphasis." She replied like this to get a reaction out of the loser with whom she chose to go for drinks with routinely due to her low self-esteem.

"And do you get to study about sex?" he asked archly.

"Yes, as matter of fact," she continued, "we get to study a lot about sex."

When she said 'sex' Christopher's tongue nearly fell out of his mouth and straight onto her lap. Assuredly, he'd already made a tent below.

"Yes, I thought it'd be more about the mind, but these psychoanalysts are mad into their sex. I like it, though, because so much of what's said shows off the futility of life. A leading psychiatrist, Lacan, is taught a lot where I go. I'm sure his madness helped him to professionally develop just like the rest of them. Madness is a prerequisite for psychoanalysts. Lacan was in love with the French word for orgasm: *Le Petit Mort*, the small death. And he believes there's no such thing as sexual union, just a hysterical act."

Lucis Diabolis, who knew Lacan for reasons other than mundane university attendance, thought what nonsense she was into at university—the writings of a demented and dead imbecile, who'd spent too much of his natural life hanging around the mentally ill and the criminally insane. Diabolis had, when he got bored, broken into libraries and read authors in various disciplines. He was most fascinated with what mortals made of the mystery that was the human mind, a faculty he rarely saw any of them properly use.

"You have it wrong," Lucis Diabolis interrupted, as if invited into the conversation. (In this case invitation did not matter. He felt compelled to intervene.) "There is no death in orgasm."

When he said these words to this young beauty, he could see the blood pumping in her neck. Christopher, her company for the night, decided to intervene and remind him of his position here. "Sorry, but we *weren't* talking to you," he growled, sure that the interrupter would see how stupid he was, succumb to nervous embarrassment, and shove off.

Lucis Diabolis eyed Christopher as if this sorry excuse of a man would be bent out of shape like a twig in his hands in any fight.

"No, let him continue," said Deborah, and gestured as if she wanted Christopher out of her sight. To distract him, she motioned toward the busy bar and told him, "Please order three beers."

"*Three?*" Christopher said, his voice cracking in surprise.

"Yes. I'm thirsty." Once she said this he felt dislodged from his position of exclusive conversations with her on this night. He took a twenty out of his pocket and strutted stiffly to the bar, expecting that when he returned there'd be no more interruptions, just pure conversation between them.

"There is no small death in orgasm. That is totally incorrect," Diabolis said. "There is a window of opportunity. It is the one deposit of life mortals have, which they should cherish and hold onto before it's too late. We are always reminded of how this cannot be a small death once it is too late. For when *real* death has visited us, it becomes all too apparent." Lucis Diabolis here betrayed a gothic like sorrow.

The marvellous creature turned toward him. He was speaking her language, and this, for her, was the language of love, hypnotizing sultry love, the type that binds, and where she ever so easily could envision making love to him. She hoped he could feel her sexual energy flowing like a river at its most powerful stage. When not in depression, she loved to romp...endlessly, frequently, promiscuously, experimentally, and as urgently as if her life depended on it. Not to romp was to cut off the one precious tether holding her life force.

Unlike Christopher, Lucis Diabolis' face did not blush at the mention of human intimacy. Deborah was finally roused from the depths of depression, where she had languished so long. A bell rang in her brain to ring out her renewed interest in love. Alienating chemicals stopped drowning her natural instincts. Those morose initiators of clinical disorder had been ferociously raging without opposition like a flood down the Grand Canyon. Now they ceased, leaving her free to embrace life through the elated chemicals within her erogenous zones. She would demand to be taken, over and over again.

Erotic cascades counteracted the cataracts of negative disorder. When she saw Christopher returning with their drinks, it finally dawned on her what a pathetic, scrawny loser she'd been wasting time with. This was a signal to her of her depression. *What do I want with this puny runt, whose penis could not grow more than the size of my little finger?* She knew this from the times on the bus she'd bumped against it. She was acutely aware that what was in the vicinity of his trousers was no help to her depression.

Christopher set the drinks down on the table, but she remained turned away from him and continued listening to Lucis, who had far more interesting things to say than Christopher ever could. She responded to him, eye-to-eye, and Lucis felt every erotic tension that he had in his mortal days returning.

Christopher's blazing forehead signalled a rage that grew in his insides as he watched the woman with whom, for the past year, he'd wanted to have intercourse. She was rubbing against a stranger's leg. Christopher, a shy human specimen, was, in spite of his inhibitions and poor seductive techniques, still capable of knowing when a girl was interested in a man, and when she simply was not. He'd spent a long time observing Deborah and never knew her to be much interested in anyone. He'd believed that if he just hung around her like a fly would on filth, he would grow on her. The two would then, by default, become an item.

His pupils were dilating in anger and his frustrated pout grew. Christopher looked at Lucis as if he wanted to disembowel him. It amused Lucis to see the aggression written all over Christopher's face. And knowing that Christopher had no ability to back up this expression made it even more delightful. Yet, there was one more absolutely exquisite thing he could do to really make skin burn and eyes bulge. Lucis felt the strength that a young man must feel to carry out this elating element right in front of Christopher.

*Yes*, Lucis thought, and he could feel her entire body amassing sexual energy. Christopher had obviously expected to be The One who'd help Deborah's suppressed sexuality emerge. But he'd failed miserably. He could easily confirm this by the fact that with a single, brief conversation, a total stranger had aroused Deborah. How ghastly this would be for Christopher.

"I like to study sexuality," she told the weird, handsome stranger, leaning closer to him. Then she stroked his crotch and whispered, "But, I also feel that *practical* experience is very important. Try this," she said, popping a tablet into his mouth and offering him the pint of beer in her hands.

Blood-thirst coincided with sexual drive. He wanted to conquer this woman, enter her completely, *and* tap her veins like a feeding, hungry newborn. He would couple with her—but not here or now—for haste would not bring him release. It was better to do this totally in private. The vampire still belonged to that age where one should never be open with their sexuality, unlike modern folk, who think nothing of being lewd in public.

He lifted her hands from his lap and kissed them. What would happen next? (After all, what else could he say, "My tomb or yours?") Diabolis sipped the beer, hoping she would not go on about psychoanalysis, sexuality, or anything else of that ilk. For what he'd said about orgasm was all he wished to say. There was nothing more he wished to impart to her on this issue, erudite or not.

The splendid gothic creature could not keep her eyes off the vampire. He was totally unique in comparison to every other guy she'd been or ever wanted to be with. He seemed the epitome of anything romantic she read in the books she bought, not to mention the erotic art she wished she could draw to match those sizzling words.

Deborah was in love with the idea of defying the conventions society imposed on people her age—that they needed to study hard in a field suiting the needs of the job market. This was precisely something she was not doing. Within her was a rebellious spirit with no probable cause save the youthful discontent that makes young mortals naturally erratic and dangerously adventurous. Venturing too far into the arts, humanities, and various philosophies (which guaranteed that one would develop a mind able to operate analytically and think deeply and broadly), was strongly discouraged when it did not guarantee gainful employment.

Looking at Lucis Diabolis made her want to fall into his arms, let his hot response fuse her creativity and sexuality, and, in so doing, finally feel complete.

She assumed his thinking aligned with hers, but he was actually wondering about her blood line. He recognized that she was of good, educated stock and reared in relatively affluent surroundings. This told him that she would have good enough blood for him. It assuaged his fear that the tainted blood he had so impulsively consumed on Byrnes Lane and under Dame Street Archway would ultimately ruin him.

# III

## Arousal

Lucis Diabolis felt his lust rising. Before, hunger for dead life and curiosity about the walking dead of the city had misled him. What had replaced those was an arousal that would not let him rest safely in his tomb despite the approach of day.

Deborah was agreeable. She'd send her male company on another errand and use the occasion of his departure to leave with Diabolis. *Yes, I'll ask Christopher to buy an extra pint…one of the loneliest pints he'll ever purchase. What a hilariously naughty way to make this a truly memorable night for him!* So, the Goth Girl told the student who thought he was master of her heart and the answer to her psychological problems to buy two Heinekens, assuring him it was for the two of them.

Christopher, not even pretending to be civil, didn't think to inquire, "And will our guest be joining us in further libations?" He marched to the counter and awaited his turn to be served, his back to Deborah and Diabolis, his mind on those two pints as his hand reached into his pocket for payment.

Pints in hand, Christopher contemplated how he'd go about seizing the night from the man who'd interrupted it. This wasn't the first time he'd been out with Deborah in the hope of taking their platonic relationship to the next level. Tonight he'd rescue her, not let her be seduced by the stranger's charms.

Assuming he knew Deborah well, Christopher had created a mental myth about her: She was relatively and, perhaps abnormally, disinterested in sex. She was not representative of the youthful masses, and, therefore, not free or cheap or easy (the cultural straightjacket represented in the music and discourse of the modern age). She needed to be aesthetically courted for months prior to a serious relationship. She was very intellectual, craving the fruits of human knowledge. Her depression was caused by her high-strung, civilized character, which was totally out of sync with the reality around her.

Was *any* of this true of Deborah? The answer was unknown by the person who'd created this analysis. Christopher considered it his duty to protect the romantic purity of Deborah from this charismatic stranger. The stranger's mind control could mesmerize a woman who had little control over her own actions. This was the fantasy to which Christopher clung. His date was uni-dimensional, without ambivalent feelings, emotions, or a rounded character. Clutching the two glasses of beer in his hands, he turned around expecting to see Deborah and his rival. But, to his surprise and disgruntlement, she was not there and neither was the stranger!

Lucis Diabolis, Deborah's hand in his, walked with her to Saint Stephen's Green. He stared into her eyes. Deborah was catapulted into blissful sexual surrender. Her eyes consented to him, as did her body. He held her waist, drew her close, and kissed her lips softly, as if making love to a woman for the first time. Diabolis saw in her eyes that her depression had been overwhelmed by her appetite. He well understood that this urgency was not about food but could kill your spirit if you did not satiate it.

Around him he observed the lost men roaming Dublin's streets, denied gratification, breaking the glass of telephone booths, smashing bottles, and viciously assaulting one another, having no other outlet but violence. Their female counterparts were to be found curled up drunk and crying to a friend, or wrecking their young lives in far worse ways.

Deborah welcomed her hunger. Before her was an outlet and relief from the stirrings of excitement first revealed in her pubescence. She felt again the exquisite torment of utter insatiability. The first time she'd actually dared to see the logical conclusion of her desires through had been as an awkward thirteen-year-old. Her libido, once ignited, cried out to be released, again and again, ad infinitum.

Diabolis, who knew the inner workings of mortals, was aware of her intense craving and understood the urgent need for that satiation matched by his own. Vampirism was a kindred state. To be without want and need meant extinction. It drove him to feed and kept him alive beyond his allotted span. Without it, the break from immortality was imminent.

Deborah suspected that depression was the other side of this coin. She felt the dice had already been loaded for her at age eleven; her puberty had been of the most awkward type. Like so many of her generation, her episodic depression was a reaction to an outer world and an inner nature beyond her control. To her, the only thing worse than sexual precocity would have been a delayed puberty. She experienced herself as more sexual than most, and gratification a mysterious subterranean labyrinth she had not yet fully explored. Tonight it was time for *sexploration*. Depression had kept her sexuality dormant, revealing it only in dreams—a sleeping beast inside her that grumbled, its claws scraping, not knowing how to escape. This suppression drained her energies.

The girl Christopher knew—entranced by decadent, depressive art and music, and cynically oriented towards bleakness—was not the one in front of Lucis Diabolis. Her sexuality and capacity for sexual attraction was finally awake. The former girl was the prototype, the carbon copy of a girl Christopher imagined. This was precisely why she could never fall for him. Christopher had typecast her. Lucis did not.

Lucis had overthrown his own humanity. Any typecasting that might have existed in his mind of a person was obsolete. Human beings were a mystery he wished to explore in terms of the life-giving river which flowed within them.

Deborah knew that this stranger could have all of her, and repeatedly at that.

Lucis Diabolis kissed her on the left cheek. "Let's walk for a while," he said in a commanding voice, "and when you get tired you are not to worry yourself, for I have a driver on standby."

She was putty in his hands. Her heart throbbed with anticipation. Yes, a walk would quieten her and help her collect herself. "You have a driver?"

"Well, most certainly."

"Most certainly," she repeated, as if she could not quite believe it.

The two strolled the periphery of Saint Stephen's Green Park, enjoying what Diabolis remembered as one of the more aristocratic parts of Old Dublin. Holding the hand of the splendid, young creature in his, he pictured her clad as a lady of two hundred years ago. Females had dressed less overtly, yet, to him, more sensually and seductively, the secrets under their gowns left to the imagination.

Buildings surrounding the Green replicated the old Georgian style, reminding Diabolis of his glorious past. *Oh, to relive that era in this very neighbourhood as a vampire, roaming Dublin ravenous as a werewolf, cunning as a fox, but as wisely selective as an owl!* Being in the vicinity of the best quality blood source for those times, he could have existed as a contented immortal.

Unfortunately, for Diabolis, the only thing that truly stayed the same was change. St. Stephen's Green had been surrounded by walls when he was a child. To his grave distress, those boundaries of the park had since been replaced in a way that insulted his senses. This alone reminded him that his will couldn't overcome reality.

The couple paused for a moment beside The Fusiliers' Arch, built in 1907 as a dedication to the officers commissioned by The Royal Fusiliers of Dublin who fought and died in The Second Boer War of 1899-1900. Diabolis and Deborah kissed passionately beside the granite construction inspired by the best ancient source of them all—The Arch of Titus built in old Rome. His mind was seduced into thinking that he had returned to old Dublin. The Goth Girl's blood, he fantasized, was potentially going to provide an oasis in the deep desert of his need. Satisfaction was waiting within her veins.

*Deborah's blood must truly be derived from an aristocratic source.* Maybe it was the clever books she read, or how she spoke so beautifully about the art housed in the National Gallery (which he'd never cared for until he heard her lips articulate their history—who had painted them and in what style and in what texture and in what era and spirit).

To Deborah, his touch on her throat felt as soft as a feather. He was so calm, looked so tender and dear to her, that she knew he meant her no harm. Holding Diabolis felt akin to cradling a robin (in contrast to the type of bird his maker deemed him—neither sweet nor tiny, but more like one of the Eurasian Griffon Vultures that scavenge carcasses of dead animals on Africa's plains).

Diabolis' tongue met hers, and he thought: *She is certainly the one.* Behind her cold exterior was a hot-blooded creature full of the noble nutrition his nature needed. He did not bite down on her lips or tongue, not yet. He wanted to optimize her erogenous experience. It would be vulgar to do otherwise. Diabolis knew how to attain his goal with finesse, unlike moderns' artless seductions, going off with all guns blazing as if two people melding could never be anything more than submission to instant gratification.

97

His back to the archway, the vampire noticed Christopher eyeing him as if he'd like to rip his face off. Diabolis remained quiet, watching Christopher standing outside the Saint Stephen's Green Shopping Centre.

Christopher mistook his rival's posture for weakness, sure that he'd easily win Deborah back.

Diabolis wished this Reek gone. Christopher stayed put. Diabolis smiled at this wimp whose ego fed off someone in a vulnerable psychological state. Diabolis knew how to control the situation without saying a word. He moved his mouth away from Deborah's and held her head to his chest so that she could not see her intrusive and annoying friend.

The vampire turned his eyes to the trees and the birds resting there. He awoke and evoked the right type of emotion in these birds who had been in deep slumber. Panicked and aggressive, the birds looked at Lucis Diabolis, who pointed his finger at Christopher. Five pigeons left the tree where they had settled for the night.

Christopher, about to cross the street to intercept the couple, saw Diabolis escorting Deborah towards the Shelbourne Hotel. But then his attention shifted to the birds. Another bevy joined the pigeons and the group then descended on Christopher, pecked him, and soiled his hair, jacket, and trousers.

Diabolis glanced behind and grinned with satisfaction. The way Christopher now smelled and looked defeated him. The bleeding wound on his pimply cheek and the chalky excrement all over him left him simply unfit to go anywhere near Deborah.

Regret for a love thwarted overcame Christopher. He finally realised he had deviated from logic toward the foolish folly of unconsummated, one-sided love. Christopher raised his fists to the sky and screamed in outraged frustration. But a passing bus drowned his thin cries and splashed his shoes and socks with muddy water.

"Where to now?" Tired of hanging out, Deborah felt ready for the next stage.

"What would you like to do?" Lucis responded, as if he had no idea what she was about.

"Oh, I think you know," she said with a wink.

*Could she possibly be so attuned?*

"Yes," she said, circling and sizing him up with an appraising eye, "I've seen how you look at me."

"My kind—" he began.

"Yes, the kind who look at you as if they could swallow you whole. I should have known what my cure was all along".

"Cure?" he said curiously. "What else do you know? What other things are you interested in?"

"Well, if you look at me you'll probably guess."

"What if I'm curious to know what makes you tick and wish exceedingly to find out more?"

"Then you'd have to come into *my* world." That made his icy skin burn. "But I'd have to *invite* you in, wouldn't I?" she said.

Suspense climbed. The summit where she resided remained distant. "The question is, will I let you in? Will I? Will I invite you into my space, to where I rest and belong?"

Why was she talking as if, although *she* was not one of them, she knew the undead very well? If she was aware of his kind, it would be awkward. He thought he knew enough about his own to identify them readily.

Her manner of speaking was disquieting. Had he done something to give himself away? Who could accept the truth of who he was? He very definitely wanted to be the only one of his kind to live in this neck of the woods. Yet…she was so very seductive. For a vampire what could be more perfect than a reclusive, morbid, negatively depressive *gothess*? What could be more wonderfully ideal for him…unless, of course, her secret was that she knew others of his kind? This would not do

99

at all. Could he stand not being so unique? *I must find out, once and for all.*

"Would you like to spend the night with me?"

"Yes," she said.

"But I feel *you* may have the more suitable accommodation."

"I might…"

"I'll give my driver a ring."

"I don't often do this."

"I can tell," he replied.

"A woman must be selective about who she lets in."

# IV

## Completion

Lucis Diabolis sat back in his limousine with his arm around Deborah. He had ordered his driver to go in the direction the girl indicated, which turned out to be only a stone's throw away from his own cemetery digs. *How odd, he thought, that I did not even know she was my neighbour all this time.*

He kept thinking how absurd his notion was that she might be a blood drinker too. Unless she had been supernaturally inducted into vampirism, she could not possibly live as he did without developing some blood-borne disease, heart or liver failure (mostly through hemochromatosis), cancer, or all of these. Alex Leman had trained him to distinguish between an actual vampire and a mortal simply in love with the idea of being one.

*The consumption of blood overloads a mortal's fragile systems with iron. Blood is not the same to a mortal as to an immortal, nor can a mortal ever know how delectable blood is as it improves in quality, the blood of the nobility being the rarest life-source on earth. The true vampire who possesses and understands his powers has total immunity from the high level of iron in blood. Feeding on quality blood is a ticket to eternity; the richer the blood, the more vital it is to seize and hold onto it.*

For a vampire, the place where Deborah lived, although not a tomb, was exquisite. Lucis appreciated the attention put into it to provide adequate 'living conditions' for one of the un-dead. "Splendid," he announced, after looking around, "most spending indeed."

Delightfully, there were no dreaded windows, those whores of natural light, letting the sun's vampire- burning essence in. As for a front door, this was also denied in favour of a blank brick wall.

Deborah was a temptress, an arch seducer, a gothic creature, who lived by the type of art portrayed in the published myths that she had grown up with and learned to love. *Why*, he wondered, *have I not come across this siren before?* He could tell that she did not suffer from the misunderstandings and objections of mainstream, conventional young women.

"I," Deborah announced (as if she could read his thoughts), "despise convention and 'looking on the bright side'. Having always been drawn to darkness, I do not believe in the benefits of light and do my utmost to avoid it, leaving the house only when it is dark, unless for studies. Then I always wear sunglasses to keep the light from burning my eyes."

Lucis, whose name meant *light*, had not given it up willingly. He was compelled to avoid it in favour of the darkness she embraced darkness from desire. He had accepted his situation, until technology enabled him to watch movies and television programs which featured daylight through the eye of the camera lens. At first cinematography had made no impression on him. But the dreams inspired by it left him longing for daylight and the natural world seen then.

The vampire had not reached a long life in mortality and so was now amassing, not by voluntary omission but necessity, a lifetime of memories which owed themselves to *night*. He had thought she might empathise and understand his darkness. She could not, and did not appreciate that what she wanted was not desirable. He knew from a lifetime of this dreary, isolated, alien life that being a creature of darkness sets one apart from everyone else in a very bad way. He could not bring himself to tell her how being thus was not so wonderful. She was more in love with darkness than any creature he had ever met. And she liked him. If he told her the awful truth, he would create friction. The goal here was union without friction, and complete consummation.

Her 'garden' was weeds. The exterior of the house and its grounds proclaimed it a monument to darkness. He could not ask for more, although he might have preferred acceptance by someone who was beautiful, yet conventional and normal.

"Shall we open this bottle of champagne inside?" she asked, taking his hand.

"Yes," he replied gratefully, his hand closing around hers.

A sensation filled his body, as if a draught of her blood, drunk straight then and there, had revived him. The mechanics of this process would end shortly. He had been officially invited into her lair, although this was not required for him to enter any dwelling. If one is hungry one will eat just about anything, anywhere. If one's blood is running low, as was Lucis', then convention-be-damned! But it was more pleasant to the senses to consume after being asked inside. When one is invited in for dinner, its flavour can be savoured, unlike the situation where one has to steal inside for a meal.

She escorted him to the rear of the house via a brick walkway. Again, there were no doors here; he was perplexed. *Is this place hers, and is there a way to enter this house like any normal house?*

Deborah walked up to the back wall of her house, where, on the ground, there was a large steel lid. She pulled on a metal ring to release the lid and said, "I like to live underground… where I will be when I die."

Inside, diabolic symbols and drawings covered the walls, which were painted red. The ceiling was black. "I've never been to hell," she said, squeezing his hand. Diabolis thought, *neither have I. This earth is my hell.* "But it must be more fun than the other place where one is required to be ethical and noble. Though, I must admit, I do pay my taxes, go to work, and because it is uncouth and for the ignorant, seldom curse. Nor have I hurt anyone out of spite. I've just never felt a need for The Light. People shun me, but darkness nurtures me.

"We both know you are not here for champagne. I know what you want. Past experience has shown me that it is better to let the tension build. Once you increase tension, the release is amazing."

"How very observant and erudite of you," he said, "but waiting is usually only an exercise in futility. When I want something, I simply take it."

Diabolis' body was prepared for her…almost. He adhered to the tenets of Emile Coues' teachings on the mind and his self-improvement maxims: *Everything the mind perceives it will achieve, because, every day in every possible way I am getting better and better.* Just as the emerging male adolescent who is intelligent and cultivated must learn phallic control, Diabolis exercised control of his fangs and the urge to drain her dry.

Deborah escorted him to her bed. "I can render you real satisfaction in this experience, if you let me."

"Within reason," he responded, believing that she was about to do something peculiar to the 'fifty shades' series, or alternative sexuality involving domination and submission. He was simply not interested in helping her worship at the altar of de Sade. "I only wish to feel who I truly am and wish to be."

"Wait here," she said, "do not budge." She smiled at Diabolis, but all he did was nod without smiling.

After centuries of exsanguinations, it would not do to act shy and retiring. He watched her walk into her bathroom to prepare herself exactly as her mind wished for her to be visually presented to him. This was important to her sense of identity and hyper-sexuality—the maintenance and lively gratifying of it.

She wanted to smell like a flower in full bloom, and to accentuate her most agreeably attractive parts. "Undress and lie back," she called. When he said nothing, her next order was: "Let me be your fantasy."

She powdered her face, and blackened her eyelashes to flatter her ashen skin. "Be patient, my love," she said, anticipating the passion awakened by overanxious waiting.

*Not only is patience a virtue, but most rewarding when its goal is delivered*, she thought, admiring her attributes. She saw exquisite results: a black-leather bra highlighted her bosom and leather cupped her bottom; red tights came just over each knee; perfectly dressed for the occasion, her present gaiety defeated every ounce of her former misery. She emerged from the bathroom, smiled to expose her perfect teeth, and decided to wax poetic. "I am a thousand blooming flowers."

Lucis Diabolis did not know how to respond. "You look…" He could not finish, for it was tragic to state the truth: beauty like Deborah's does not last.

"I embody the spirit of the swan, which, all its life, is silent. When swans reach their end, they know, and sing the only song that they will ever sing in their entire life. Theirs is the most beautiful song of any bird."

This was so touching that, if Diabolis' eyes could have shed salty mortal tears, they would have. *Will she sing the most beautiful song I've ever heard before I take her young life?*

While he struggled with what to do next, she approached him, held his strong body to her, and kissed it. She kissed his body like no woman had before—his stomach, arms, back, legs, genitals, and face. Then she invited him to kiss her.

His mouth tingled, warning him he could not have normal intercourse, so he opted for a more dexterous approach. Amazingly, his mouth still looked normal. But, when he looked at the ceiling, he noticed something—revealed to him but not yet to her. She was aware of the mirror on her bedroom ceiling, but not the other thing going on in the mirror. The more she made love to Lucis—whether it was the soulfulness or the intimacy of it (this touching the core of the human being as one of the highest forms of ecstasy)—the less he saw of his own reflection. Her actions were depleting him—making less, not more of him.

Maybe she did not see what he saw. But *he* certainly saw it. He watched his bestial, more supernatural nature unfold, especially as he entered the mouth of her womb. She was too invested in her own pleasure to notice this, since her eyes remained closed, as he strove for completion.

But, "More" she demanded, "more!" What she was sure she required was draining her body of the depressive toxins wired from her brain. She craved orgasm the way a junkie craves hits, an alcoholic craves to be locked in a brewery, and a gambler craves piles of money to wager.

When she discovered that he had superhuman strength, she cried, "This is amazing! I feel *so* good."

He lay atop her as her eyelids fluttered, and in the mirror he noticed that his supernatural appearance had subsided. His fangs had submerged, his eyes had stopped glowing, and the whites had lost their crimson pigmentation. His hair had given up its spun-glass texture. He was relieved that he looked normal again.

In this age of anti-depressives, anxiolytics, anti-elation tablets, and all those other legal, mental health drugs, Lucis Diabolis' body was the drug of choice. Yes! She would be his nymph and do anything he wished her to do. She was his playmate to handle however he wished. She would not object at all. If she saw him in his more supernatural manifestations it would actually want make her want him more! His body would be her psychiatric treatment. It would fortify her against the demons of psychological lows. No one could deny her need for the supernatural stranger who had come to her on this night.

Then his true nature emerged, and most viciously. In response to her arousal Lucis Diabolis grabbed her mane of gorgeous white-blond hair, pulled it back, and sank his fangs into her throat.

"Yes," she said then, "yes, I know who you are and exactly *what* you are!"

"What am I then?" he said, interrupted in his feeding frenzy.

"You are the handsome and bestial 'Vrykolakas' I've longed all my life to meet. Feed on me. I desire you to do so. I've always wanted it. I love it, even if it is perverted and abnormal."

As he gorged on her neck like a ravenous lion she screamed, "But make sure you turn me!"

He was not sure that he could. Her blood was delicious, almost like the blood of those bygone landed gentry who had plenty of wealth and not a clue what to do with it. It was probably only ninety-five percent noble, but nice enough. And, although she was an exquisite playmate, she made a far better meal.

There was the question of turning her. He had never wanted any of his kind to share the streets of Dublin. It would degrade his status to be less than unique. He deserved to be the Blood King. He drank her almost dry, and it was a most beneficial feed. He felt it doing his system so much good, cleansing and ridding his body, like a miracle medicine, of the tainted blood he had recently consumed.

And, as Deborah grew limp before passing into that place called death, he realized that she reminded him of someone he once knew. The resemblance was so uncanny, it shook his senses. It reminded him that he had a mindset, almost fully aborted, but enough to connect him, no matter how tenuously, to his human nature.

If he was to make a vampire he would have to move quickly. But did he really want to do something he had never done before? He sensed her breathing and her wish, and knew from decades of doing this that she was about to be rendered speechless before she could beg in words he knew all too well, "Make me one of you. I've always dreamed of being just like you."

If her life was a quill on paper, it would barely have gotten the last word on the page before the ink ran dry. An icy tear of blood, so out of place on the face of Lucis Diabolis, dropped from his eye.

That Deborah looked exactly like Monica Westard to him frightened him. He could not let her die; she was too precious to him. Her alikeness before him, he could not condemn her to rot. But was it any better to condemn her to a life with blood as the staple of a most antisocial, antihuman diet, and make her an outcast?

Time was pressing like a grinding axe against his head. His head was bursting with the ache of having to make a decision as she lay near death. *If my head bursts, will all the blood I've consumed gush from me?*

Diabolis always looked diabolical when anxious. But his appearance changed completely to that of an ancient. He had lost the youthful essence he'd had when he first arrived. His nails were now claws. He walked over to the mirror while she lay near death. The stress had really gotten to him. Stress ages one. He was horrified at what he saw: a Methuselah with falling hair and opaque eyes; while most of his hair had gone from the top of his head, the rest grew wildly from the back. Instead of being a tall, well-built man, he'd become the complete opposite. His spine was twisted. Doubled over, he hobbled like an elderly mortal, and it disgusted him. *Better to let her die and not give in to her dying wish than to let her become a monstrous creature.*

But selfishness persuaded him. He did not want to be alone. He walked back to her in the laboured way of an old, crippled man. She was so young, nubile, and fresh, her body still fragrant from feminine arousal.

His existence hinged solely on the attainment of pleasure and the elimination of the tension that is pleasure funnelled out of one's own system. He had to keep her. He knew this now. He had never looked so unmasculine. What a contrast! How could this ruin he had become be the same man who had just pleasured her? Having left her body bereft of its flowing rivers of blood, he could not assent to her death.

His body aching with arthritic sensations, he took hold of her mouth and said in a quiet, choked voice, "Open your mouth." When she obeyed him like a lamb does a shepherd, "Drink," he ordered, "drink," and she did so, as if it were the first drink she'd had all night.

He would be destroyed if he could not turn her. What is the title of a vampire who can't make another vampire? Eunuch! So what if he was sure that he was the only one of his kind in Ireland? As a vampire he'd had enough decades to get used to it. Loneliness was a companion, a way of reminding him that he stood apart. He did not want to initiate anyone into vampirism, but tonight he had no choice. This would be his what? *First born* was hardly the right term, but it did not matter to him. Her survival was all that mattered.

He rose from the bed. He could not go anywhere, since it was already daylight. Besides feeling perturbed, the only thing he could do was stay here. There was no sign of life in her. Not only was he the strongest, most powerful, and only vampire in Ireland, he was flawed. He wanted to vomit at the realisation.

So he stood in this blessed, daylight-proof home. The floor was barren of carpet and absent of nonessential furniture, the interior designed as if she'd attended classes on the minimalist style. The recently deceased occupant had decided that it was good to leave out excess furniture in favour of more space. Space was of premium value to her. It presented a less cluttered view of the world. She valued space because her neurotic mother was an obsessive-compulsive, whose hoarding had deprived her of space. Hence, her aim on entering her teen years had been to work hard and move out, to a place where she could at last indulge in her lust for space.

The screaming started inside the abyss that passed for a soul in Diabolis.

Everyone would have laughed at the vampire knowing this. But, not everyone is born with a silver spoon. Lucis wanted to hold onto the silver spoon he had been born with. But his felt like it was rusted, falling apart, and actually aging from the rust. He wanted to do more than just bury his decayed masculine essence in some young feminine creature, though no doubt that could offer some relief.

He'd once wanted to be a wild stud, sowing his seed without care, like an American slave owner who fathered children indiscriminately with slave women, or the Latin lover who impregnated enough women to fill a village. He'd wanted to procreate senselessly with impressionable, vulnerable, poor women without authority or status. When the going was good this lust monster made any woman an object of desire and open to the moves that he put on her. Not a care went into preventing impregnation. Children would be born and thrown to hellholes of orphanages, reared in odious conditions, or simply destroyed by the hands of some back street abortionist. He did not care if his own seed ended up in some shrine of abuse, which was another term for an Irish, state-sanctioned refuge for the unwanted and misbegotten.

Lucis Diabolis, before Mona, was no stranger to brothels. Buried under anonymous sheets, he did not care if he made a baby with someone whose name he'd rarely remember or even asked during the conception, unless knowing it would speed the seduction. This age thinks it has a monopoly on hasty, thoughtless sex. But such has always been the case, and Lucis knew how to bed and take the ladies where he wanted them to go.

# V

## Betrayal

Diabolis' situation was a deterrent to sleep. He could have treated his head like a rock and bounced it against the walls, the floor, the ceiling, or rolled his eyes out of their sockets with anger, or wrenched his hair out—especially since it had started painfully pricking his scalp. Self-destructive as these actions would have been, he knew he could end his misery more quickly by simply going outside. But the photo-toxicity to which the vampire condition is heir was not an escape, merely an end from which there'd be no awakening. Vampires were one of the few creatures that could be buried underground and still survive; to expose themselves to the light of day was lethal, a court of law which judged their actions harshly enough to merit damnation.

Was the suicidal urge growing within him? It was, indeed, like the only truly booming industry in Ireland: killing. Why should a horror of self-destruction stop a vampire from acting on his own negative ideations?

Diabolis yet lived because he had one hope. Tenuous at best, this hope was what all scientific research rests its investigative work on: the hypothesis. His was based upon a guess that noble blood would save him. There was, however, no certainty that the procurement of pure noble blood would achieve his intended goal of replenishing him enough to make another vampire.

The vampire condition Leman had shared with him was bound to have always been there in the history of the world, but how and why was a mystery. Perhaps Leman had intentionally made Diabolis an impotent vampire. Or, maybe Diabolis' impotent mortal DNA continued into his vampire existence.

*Is there no exact way in this scientific age to find this out why I have vampire impotency? Mortals go to V.D. clinics to discover if they have diseases: H.I.V.-A.I.D.S., syphilis, and so on. Except, mine is not a disease, but a condition. How does a vampire discern if his mortal DNA was corrupted and corrupted his immortality?*

His mind danced around the problem with the use of invented theories as he gently picked up Deborah's corpse. In his head sensual jazz played. He'd first heard that type of music in the early 1900s (while sucking the life out of Irishmen whose rivers of blood from drunken brawls delighted him as he pounced). The sound was so erotic to his ears that he felt it could help infuse her cold corpse with supernatural life.

He started to dance with the corpse. Though this was hilarious to see, it was one swan song he personally enjoyed. Instead of going to his rest, he spent the whole day treating Deborah as though she were alive. He sat her down and spoke to her about his entire life and the responsibilities involved in being a vampire.

"Most of all," he announced, "the night life isn't what gets you down. You catch the drift after awhile; you must only work and be at night, and live by day in cool, dark places just like this room you've so nicely arranged to bar daylight. But a solitary existence can hurt you. At first it seems fine, when you're a young vampire, only a few years into this draining game. You think this whole business frees you from everyone else."

Deborah looked mesmerized by his conversation. He perceived that her mind was totally absorbed in every part of a word, never mind whole words, and was excited by this delusion.

"Pardon me," he said wholeheartedly. "Where are a gentleman's manners when they are required? You're obviously watching me smoke and asking yourself: *Why did he not offer me any?* No, you do not feel like smoking? Oh, you vixen, is it because you want your lungs open for when we enjoy ourselves again, so you can moan like a Banshee?"

Diabolis laughed at this. He laughed so much that he cried, and then laughed some more. His skin turned ice-cold, his pupils dilated to exclude the whites, and his hair greyed.

"Look at me now, Deborah, my dead beauty."

His back was humped. When he moved to a night-black couch nearby, he felt utterly ridiculous. *Look at me now.* He sensed how ugly he was, ugly beyond belief. His eyes were marble black, his face was creased with a thousand lines, and his mottled skin was cold enough to freeze a mortal's touch.

"Yes, loneliness is a killer. Sometimes I just want to talk to someone else, who knows what it is to have to drink blood, how closely I am embraced by the hell within me."

He laughed. *She's not the vamp she wished to be, and more ready for rotting than for living death.* His wheezing laughter was a wolf's wails, not a human's glee. It was insane emotional release. The sane part of him realised that he was having a one-sided conversation with a corpse.

He knew he ought to, but did not want to sleep. He resisted the natural forces within him and walked around exploring Deborah's sanctum like a tourist in a foreign land would a museum. He wanted to know something about her life. He expected to find family pictures, but found none—neither parents, nor siblings, nor other relatives or past lovers (if, indeed, there were any). Just like him, Deborah knew what isolation was, and ended her life in the isolation of failure. Immortality, which she could not have fully understood, but which he knew she badly wanted, was something he could not give her.

113

When he entered what appeared to be a guest room, a ghastly odor choked him. His black eyes flared red. He fell to the floor, writhing in pain, and then went stiff. He did everything he could to move away from the sight of the truest horror he'd ever met. Garlic hung there, from the ceiling, and it was fresh! He knew that type: *The Great Satan of Garlic*, and, to humans, the largest, tastiest, gourmet, organic, and most expensive kind.

Its pungency made him feel as if he'd been caught in the middle of a furnace with no escape. Where had it come from? Had this vampire poison been growing right outside in her garden?

Diabolis' whole exterior was assaulted by the foul weed humans called a flower. Every part of his skin erupted in sores. His organs felt like they were undergoing dissolution; his heart was full of bulging spots. A needle puncture would reduce him to a pile of putrescence. Those big cloves were like an anti-terror squad that has hunted and finally found the subversives they were after, and then exacted the severest punishment possible.

As a blood hunter, he could not stand the humiliation of being broken by a mere vegetable, and later found in a state much lower than a germ. *If only I could worm myself out of this mess! But how can I?* Finally, he knew what people feel who are devastated by the misfortune of being incapacitated from the neck down.

His elbows had some strength in them, so he successfully managed to hold his nose; but he felt he was soon going to self-immolate. He hated the idea that his immortality, which enabled his mastery over the living creatures around him, would be lost, thanks to a bunch of garlic.

Potential humiliation goaded him. Visualising being destroyed was a strong motivation. Who would discover him? Would he be lower than bacteria once his body was utterly destroyed? He'd escaped destruction once before at the hands of the law, but he was not certain he would escape this. He dragged his body forward; three more drags and he would be out the door; hopefully, the door would close behind him, and separate him from this torment.

He reached the outside of the deadly zone and kicked the door closed behind him. He lay gasping on the wooden varnished floor outside. His skin was a hive of sores, his already ugly human semblance destroyed. He felt that there simply was no more reason to go on. He tried to stand up, but his legs would not support him.

Squirming from skin still bubbling in reaction to the toxic garlic, he tore off all his clothes. Burning and itching from the inside out, he clawed himself. He still could not stand up. His hide felt like it had been attacked by killer bees, or was lunch for a host of scarab beetles delighted to find bones to pick clean of skin.

*This intense pain might be divine retribution, deserved for my doing such terrible things to other people through the years. But I had to feed. For my prey to judge me based on their own standards is not their right; mortals are flawed as well.*

After two hours of rending his flesh and screaming in pain, Diabolis finally stopped moving. For the first time in all his vampire years, he fell asleep at night. His body grew as cold as an iceberg, oozing a slime which poured out of him. Would it end him, once and for all? If not dead, would his skin ever recover? And was he doomed to appear as ancient as he truly was? Could anything restore what he had lost?

The whole night he slept. When, at last, he stirred, he could move his body. It had changed. His skin was grey all over, except for his face. Parts of his face had small black spots, but nothing that makeup could not erase. He wanted to leave Effra Road, but night had given way to the brightest of days. What was only a ten-minute walk to his tomb was too far for survival. He decided not to explore the rest of this house, just in case other nasty surprises awaited him.

Diabolis lay there on the second floor of the house. He who could control man and beast alike, and fly and change shape, was shaken to his very core and just wanted to recover his senses in peace.

# VI

## HORROR STOP

On Effra Road lived a man in a flat he could just about swing a cat in. Life depressed him. His stinking apartment was a sty where he'd had no guests in years. The clothes he wore to work were clean enough, but hid the truth, for he showered at work, never at home, and shaved there also. He had the kind of home that would be the envy of reality-TV garbage hoarders. Frank was not yet an alcoholic. But, work hard enough on something and it becomes self-fulfilling, proficiency at it increases, and behaviour matches the predicted path. Alcoholism is not just the disease of needing drink; it is the end result of a demon-tormented soul. Frank's demon was his job. Rather than admit what depressed him, he drank this truth about his life down to the bottom, and left the empties lying around his apartment.

Contagion and disease grow where a space for them has been created. His space was at home and at work. He ate alone, drank alone, and took lunch on his own. His weekends were spent squarely in his small flat, where it was so quiet that, if he died there, no one would know for weeks.

Frank worked at what he called (unofficially to those who did not matter, never to those who did) The Horror Stop. At The Horror Stop, those who mattered and were well off, expected everyone else to adore their job like some false god. The workers figuratively fell prostrate before an effigy of the living leader of The Horror Stop to show true veneration towards him and his managerial hierarchy.

His job contributed to Frank's utterly boring life. It was like a road sign that says STOP. But, instead of only saying STOP, his job description could have read: **HORROR STOP**. Yet The Horror Stop job, ironically, did have one thing going for it: it was a job. In the West having a job was never a certainty or a right, and the West's masses believed giving profit to the few and little to the many was honourable. The dissolution of the trade unions was considered progress by the power brokers who saw no need for their minions to ever unite for a better life, because the powerful had historically been and always would be in the right.

*To acquire the job Frank had lied.* He'd padded his Curriculum Vitae, which, together with his job interview, followed the current dictum for employment by taking time to brag. Frank was aware that he had nothing in this world to brag about. His true CV would not even qualify him for an entry-level job. The basic requirement was a steady record of employment. Frank, who had not been drinking much at this stage of his life, had encountered his fair share of hardship and bad luck with sadistic employers. Those worthies were more than capable of making life miserable and being excellent at hire-and-fire. The least irritation from others, and he was straight out the door. The nervous man could not defend himself against elements obstructing his professional life, which injured his chances of getting, let alone keeping, gainful and meaningful employment. He had to have his freedom at all cost.

And freedom is exactly what Frank got at work. He was one of the least notable people there. Given his nervous disposition and low self-esteem, the greatest challenge he faced was filling in the empty hours. All day long at The Horror Stop he felt uni-dimensional and strange; the granules of his life were slipping through an hour-glass in painful slow motion. The clock kept ticking, like the hammer of a heart, while he sat, and with the passing of every day, transformed into a vegetable suitable for boredom stew. Frank had once been told by an erudite young entrant (who always spoke over his head) that boredom was a form of unconscious aggression. Frank did not understand this comment and simply vowed not to talk to this co-worker anymore.

It was not exactly his boredom which irritated him most. He saw it as his duty to manage his emotions—the same way that a gardener has a duty to look after weeds by pulling them out. One could sprinkle weed killer on the ground. But underlying this activity is a duty of care. It has been said that plants are like people: they have souls to be nourished. This was how Frank explained his emotions and his duty to manage them. The world, however, was populated by numerous souls, clueless about his duty to manage his emotions…or theirs.

Frank was always at the receiving end of other people's bored reactions, and this abuse piled on just like the empties in his apartment.

Today would be very different, though. He was contemplating accepting an invitation from one of the organisers of The Bram Stoker Festival to produce paintings before the start slated for the end of the month. His task was to create a poster with a definite gothic character which would appeal to the organisers and the tastes of those who would attend.

In the first five hours of this day, his surroundings depressed him. He smelled the garbage strewn about and, from among the lost souls plaguing Dublin, the odd one who popped into the building. The effect enforced the belief that this was a measurement of his life's worth. The clock in the reception area was large; its blade-shaped hands could have snipped his head off.

Frank had taken this job because he wanted secure employment that paid more than the allowance afforded by the Department of Social Welfare's Job Seeking Allowance. This job afforded his life that much, but he'd also inherited the dirge of empty hours.

*Direct my way in your sight, O Lord.* This dirge expressed his grief at so much time wasted. The dirge trapped itself inside him.

He had no one with whom he could share his thoughts because of the systematic reinforcement of professional status one dons at work. At an unspoken level, some people are more, some greater, some terribly important, and others are less so, as one goes down the work place ladder. The empty space of insignificance is allotted those invisible souls who enter The Horror Stop. The majority, even those who wear the garb and embody professionalism, are preoccupied with the very reality which creates the dirge within them. Instead of singing so others can hear the lyrics, they trap this nervous energy inside, where no one may ever hear what, by grace, those who have eyes may see.

By ten o'clock Frank's brain wore a crown of thorns. The "lucky to have a job" sword had penetrated his side. The condemned man smoked on the roof balcony, believing he'd done nothing with his life. And the more he admitted this to himself, the worse he felt. Then, his break time having elapsed, he left the roof, head low. He felt so devalued that he wondered how he could possibly continue living such a meaningless existence. Dwarfed by the waves of this negative thinking, he entered the lift and pressed *zero.*

Inspiration flashed through Frank's mind. *10:20—time to fight back.* But having the desire to act is one issue; having the means of escaping the emptiness he found himself falling into was another.

His breath stuck in his upper chest. Anticipation was followed by no answers as to how he would go about just making a mark on the sand before leaving this earth. He visualized the gothic girl, and thought maybe he should go visit her. He had to see her tonight and would show her samples of the surrealist art which had gained him the request to contribute a work to the Bram Stoker Festival. The man who requested the art was of noble origin. His opinion held weight amongst those who cared to project their precious feelings and emotions onto a canvas, or to allow their mental space to be filled with the discourse of art history and famous artists, and the ability to compare one piece of art to another. This talent goes all the way back to the early times when humans lived in and drew on the walls of caves.

His neighbour Deborah, a splendid looking creature, would be ideal. She would be the subject that he would place on canvas. She had the power to make his life more interesting, less ordinary.

The Horror Stop did not brighten up. Outside, junkie hordes gathered, some to deal drugs, others just to curse and brawl, while the law-abiding citizens of Dublin went about their business.

On streets like Parnell, O'Connell, Middle Abbey, and North Great Frederick Street, visions of syringes marched like toy soldiers, like the 1994 movie *The Mask* with Jim Carrey. (When under attack The Mask character displays a thousand guns pointing outwards, ready to attack the enemy, in a piece of surrealism at its hilarious supreme.) In this context, syringe armies paraded Dublin's streets. Once they found their suitable mate, they arrived like a flurry of darts hitting targets throughout the body. The results were devastating.

A drugged man in a car, driving the wrong way on a one-way street, ploughed into a group of pedestrians, mangling one. That fifty-two-year-old lady, he left as dead as a doornail. Within minutes of this incident, came ambulance after ambulance, along with fire engines, sirens blaring. When Frank stepped outside his workplace he captured the tail end of the episode, with the poor woman's body fastened to and borne away on a stretcher. He knew that, when the hour ended, her death would be broadcast on state and electronic media, and television.

What did her swift, violent end do to Frank? It shook him, and made him aware of how the slow kill of boredom at The Horror Stop had succeeded in strangling the quality of his life. Death, as was seen with this mangled lady, can happen like a snap and you are gone. This was the cruel reality.

This job was devouring the quality of whatever years Frank had. He became aware of something deeper embedded in the story of his life. Boredom, like crawling insects, was creeping into the personalities of his fellow workers. The insects, though invisible, were none the less real. They gave people in the building various allergic reactions—depression, or at least melancholia. The manifestations of the infestation in many included after-work alcoholism and drug abuse, could have a violent effect on others, and could infect others.

The infection could be like eating meat from an animal infected with Creutzfeldt-Jakob—madness would muddy your mind quicker than you could say Bovine Spongiform Encephalopathy. Death snuck in gradually. In this institution you might think that a normal person would die quicker than they could say BSE, a condition as progressive and degenerative as institutionally-cultivated boredom.

Once a worker realised how unfulfilled they were, their inner chaos might lead to self harm. Peaceful people could alienate their spouses and children, followed by other forms of destruction. Boredom's evil pervaded the workers and eroded their intelligence. It turned progress to childish regression and loss of the caring they may have learned while maturing. It made plain into ugly, passive into aggressive, proud into peculiar, power-disordered into crazed and deluded. Such was the potential of the boredom infestation that the end-products

122

might be: thieves, gamblers, deviants, perverts, fraudsters, and even murderers. Institutionalized boredom lulled some into villainy, where they played around in a tide of their own filth like a pig in mud.

If Frank had not been aware of these boredom insects devouring the souls of those around him or the soul within him, now he was. He spent his lunch hour walking the streets of Dublin.

Just as human nature has a sexual drive that burns like a furnace causing and constructing life, we have a psychology that brims with living impulses, from the breathing heart to the fantastic structure of the brain, to the system of our imagination, which bursts forth creative energies. We are designed to think of life and survive in a world where life exists, yet often confuses us with obstacles. Frank was embracing what he could do with the life energy that had been a sacrificial lamb roasted over the banal coals of his duties. His duties were a form of subordination and pressure, producing nothing but nervous exhaustion.

He sought out a space in Dublin's Inner City where he could turn his mind toward creating beauty. Though, to the casual observer, it was not beauty, it was so from his perspective. He looked for peace, but found himself walking past places estranged from peace. He walked past Ireland's Forecourts which housed cases of her most traumatizing genres. He went where the smells from The Guinness Brewery teased his nostrils. Then it was on to St. Patrick's Hospital. John Dean Swift, who wrote books like *Gulliver's Travels*, had handed his estate over to become a place of care for dipsomaniacs and the poor. St. Patrick's Hospital, one of the finest psychiatric facilities in Western Europe, did its best for Ireland's mentally ill, alcoholics, and drug addicts.

At St. Patrick's, the visceral truth was cigarettes stamped out on veins—hallucinations terrifying their sufferers with nonsensical, paranoid delusions. Was their mother or father plotting to kill them? Are they God, or God's chosen instrument? Do their voices threaten ridiculous things or warn them that the IRA is after them, order them to harm someone or do something like burn down a building?

The IRA always played a major role in the mind of the Irish psychotic, manifesting in total paranoia. In the minds of the mentally ill, a persecutor, or even an imaginary friend, tends to exist as a destructive force. Often, Irish psychotics either believe they know and have as an advocate a member of the IRA, or that the IRA was plotting some bomb and it was their duty to warn people, or, was somehow after them. The ill person would say they were a member of a secretive organisation, or privy to the inner workings of the IRA.

Frank tuned into all of this suffering. He saw bodies mutilated by knife cuts. Some souls were as gentle as lambs and fearful as a cat which just caught a glimpse of a big, angry dog. Others were growling as if the lion or tiger within them was ready to prowl, scream, and claw into anyone. Others, in the heart of their schizophrenia, believed firmly that they were God.

But hordes of sufferers did not make it to this institution. The streets were the only refuge for the homeless ones, bar hostels. The hostel scene was renowned for sinister elements and unsanitary conditions. The unwell unable to afford private health insurance were too sick to leave their homes.

Frank returned to work. He did not want to be there. For the new entrant to the world of the dead, the female accident victim, entrance had occurred just outside his door. The street was blocked by unarmed Garda who had placed boundaries where the incident had taken place. But how cheap life is where selfishness reigns supreme. A woman totally ignored a Garda who told her that it was prohibited to pass through this area. She went underneath the plastic rope and proceeded on her way, heedlessly.

The hours had to be passed. Frank fantasized about the rich changes he was about to experience. His painting would be executed to suit the style at the heart of The Bram Stoker Festival, a venue which would proudly display his artistic dedication to the morose and the macabre.

He saw himself taking his time and having a truly meaningful experience passing the hours of his life in artistic and total creativity. He would enter a world of artistic, creative flow. It was frustrating him, just being here at work, sitting doing nothing, when he so desperately wanted to start creating. His skin prickled from utter frustration. He had no painting utensils or subject here. His inactivity in relation to his artistic desire was simply rotting him to pieces.

A man he just knew as Robert—a pale and emaciated asthmatic whose reeking casual clothing revealed him to be a chain smoker—stood there holding a cup of Earl Grey tea. "I'm having a cigarette," Robert said invitingly. "Why not come outside with me and we'll have a chat?"

"Sure, why not? Won't it kill the time at the very least?"

When the two men went outside, Robert lit a match and held his cigarette to it. As his cigarette started glowing, he noticed two vans parked in the laneway within which were two junkies shooting up. The first had his grey trousers down and was injecting his groin. The other was holding fast food in his left hand and lifting his jumper up to inject his stomach.

"Not to worry," Robert said, "it's daytime. But I am hearing the ones who inject at night have changed."

"Changed?" Frank said, laughing.

"Yeah, between you and me," Robert said in a soft voice, "they are getting vicious."

"But sure, with heroin, aren't they more docile?"

"Not the ones at night time. They've attacked a few, say friends of friends".

"Attacked? What do you mean? I pass them every day and

they are too out of it to attack anyone—I mean, of the general public."

"Well, these people for some reason have not reported to the police that they have been bitten."

"Bitten?"

"Yeah, properly bitten on arms, upper arms, inner thighs, or throats…anywhere there's a bit of a vein with blood in it."

"Why?"

"Something peculiar went on here one night and, ever since, things have gotten very vicious."

"But sure, you always get a bit of viciousness in the city?"

"Well, I am talking more vicious than usual."

"Yeah?"

"Oh yes, indeed. I mean they've always been like zombies. But they are now like vampires whose brains have been sucked out. You know…it's weird. They're like decomposed vegetables who have awakened and smelled some kind of stimulant and decided it was blood. I know you don't believe in that shit, and what normal person would?"

"That is fucked up!"

"Well, they are selling drugs out there with all kinds of stuff in them, so maybe they've developed stuff that has made people hyper violent."

"Look, no one believes in vampires. If I am mad, I am mad. One night I got very drunk. I slept right here in this lane behind garbage bins."

"When was this?"

"Just a couple of days ago."

"A couple?"

"Yeah, not long ago. Maybe the old gargle I drank was spiked. Maybe I was not the old May West. I was in a desperate mood for a couple of gargles. The wife was stressing me and I just needed to get the fuck away.

"There was junkies shooting up not far from me—mean fuckers by the sounds of things—so I decided to keep my mouth shut. They were not like the passive type of homeless people, but the type that would feed off the most vulnerable.

"This was a shitty place to be sleeping—beer cans, syringes, used condoms on the ground, weeds growing everywhere, shit and piss all over the joint. Sure, this is their toilet. Pubs, clubs, and restaurants won't have them. The council has closed down their public toilets. Sometimes, I've even thought that if you stick the tip of the syringe into the ground here it will fertilize the weeds. Then I saw this big thing come out of the sky."

"What? Something come out of the sky?"

"Weird, yeah?"

"Fuck, yeah, it's weird."

"This thing viciously attacked and bit the junkies. I was too scared to say anything to anyone or see what the CCTV footage reported. I have my suspicions that my drink was spiked. I heard nothing in the papers. Must have been some good shit in that beer."

"Or bad shit?"

"Exactly."

# VII

## Frank Meets Fangs

Frank felt great relief when the hours finally passed. At seven o clock, with darkness in the sky, he left the building through the rear exit. Too much fighting at the Luas stop made it unsafe for him to leave via the front door. On his way out of the building, as he locked it, hoping he'd set the alarm properly. He did not want its blare to delay his going where he needed to go. He switched off his mobile phone so that no one could ring or text him. He approached a huddle of black bins and the familiar sight of every type of filth imaginable.

As he walked past the bins, a girl—tall, skinny, wearing a filthy track suit—emerged from among them with a sleeping bag. She walked past him, never looking at him, as if he didn't exist. Her clothes stank and her bruised face was covered with mud.

It took him forty-five minutes to reach the area of Harold's Cross. When he arrived there, the first thing he did was go to his flat on Effra Road. Frank was so anxious about wasting time that he almost forgot what he was supposed to do with the time!

When he reached the gothic girl's house he was perspiring from nervously trying to recall where the entry was and how to get the occupant's attention. He found what appeared to be a bell and rang it. At that exact time a light switched on, enabling anyone within to see the visitor through a peek hole.

Diabolis was angry with the dead proprietor of this establishment whose fault it was that his face and body were riddled with pain. *What kind of subhuman collects the most hideous vegetable known to vampire-kind and stores it in a room of their house knowing full well that her attachments and declared interests are creatures who have a peculiar aversion to this kind of thing? She deserved my drinking her to death.*

Someone was at the trap door, most likely to see Deborah, which caused his fangs to emerge. The visitor was an intruder in his space—defiling his present refuge. What possible right could they have to be here?

Maybe it was that degenerate boy the birds had sorted out on St. Stephen's Green. Maybe he was coming to Deborah's home in hopes of renewing some form of a relationship.

Diabolis swore that if this were the case, if this man could not know when he lost and when he won in life, he would rip him to shreds, no questions asked, to teach him what Deborah had learned too late.

Even if half of Dublin witnessed it why should he care? He could evaporate into a cloud and travel through the sewers; if the powers that be dared track him down, he'd leave them swimming in a sea of their own blood.

This rage assured that he was highly overwrought. In this state, he approached the door, only to find a glass key hole he could peer through. Diabolis bent down to the keyhole and saw before him a man who looked to be in his late forties. Unappetizing, he observed, *His blood—oh goodness!—I could not drink that swill in a million years.*

"Who are you?" he said in a virile voice, as he covered the damaged side of his face and neck with a scarf.

"I'm just here to talk to Deborah."

129

This peculiar looking intruder displayed a puffed face with fake tan, the stench of a bottle of fake tan. His hair was peculiarly dyed, as if he was trying to hide the damage done by a combination of unhealthy living and aging. He hid them as carefully as a well-endowed woman might hide the obvious by wearing a see-through bra.

With his dyed hair, his fingers cluttered with gold rings, and his wrists and neck with jewellery, he looked as common as the day he was born. This specimen reminded Diabolis of those inbred clans his maker had informed him about from his 1800s travels State-side. Leman admitted he'd never met their like, after coming across the Jukes and the Kalikaks, their white-trash blood a eugenicist's wet dream.

This simpleton, Diabolis thought, was possibly the genetic end result going back through the swamps of time, and the kind of waste eliminated onto the plains of the New World that even the Old World's rejected.

"What do you want here?" Diabolis demanded.

"Please let me in. I wish to speak to Deborah about something I consider important."

"Important to you!" the vampire replied, almost spitting the words. *How dare he act as if anything important to him, anything he could ever value, could possibly be valued by anyone else.* "Very well," he growled.

Why had Diabolis consented to allowing this vile thing entry? Had he lost his mind from skipping a day of rest in the coffin? Or had he decided to withhold his initial judgement of the intruder, as in 'You should not judge a book by its cover'? A cover, however, is a novel's most valuable asset, and people *do* judge books by their covers. So why not judge others by their covers?

Human creatures, things who think so highly of themselves, but whose value to a superior being may amount to no more than a pawn on a chessboard, were, for Lucis Diabolis, simply food. He judged his meat as he saw it, regardless of silly human expressions. If the meat a human intends to eat looks or smells off, as if tainted by unhealthy germs, would they still say, 'Do not judge a book by its cover,' and consume it?

A vampire, likewise, must be judgemental and analytical about the stuff they feed on, with the odd consumption of, perhaps, a slight bit of flesh and bone, and other non-blood related material.

To Frank, once inside, Diabolis looked utterly strange. Frank could see the disfiguring growths on his face which Diabolis had tried, unsuccessfully, to hide. He was not here, however, to focus on how weird Diabolis looked, but on how he could get his ambitions achieved.

Thanks to the Horror Stop job, Frank knew how to lie to this hideous excuse for a man without displaying any of the bodily signs of disgust. But Diabolis had *centuries* of experience in hiding his disdain for the refuse of humanity. His words left Frank in no doubt that Deborah was not and would not be home for some time.

"But is there anything I can help you with?" Diabolis asked, hopeful that this social interlude would end, and this foul creature would leave, so he could return to his coffin at the cemetery.

Instead, the man, frustrated that he could not get what he wanted, insisted on hanging around, assured only within himself that this was a Shangri-La in comparison to his place of work. "Nice home you have here," he said, as a storm of envy erupted in his body. He was mentally doing the arithmetic and figuring out what item 'A' cost, then item 'B', and so on.

Frank lived in a one-room flat where he could just about flap his wings, though his feathers prohibited him from flying. His cluelessness did not even require the classical vampire activity of mesmerism. He was a smelly creature, who reeked

131

of the dampness of his cave-like abode. He was so odd looking that Diabolis wanted to laugh, then maybe disable him and
engage in taxidermy on a live subject, so that if, at any stage he
needed an object worse off than himself, he had this creature
to show what low depths humans could plumb.

What on earth had Frank to offer him? What business did
such a loser have with Lucis Diabolis? He was standing in front
of Diabolis, all blank in the head, and could not say a word. He
stared at Diabolis with his dull grey eyes, set in a balding head
that looked about to sprout antennas and start broadcasting to
planet Mars. Plus, the man, who might have been tall, was wid-
ened instead from his daytime desk job and too many nights
perched on a bar stool. Frank's mouth stayed open, waiting to
catch flies, until he stuttered out something inarticulate.

Diabolis had no patience for impaired speech. Either you
spoke clearly, the way the Queen's English was meant to be
spoken, or you kept your mouth shut, except to eat.

"Just sit down," Diabolis said, irritated by the zigzagging
of words incapable of forming a proper sentence. Just listening
to the hideous deformation of Frank's speech, the putrescent
elocution, the way his utterances were sliced as if by a meat
cutter, he wished he could sever and feed Frank's tongue to the
dogs outside.

The easily frightened, nervous guest felt the unwanted
vibes acutely, as they poured out of Diabolis, who was doing
all he could to make Frank uncomfortable.

"Yes, I will sit down, thank you." Frank bleated.

Lucis Diabolis could smell the timidity. Frank smelled like
prey, but not prime; to consume the red liquid which pervaded
his flesh would be like consuming offal.

"I'm looking for help with something," he began, somehow aware deep within him that asking Diabolis for help was
futile. Frank's gaze met profound darkness. "I'm an artist," he
dared admit to those soulless eyes.

While being in the presence of Diabolis for mere minutes, Frank had regressed in both stature and status. There was something Darwinian about this situation, more helpless than pathetic Oliver asking in his feeble voice, "Please, sir, may I have some more." His vulnerability was like the sickly child who never develops and reaches late adolescence to become nothing but raw meat for the high school bullies.

"I've been asked to do something important by The Bram Stoker Festival's most prominent organizer. He will provide excellent finances, for he is a man of wealth and power, and wants me to draw a picture for them which would suit this type of festival."

"Oh," Diabolis said, as if to a child who reads his horror comics under his sheets late into the night. "So, I see that you like your vampires," he croaked in a voice like that of the centenarian he appeared to be.

"Ah…yes…I do, which is why I'd like to talk to Deborah. I'd like her to be my model; she is perfect. Look, please just let me speak to her."

"Deborah," Diabolis smirked as if Frank's request was the funniest he'd ever heard. Okay, I'll call her—seriously—I will…or maybe we should go see her." He pointed to the room where her corpse was stationed. "Deborah…oh, Deborah!" he called into the silence.

At this, Diabolis chuckled, and then added something which startled Frank. "Certain people would be inclined to think that I would make a most authentic looking subject for this genre of yours."

Frank examined his face, build, and clothing. "No," Frank said, shaking his head in negation.

"*What?* Diabolis squeaked, hiding to the best of his ability his chagrin.

"You could not possibly be a vampire. You're old, but that does not make you scary." Frank laughed.

"Yes," Diabolis agreed, "you *are* perceptive, aren't you? I think that Deborah is pretending she's not in the house. She's very playful. You know the type. People who think they are vampires are excellent at make believe. Their imaginations run away with them. So…let's see if she is playing hide-and-seek. I can see how determined you are to paint her." Diabolis opened the white wooden door and said politely, "After you, good sir."

"A vampire should look menacing, cold, macabre, and frightful, as if he could gnaw your veins and suck them dry. Vamps should look like Deborah, a gothic, pale mannequin who has a mysterious, creepy side to her," Frank lectured Diabolis.

"You seem to be quite the vampire expert."

"I've examined vampire history, especially in film. I really have a strong mental image of how they should look. I've been thinking all day about Deborah."

"Well, if you turn around, Frank, you'll see her."

"Oh, excellent!"

"Yes, it is wonderful that you have such an interest in vampires," muttered Diabolis.

"Oh," Frank shrieked when he turned around, "what is *this*?"

"It's Deborah," Diabolis said, laughing when Frank almost fell to the floor.

"I do not look like a vampire?" Diabolis mocked, his face suffused with anger. "I do not cut the grade…am not vampire-looking enough for you?"

Frank wept, frozen in terror. *What have I done? Trying to better my lot in life has led to this dark and demented end.*

The muscles in Diabolis' arms swelled. He picked Frank up with one hand, lifting him until Frank's head banged against the ceiling. Then he threw him back down as if he weighed no more than a basketball. He sliced Frank's neck open with his long nails, tasted a sample, and quickly spat it out like it was piss.

"I am not the vampire type, am I, Frank?" he said, and walked out the door. "Well, this vampire type would never drink from you." Frank squirmed—a dying fish in a pool of his own blood.

Diabolis walked back in and severed Frank's head with one blow. He placed the head on the table like a centrepiece and lit a cigarette while he watched blood gush out to dye the white tablecloth crimson.

# VIII

## Talk Therapy

Diabolis slept well because he'd disposed of the human garbage which stopped him from being able to do what he would normally do at night. The key to his success was keeping human creatures at a distance. They did not understand him. He did not understand them.

When he awoke at eight, as usual, he touched his bodily semblance. His skin felt clearer—the garlic- induced allergy would not leave a lasting impression on his face. What about his mind? The key to excellent vampire mental hygiene simply followed one rule: Never be socially intimate with your food, which you must inevitably destroy to consume. Besides, humans were rarely affable, especially when they had such a fantastic penchant for making everything so difficult to follow. Yet, that did not mean becoming agoraphobic and isolating oneself in a tomb, which could induce claustrophobia and lead to eating disorders.

The only mortal who could tolerate his presence enough to allow Diabolis to open up his unconscious mind had been one Doctor Rosenthal. At the termination of analysis with Rosenthal Diabolis had concluded many things, one of which was that his split personality caused him grave tension and inner conflict.

An inability to link his inner mental identity with his odiously immoral immortal identity defined his mental instability.

136

This caused Diabolis to be muddled, profoundly confused, and upset. So he'd ended up going to and ultimately rejecting the descriptively-based psychiatrist for an analytical, non-judgemental listener.

He sat on the Boardwalk of Dublin beside the Liffey River; its full tide was, to Diabolis, akin to his own energetic flow. Here he pondered in minute detail the deeply personal analysis of which he'd been an active part. He'd found Doctor Rosenthal different than other humans. For exactly sixty minutes, three times a week, the psychoanalyst encouraged him to be just who he was, to embrace—not reject—his very nature. (Doctor Rosenthal, of course, realized and accepted that his neck was on the line if his treatment was less than perfect.)

"I came across the literature of your profession when I was breaking into a blood bank in Trinity College, Dublin. *Very interesting* I thought. You doctors potentially have the capability of comprehending the truest, deepest part of the human mind, since you're trained to be excellent observers of it's workings. I won't keep secret what and who I am. I'll know if you snitch on me to anyone, and will show you and the one you confided in just how bloody tasty your tongue can be when it is prevented from running wild."

Judging by the first ten sessions, the doctor could almost forget he was treating a vampire. Diabolis described the most mundane aspects of his life, such as how he read a paper, what he thought of that reading, and how unkind society was to people it considered an inconvenience.

Diabolis even came across as sensitive. He would talk about the loneliness of strange people, or the suffering of disabled people. He had ethics. He never bothered the strange or disabled. Doctor Rosenthal was starting to believe that the patient was suffering from a Vampire/Fantasy complex. The analysis was going along in a surprisingly mundane fashion. Diabolis described how he sustained himself in such logical terms that there was no question that, being well endowed with cash and valuables, he had plenty of time on his hands.

Questions concerning how far he was removed from humans, however, could not be dismissed. Everything Diabolis described was solitary. He was definitely an island, unconcerned about political events. A liberal at times, he expounded on how the insane were once treated like circus entertainment, to the point where Bedlam earned a fortune. This seemed to disperse anxiety in his system. He kept discussing the need for understanding towards people who were different. Was there psychoanalytical substance in this? The goal was to start moving away from this cerebral conversation and discover what was at the root of his complex.

After all those sessions of his client's letting off the steam of built-up frustration experienced living this life, Doctor Rosenthal finally began to hear evidence that Diabolis was not as ordinary as he first might have perceived, preoccupied as he was with an overly distracted social conscience.

"When I first started out as a vampire," Diabolis confessed, "it felt like being a child all over again. It was the helpless feeling of one who does not know the first thing about survival, independence, or how to make the most of this existence. Being around Alex Leman felt like this."

"Of whom did Alex Leman, in your life as a vampire, or as a mortal, most remind you?"

"Who did he remind me of?" Diabolis said, taken aback by the weirdness of this probing question. "He was like my older brother, who was seven years my senior. I always felt inferior and inept in his presence. I was always in his shadow."

Diabolis learned why it was intolerable to be near his maker: Leman regressed him and made him feel inadequate, just as his brother had.

Over the years of analysis Diabolis' head cleared as he

unloaded what was stored in his unconscious mind; this had a therapeutic effect. Diabolis learned to understand his dual vampire and human natures. His human nature was behind him. Although he could never come to terms with the humans around him, he could learn how to operate in and around them. In both natures, human and vampire, he shared intense vulnerabilities.

For a full month in the third year of analysis Diabolis focussed on suicide. At first, he was philosophical and intellectual. (Just because a subject talks cerebrally or abstractly about something does not mean that their own complexes are not stored within this discussion. It infers only that the subject wishes to talk intellectually about a traumatic issue like suicide because they do not yet have the capacity to discuss these things at a more personal level. To say, "Then he disclosed how a vampire could self-destruct." and "Next, he moved on to discussing how he might do so." is a rather blunt description of how truths emerged.)

[Talking intellectually about suicide, and how a vampire might do so, is like putting raw meat on a fire. You're not going to eat the meat right away, but must prepare it. This is how things work with the mind and with people. You can never treat the patient subject the way a KGB officer or a probing journalist might. The analyst directs the subject to spill what makes their lives miserable and filled with discontent. But the subject is not resisting revealing their more painful material because they are lazy or need to be probed. The patient stalls until it's the right time for them to convey what is hurting them, due to the powerful resistance of their ego. Intellectualization, rationalization, transference, and denial stop one from being able to get at the nucleus of neurosis.]

When Diabolis talked suicide he could not stop. He expounded at length and in depth. Doctor Rosenthal was sure that by the following month Diabolis would no longer be under his care—life had certainly lost all value. What you think a vampire would just get used to and take for granted was utterly annoying, irritating, and frustrating him. One troubling certainty loomed over his life: that every day he only could exist under a black sky. This would always remind him he had died and, thus, lost all ability to make a humane connection with the living. During his month of suicidal ideation, the vampire did not drink a drop of blood or go near a living creature. He confessed to an overwhelming morbid feeling of childlike vulnerability.

The reason for his excursion into suicidal ideations was a mystery. When asked, he gave Rosenthal no reply. A lack of insight is related to the psychotic condition to which sane neurotic folk can graduate. Doctor Rosenthal was prepared to reject any notion that Diabolis was psychotic. Yes, he entertained some psychotic, paranoid tendencies and was asocial, but this did not seem to be true psychosis. Diabolis was not divorced from reality, although the reality with which he was engaged was difficult to relate to, but this was why he was in analysis. Doctor Rosenthal believed that Diabolis was actually about to have a breakthrough which would leave him feeling much better about who he was.

After thirty-one sleepless days in the tomb during an exceedingly warm August, Diabolis seriously contemplated going outside in broad daylight and burning to death. His body began to disintegrate; he started to become emaciated and shrivel up into a bent, weak, very old man. His fangs even decayed.

It was extremely weird to be treating a man who thirty-one days ago had appeared to be in his late twenties, and then, over the course of thirty days, began to look like he'd aged a century. The subject's appearance brought home to Doctor Rosenthal that he was dealing with a supernatural creature.

Diabolis would look back on this transformation and recall how his doctor still treated him with total professionalism. It helped Diabolis to fully realize that he was in the company of a consummate professional.

Throughout this process, Doctor Rosenthal, who kept meticulous notes about his own reactions to this therapeutic process, maintained that he felt relaxed, calm, and completely in control. He was looking forward to working through the analysis issues to see what was lurking behind Diabolis' acting out. He deemed 'acting out' his suicidal ideations and dramatic weight loss because what lurked behind these manifestations of his symptoms were deeper truths.

"I would end it all," was the subject's brief remark about his hopelessness.

Doctor Rosenthal drank from his coffee cup and placed it on the saucer. He was a man of forty-five, but vastly more intelligent than his years. He was a professional, yet a renegade who disobeyed the unwritten rule for academics: *publish or perish.* After training, he neither published nor perished; his practise thrived, mainly via word of mouth. A poorly trained analyst with unaddressed personal issues would have given in to their patient at 'the level of demand'; they would have broken the established boundaries of psychoanalysis and tried to be more than one thing for their patient. He had simply concluded that, just as an infant needs to be fed, this client was in a state of need.

Doctor Rosenthal, with his youthful face, tanned skin, and black hair (balding on top), listened patiently, not for what was being said, but for what Diabolis was *not* saying. He discovered a great deal about Diabolis' needy state. Where an unskilled thera-pist would have adopted an overly involved role, he remained stoic when Diabolis became ravenous. Confident that he could manage the client's negative transference, he calmly said, "If your fangs could talk and you were patient enough to listen, what would they say? Use your imagination."

"They would say something absurd about how much you remind me of both my brother and my maker, although you resemble neither of them. Those two belong to a different century. It is idiotic that I should have this negative reaction to you."

"But the emergence of your fangs tells me otherwise."

"I'm running on low, having become anaemic from a self-denial which has never been a feature of my existence. Existing under a black sky with but one form of relief—stars and moon—and knowing there never can be a variation of this, reminds me of my mortal morbidity, and this depresses me."

On the thirty-second day of his blood fast, Diabolis skipped analysis (having sent by messenger the full fee for analysis, plus sixty percent extra). He broke into a Blood Bank, predictably on the affluent side of town—Chelsea. The timing of this break in was excellent. It was closed Friday night, all day Saturday, Sunday, and Monday. Where the blood was stored neither daylight nor windows intruded; it was totally divorced from the outside world. After realizing that his entertainment of self-destruction was formed around an insane hatred of others turned inward, the hatred which he had directed towards himself simply stopped.

*Self starvation is deplorable. If one has enough to eat one should respect that.*

Diabolis burst into laughter at the thought of a blood donor board holding blood for a starving vampire. He got a glass out of a bag he'd brought with him. Dressed like a nobleman in a spectacular, dazzling-white shirt and black tie, and polished black shoes, he filled the pint glass with blood. Not a chance in Hell did he want to raise a toast; no sooner had he downed that blood than he began to feel renewed.

His appetite was back with a vengeance. He needed a refill. On the second pint he raised the glass. "To the donors," he said, "who understand the value of life so much that they would literally give their blood just to see another survive. We vampires are deeply touched by such sentiments!"

142

On Tuesday morning at four am, having drunk the blood supply dry, he came out of the clinic looking young again, albeit a bit bloated. This was as glorious a high as that of a herd of drugstore cowboys with free access to the local chemist shop for three days. Such a bunch would leave feeling as if they'd been transported to a different plane of existence, to the fifth dimension and beyond.

Usually a young drug user starts out looking youthful and relatively healthy. If they are a recreational, non addicted user, this can continue. However, a habitual user develops tolerance for higher doses, then experiences horrid withdrawal symptoms, and thus needs a higher amount of drug to get any relief. They can end up looking like hellish zombies. But blood, being more than a drug for Diabolis, had him looking, depending on the quality of the blood and his mood, positively preternatural.

When Diabolis returned to analysis, he was a new man, whose youthful vigour has been restored. Of course, the danger for Doctor Rosenthal was all too predictable. The veil that divides opposites, such as love and hate, good and evil, sanity and madness, is very thin. These opposites can be interchanged within a person over time. So, just as Diabolis had unconscious hatred for Doctor Rosenthal before he worked through his feelings of sibling rivalry and problems with authority figures, his inner weather blew unconscious feelings of love and positivity towards Doctor Rosenthal. This actually helped the analysis to work even better.

"Over the course of existence," Diabolis added, "I've preferred the territory of my own company. You are the first person I've *really* talked to in nearly a century. I trust this is to be taken by you as the best compliment possible from a human-blood sucker. It allows me to exempt you from being the subject of a very personal, very bloody feast.

"Going to a human for professional help feels peculiar.

You go to a psychiatrist feeling that they want to perversely experiment with some Frankenstein-like cure. You're never asked about anything beyond surface details. The outlook is grim. They either tie you up in restraints, fry your organic brain using a so-called therapeutic procedure—Electro Convulsive Therapy, E.C.T. for short—or they want to be brain butchers. They play around with your head, carving your frontal lobes, so that, thanks to lobotomy, any semblance of your character is erased. What I initially wanted, as far as psychiatry is concerned, simply never mattered. I was just never asked or allowed to speak."

"Mr. Diabolis, what do you really want?"

"I want self knowledge, to understand just a little bit more the vampire part of me and the part of me which was once human. If I could just understand the eccentricity of this position I would be more at ease with myself. I could get on with my immortality."

"You've only lived once with another vampire. You reject the company of others. Does this feel like what your life should be like," the doctor inquired, leaning forward toward the leather sofa. When he was done speaking he leaned back in the chair and looked at Diabolis in a way that made him feel warmly engaged and less paranoid. Diabolis felt that the territory of his mind, a previously private and confidential place, was not hidden behind an opaque barrier, but was so open that Doctor Rosenthal could look straight at it.

"But what other life could there be for me? Vampires have always followed blood lettings, be that the guillotine or the hangman's noose...or war. The popularity of the book by Reverends Heinrich Kramer and Jacob Sprenger in the era of the late Middle Ages—*The Malleus Maleficarum (The Witches' Hammer)* written in 1486 and published in 1487 in Germany—saw to it that those named witches, sorcerers, or magicians would be sent to a torturous death. Vampires in hordes are like war correspondents; if it bleeds, they will come...and drink up.

"I'm content with the British Isles, especially Ireland. I had enough blood to drink in Ireland with The Easter Rising of 1916, The War of Independence, 1919 to 1921, and The Civil War from June of 1922 to May of 1923. But I've always kept my kills more domestic and local than anything to do with politics, which I simply do not care for.

"I could have had a more continental blood supply if I'd visited the trenches of Europe. But I knew these sites would only be disease-infested hellholes—odious, muddy, gaseous, pugnacious, and crowded—no place for one who likes privacy. I never take kindly to drinking blood spilled needlessly. Other vampires love to consume blood spilled this way. I prefer mine nicely stored for me, or as the fresh product of my own kill."

"It sounds," Doctor Rosenthal interjected, "like there is a state of ambivalence within your psychology. What I mean by this is two totally opposite emotions are a source of conflict within your mind. Possibly, at some level, you wish for a compatible communal life with others in different land, but you have an intolerance of mortals, despite your curiosity about them. The psychological conflict is very interesting, Mr. Lucis Diabolis, as these emotions attack you simultaneously."

"This is true," Lucis Diabolis agreed, "but I fear the group setting more than anything; any desire that I should harbour to be part of the group will always be personally sanctioned. Yes, I've dulled the quality of my life greatly by restricting my consumption solely to the blood of this land. This being the 1930's, our population is mostly Celtic and Caucasian. I yearn to sample the blood of various ethnicities; even European would do just fine. Give me anything other than the usual homogenous lot. Latin blood, I imagine, would be spicy, and would cause positive thoughts to emerge in me, keeping me a more contented, warm-blooded vampire. I've also considered consuming the blood of East Europeans and wondering what that would do for my temperament.

Sanguine Scandinavian blood from the descendants of Vikings has interested me. But Swiss blood might disappoint me; it might be too bland from being so safe, comfortable, overfed, and OCD (from hoarding the excess of other countries)."

Ultimately, as Doctor Rosenthal helped to regress the client, he found himself able to access past life and let Diabolis get in contact with his vampire DNA and, therefore, preceding generations of vampires who'd roamed the world more freely.

From this analysis Diabolis felt more secure in his decision to live as a solitary. He realized what repulsed him about the European mainland was how vampires had, through ignorance, discriminated against one another. He did not understand their logic and saw why it was best to follow his vampire nature in the Emerald Isle.

Doctor Rosenthal could easily have been Diabolis' supper. But Diabolis saw in him a doctor who felt it was paramount, before it was even considered popular, to hold an unconditional positive regard for his clients. So he paid him more than any of his other clients had, and terminated the analysis after six years, to return to Ireland.

Going into analysis he'd had no tolerance for himself. He'd despised his vampire identity as something which hijacked him, depriving him of normal mortality and the right of discovering what happens to a person when they die. The analysis taught him about this split identity within him, which caused him ambivalence, and, in turn, inner conflict and tension. He decided to continue his existence, as he understood it to be, to the best of his own ability. He had no full understanding, but was living life one day at a time. To continue he had to eat.

He believed that the vampire is indeed a peculiar, predatory, disgusting, surreally grotesque, horrific, nocturnal creature who is non-amiable most of the time, tends to be severely anti social, and is uncomfortably close to the Devil. Yet here was a creature that knows how to survive in the harshest of conditions.

When Diabolis' assistant delivered the blurbs that mainstream Irish media were producing about vampires, he wanted to scream. He was utterly disillusioned by society's inaccurate understanding of vampires and their nature. Subsumed by modern discourse on topics such as classless equality and ideal cosmetic beauty, the glorification of the vampire was the most perverse of all fictions he'd ever encountered.

# IX

## Every Dracula Needs a Renfield

The problem with any solitary lost in his own world is: nothing practical is accomplished. Diabolis had been distracted by his preoccupation with an analysis seventy years in his past.

So, the vampire made it his business to snap out of it. Walking into Temple Bar, he admonished himself: *Good heavens, you really have lost track of yourself! Your objective is to drink as many varieties of blood as possible, until you find that which will satiate you and help you to stop such frequent bouts of aging.*

He surveyed the masses that were part of this changed Dublin. There was a true variety of humanity which had come here, which made him salivate. For instance, he saw Africans around him with delicious ebony skin that only enhanced the rich, warm blood flowing within. *I suspect their blood is so fine that I wouldn't even need to consume it entirely,* he surmised. Diabolis couldn't believe he'd thus far neglected African blood, which he assumed would act upon him like a good hot whiskey. He eyed these splendid, sultry, dark products of jungles and deserts (which he'd dreamed of travelling to), and vowed to partake of this blood and lick this flesh when the depths of the Irish winter came upon him.

He was enthralled by this hypothesis: Living in a damp climate like Ireland's, where it seems like it will never stop raining and depression sets in from the worry of melting into slush, engenders an absolute horror of their weather by Ireland's natives. That same weather is a curiosity to tourists, who treat Ireland, not as some cold and dangerous swamp, but as a fabled land of lush, green beauty.

For the present, it satisfied Diabolis to stay in *Temple Bar Square*. It was a hub for various small streets which all met here, fed by the varieties of people who either lived in Dublin or were passing through. The new wave of immigrants strolled freely— Brazilians, Chinese, Poles, and Russians. Tourists who came to the city just for the weekend included: Americans, Australians, British, Canadians, French, and Germans. The sky was the limit! Diabolis could help himself to any of these foreign bloods, or simply wait for a more noble blood supply.

Frank, whose head he'd cut off and left on Deborah's table, had intimated noble blood might be in attendance at the Bram Stoker. However, he had been disappointed before in aristocratic blood that, when sampled, proved to be diluted. The aristocracy had lost their hold over Europe, and thus the potent nutritional value of their blood. Looking at this traffic of different bloods he had to acknowledge the changes that had happened in Irish society since the early 1990's. This was an excellent way to enrich the blood of the nation and make it more delectable to the likes of Diabolis.

He could find diversions in Temple Bar. To go clubbing did add the nuisances of an entry fee or of having to deal with idiotic bouncers. But, once admitted, he could find himself at close quarters with people and the delightful possibility of 'mixed drinks'—a little blood from one, and then a little from another. Or, he could just quietly observe and imbibe the atmosphere.

The busy night filled with those who lived and worshiped night life, making it their business to swarm the city's centre. After spending time hanging out, he was jaded with Temple

Bar—a box of businesses lumped together, haggling for tourists' attention. He wished to go somewhere less confining. He vacated Temple Bar and eased on over to Dawson Street's *Café En Seine*.

As he entered the café a song started playing that sounded like the lyrics were inspired by a vampire's thirst; it was the first time Diabolis had heard this song and was able to put a depth of meaning behind it. The aggressive singing matched the emerging hunger all around him. Yes, the midnight hour was coming and, gradually, 'more' was the order of the day.

Outside, where people smoked, he could see more and more entering, filling the place up. They would go to the counters and order rounds, then imbibe to the point of entering the zombie state. But he knew that alcohol alone could not be responsible for how peculiarly intoxicated these people were. Every song seemed to ease people into the herd on the dance floor. At first, there were two blondes mid-floor. But they vacated this spot in favour of a stage by the stairs, so they could display themselves to more effect. Their body language described total preoccupation with their own vanity. Nothing could get them off the high they were on, thanks to the abandon that allowed their exhibitionism. Diabolis listened to one contemporary song after another which spoke to the vanity and the sham that is night club life. And he could see, as midnight approached, the growing sexual hunger in the lonely single men. Single, but gyrating their bodies to a beat, it amused Diabolis to see them behave no differently than a beggar who holds out his cap—unabashed personal need on display.

Who was Diabolis going to choose to consume? *Decisions, decisions…* He purchased a pint of imported beer from Canada. At the counter, he felt invisible amongst the sea of people who flooded these alcoholic islands, waiting to be served, or, after being served, loitered and slowed the process of others being served.

His mind was telling him that imported mortals from foreign lands might have a more interesting and rich blood line. But he did not want to be desperate like the swarms of new arrivals to this club. This ritual was what people in this club performed faithfully every weekend. The club doors opened to the public and played music which talked of myth, so that the young could fall in love with their transient state, and those in their forties and fifties desperately trying to go back would not have to consider an increasingly unpleasant future.

These rituals were humorous and debased. Diabolis enjoyed observing them. There was the love sickness. Then there was the lust. The songs about being able to get with anyone in the club helped spur lost and lonely souls. Music promised that from all this chaos something more deep and profound would come. When the lights went down the fantasy emerged. When the lights came back on, the fantasy was frozen. And then the lights would be turned down again, and the ritual would recommence.

Diabolis went upstairs to the balcony with a pint of lager in his hands. When he got far enough, he could view the sea of humanity below. They were holding onto their pint bottles, or, having drunk them, and, if they were male, would be typically, nervously looking around for a woman to chat up. Lacking the sufficient intake of alcohol to do so, they would decide instead to join the squadrons of people on the dance floor in the hope that their desire would be sated there.

Lucis Diabolis was no different than a hormonal young adult who waits for the right one to come along. For something sweetly edible would help him feel that his night had passed most exquisitely. His eyes alone betrayed his otherworldliness. His body fooled others into thinking him one of them, but if they looked deeper, they'd know he was definitely not one of them. Yes, to the more discerning, there was something very weird about this man.

"I know ye!" said a gentleman of Ulster stock.

Balding, his hair a brownish grey, as was his full moustache, he had a shiny black walking stick and a jaded blue gaze that envied Diabolis' body strength. This thin figure swayed unsteadily before Diabolis. His facial flesh was taut and his frame took up five feet and ten inches of height, with trousers which looked like they barely fit. His clothes stated how out of place he was in the younger crowd there. On seeing Lucis Diabolis, he looked intensely relieved that someone he thought he recognised was present.

"Alex?" Lucis said, and thought, *No this could not be!* almost immediately; no way would he resemble this decayed, decidedly mortal, completely human, individual who appeared as if he was a snow man melting into sludge. No! This did not look at all like his maker, Alex Leman.

"Ah, that would be a good one, wouldn't it? Surely you did not mean Alex O'Shea, that cretin on the seventh floor? That dumb cunt...excuse my French...I meant *gentleman*...nearly cost me my job. He works in his own office because he's unable to work with others. You are *really* getting me confused. Great sense of humour, by the way. I know full well the names and jokes you deliver anytime you're at work. Now, for calling me Alex, I think you owe me a pint."

Diabolis believed the stranger made this cheap comment based upon the supposition that he probably had a phobia of putting hand into pocket. (But the opposite was true with Nigel. He spent frugally on himself, getting other people pints instead. He was renowned for buying whole crews of men alcohol. In fact, when he said, "I think you owe me a few pints," it was his way of saying I will run over and get you a refill. This was the old Irish way, the traditional way, the real Ulster way, and he was a true Irish Ulsterman.)

"Oh, I am getting you confused," said Diabolis, deploying his confessional style, so this mortal might sit near him and reveal the latest folly to visit the life of mortals on this earth. That way, he could observe and learn more about strange creatures which only got stranger to him over the long years.

"Indeed, Ray," Nigel said, his accent grating on the vampire's nerves.

Although Diabolis believed he was tolerant, his philosophy was: *It is not the sound of one's voice that matters or the colour of skin, but the content of a man's blood.*

"Surely you know me from the first floor, always letting me into the building at half-eleven on Friday night after I've had a few pints and was looking at you. And you were there complaining, 'I've got to stay here all night and you get to go out every Friday from four on.' And I tell you, 'This is what you get when you are working a nice nine to five and not having to work your anti-social, vampire hours. But, not to worry, Ray.'"

Weird, thought Diabolis, *he thinks my name is Ray.*

"I have been waiting to talk to you since ages, but sure we are here now, and isn't that the right time to be talking to you. It is the way nature intended. Now I see you are having a good old import from Canada and I will head off now and get you a refill. There is no point waiting with an empty pint of lager, Ray; you'll never pull the young girls here with that attitude. You got to look to them like you can have a few gargles and are able to enjoy yourself. I bet you are up to armpits with working only nights these past ten years. Let me treat you tonight. But here is the warning: you don't be a blood sucker of a vampire. I'm buying the gargle tonight. But just because I am not from the pale like you are doesn't mean I'm a thick man. I'll be buying the gargle here, but listen here, vampire! I know you might think, 'I will suck all the beers and spirits off this lad tonight and the next night, too.' No, Ray, *you* are buying the next night, okay?"

The stranger left Lucis and, as he was walking away, he imitated the fang motions of a vampire and shouted out loud, "You know your secret is safe with me. I see you watch those

Hammer Horrors at night time in the front reception there. Great craic, Ray, to be watching on your own there at night time; sure, I suppose it could be worse; you could be watching a dose of you-know-what, couldn't you? Now that would be something you could not get out of too easily if they found out."

*What does this guy want with me?* Diabolis wondered how he could get away from him, although his instincts told him to stay near him, to see if there was something that he could learn from him.

Diabolis would learn soon enough.

Nigel came back with two full pints of Canadian beer. "I love me few beers on a Friday. Afterwards, I go out and have myself two good, juicy hamburgers and chips. I love nice dry chips. You know I am some operator. That's me, *Nigel*, the operator where I work. Aye, you might think I'm just a simple operator because I work in an office? Well, don't you?"

"Well," Diabolis said. What more could he say to someone talking nonsense.

"Look around you, sonny," he said, sipping at his lager like it was soda. "You know, when this is finished, I'll get us both two cognacs each and we'll down them like real men. What you say, for old school sake?"

"I say, why not!" Diabolis responded.

"For old time sake," Nigel said, knocking his glass against Diabolis' glass.

"For old times' sake," Diabolis said, every word clearly enunciated like it was the King's English.

"You know, son, you've got more talents than you think. Aye, I mean you are a talented operator, you are. Now seriously, you are talented and you don't see your skills like I do. But," he said, gulping on that pint of lager and leaving traces of it on his moustache, "I see the talented operator you are. And I know talent when I see it. Surely, I do.

"Now," he said, pointing at all the people dancing, "see the people congregated here? Look at them, no, just examine them. They are a bunch of fuckin' posers, they are. I can guarantee you I made more money in one day than what any one of them would make in a year...during the Celtic Tiger."

"What were you doing, building?" Diabolis offered an educated guess.

"*Building*," Nigel sneered, as if Diabolis had said something derogatory about him.

"I was always a clever operator. I know how to make money, I do. But these other fuckers gathered here don't. They act like they do. And every girl has a price here, I guarantee you. All they want is a rich man with a fat bank account. Every woman has her price. It is as simple as that. That is what women are. Two divorces. Not one, no. Don't tell me about women. I know all there is to know about women. You are better off just shagging away everything in sight. And everything has its price. But it has a bigger one when you put a ring on it, or forget to put a rubber on. Then they take you for every pound that you earn, every miserable pound.

"I just look at a place and judge its value by where you can make a pound, and, if there's nowhere you can make a pound, that place has no fucking value. Everything I did, you know, had to have a way of making money. Aye, surely, this is the type of man I was, and more or less still am. You know everything has to have a bottom line for me—What pounds can I make here? And there has to be an answer for that."

"And so..." Diabolis encouraged, intrigued by this man who proclaimed that he was a man of means.

Diabolis was, however, never like him. Diabolis kept his business a secret. Yes, he was a man of means. But he never told anyone how he got those means. He thought it was most uncouth to talk about money, something only new rich would ever do, not those born into it and who knew the power of it all too well.

Diabolis did not know how he could just stay here and listen to this man. But he did. "Tell me how you earned your fortune."

"Well, I always knew how to make money," he said. "From the get-go I had this gift of earning money. I always liked what I did. And I always knew that I did it well. It was as simple as that. And I earned from an early age. I was always a worker. Now I will tell you more, but look at that guy over there with the tattoo and muscles."

They had a perfect view of everything below—and how he enjoyed this view because he observed clearly all that was around him. What did Nigel want with him observing the man with the tattoo?

Bouncing music played and, to be honest, it all sounded the same to Diabolis and Nigel. But the young girls took it seriously, including the two blondes he'd noticed earlier, who were miming every word of these songs, as if everyone was paying heed to their every movement.

"Do ye know what I mean about Mr. Tattoo?" Nigel said, pointing out with his head a man with tattoos dancing on the floor. "I will tell you, keep an eye on the man. He is some mover. In the meantime, I will get those hot cognacs I promised, less you start fanging like Lugosi on your late-night picture show you do be having on for me. And it's like you always say, 'You can't beat a bit of Lugosi on the weekend'."

Lucis Diabolis copped then what he was talking about, and knew within a few minutes Mr. Tattoo would be booted out of the place and told not to come back.

"Watch," Nigel told Diabolis, "he'll be chucked out of here soon."

That was because Mr. Tattoo kept dancing with a blonde girl with curly hair who was obviously spoken for and would not take no for an answer. And, true as night follows day, in went the bouncers to turf him out of the club just like Diabolis was told he would.

156

"You see! I knew he was trouble from the minute I saw him. And you know there is nothing you can do with an ignorant old whore like him, except throw him out with the garbage. Isn't that for sure?"

*Has all of Dublin fallen in love with vampires?* Diabolis asked himself. Was the reason why he thought he was the only vampire in Dublin because he was not aware of the norms of this time; perhaps the *True Blood* series was not fiction after all. Perhaps his kind had experienced a major coming-out-of-the-closet period and now lived mundane lives of total acceptance. Perhaps Diabolis was different because he just could not hack being new school, drinking animal blood, or getting a kind donor to come around, give him his fill, and say, "Good having you over; do come back for a cup of blood next day, and we shall talk about how I keep my fangs in such a healthy glow that I am practically a dentist's wet dream."

Of course, there was an unspeakable recession in Europe. Surely there were cutbacks even for vampires that caused them to be bloodthirsty again, although the running joke circulating in the pubs was that the men in parliament were taxing everything—from water, to bins, to property. The most telling part of what appeared to be a joke to most, but what Diabolis took seriously, was that the 'boys' in Leinster House were now asking for the very blood of the common man.

When Nigel came back with two glasses of hot cognac he started talking. "You see them idiots we have working in the House?"

"You mean Parliament?" Diabolis asked.

"Aye, the House of Irish Parliament—I used to know a few of them when I was working in logistics. During the boom, I brought in the money like Joe Ninety. No wonder you like them vampire movies. I understand exactly what you get out of it, surely I do. They are spot on, them flicks you watch. You see, I was like a vampire fanging for money, so I was—could not get enough of it. I'd have drunk another person's blood for money. Yeah, without a doubt, I surely would have drunk the life out of them and made them look like they were ghosts. There is nothing wrong with a man having to do what a man has got to do. Do you get me?

"The world is a bitch, though. I worked 24/7, and got nothing whatsoever to show for it, but sure it is all feedback they say, you know, and the feedback loop is where it is at.

"I bought property like a crazed fuckin' werewolf, so I did. Didn't expect the bubble would burst. You would just buy a property for sum x and, five years down the road, you'd expect there would be no bother, no bother in this God-earthly world for you to get that same property sold for twice, if not three times that amount. Thought this was the soundest economics in the world…did not know there could be something wrong. But there was something wrong with the damn system looking after the whole show. Then it was like the fucking schlocky Horror Show came to Ireland and rooted the arse out of the economy. And I nearly went broke.

"But…so did all the people here on the dance floor—yes, them, the ones I'm pointing at. Fuck them! Aye, you heard me; it is what I said. I am a true Fenian Celtic fucker, and I survived this recession because I'm a cool operator. It is why I have a job on the Dublin City Council. Oh, you're going to love the project we are working on this year. Do you want to know what it is called?"

"Yes," said Lucis Diaboli.

"I won't tell you unless you ask me."

"Okay, so what is the name of the project that you are working on this year?"

"My project? Now this is prestige personified, so it is; I'm working to organize the *Bram Stoker Festival of Dublin*! Now isn't that class?"

"It is as you implied," Diabolis replied, "class personified. It is surely. And you must tell me more about this project."

"I can show it to you on my i-pad."

"How do you mean?"

"What did I mean? Oh, is Mr. Lugosi not aware of modern technology? You are acting all aloof like you don't know that the worldwide web is even on one's cell phone."

"Please," Diabolis said, "I'd really like to know about this festival that you are helping to make happen."

"Ah, now good things happen to those who wait. You watch them vampire movies, so should know everything about the patient who goes around with his evil eye looking for a lovely damsel to bite. That is me. I am fucking delighted to be involved—it's class, so it is! To be involved in this festival is top quality, so it is! It is, surely. Now look at the quality involved; here it is on me i-pad."

He got out his i-pad and loaded the search engine for the Dublin Bram Stoker Festival. "Don't get me wrong there. I still wish I was in logistics, but that was twenty-four-hours-a-day work."

"So why did you quit?"

"Well, you fucking know that answer, don't you? The business went belly-up and I nearly lost everything, including my shirt, so off I went and decided to work on the council. I had to take a major pay decrease and be around people who think they are better than you because they have higher paying positions, but you know yourself I take it all on the chin, so I do, I do surely."

"Look, we'll be going into all kinds of laneways to see the macabre side of Dublin. And listen, Mr. Hammer Horror, we will be having lively discussions about all things vampire. I bet you have a real fetish there for talking about vampires; sure, you could lead a debate, so you could, with the organisers.

"Dublin Castle is a great setting, with Dublin's old cobblestone pavements for a play—my suggestion too, I am a powerful

159

suggestionist, so I am. I believe in the power of the unconscious mind; I am going to get a promotion after this festival because the people in power know these were all my ideas. You see, the unconscious mind is a powerful thing, so it is, absolutely powerful. And I really feel that power. Do you, young man, feel that power growing in you?"

"Not particularly."

"Not particularly—what you talking about there? You got to feel the power of the unconscious mind. I am not one of these talent merchants. I am a *true* operator. You have to get your twelve hundred hours of practise. That is how you accomplish things in life, not the other way round.

"Look. Just close your eyes and see a path. This path will show you exactly where we are going. Come now, close them eyes with me; it is great to get the old mind in proper operating gear. Aye, close them now and don't open them till I say so. It will be like Mr. Yipadoodle-Doo and his Missus Yipsi-Tripsi-Doodlie-Twipse.

"Do this now, and sure, you know it, in no time whatsoever, like Joe Ninety on his bike-a-doodle-doo, you will be imagining, with all that power of the unconscious mind, moving on and doing better, greater, more powerful things with your life.

"So, what is happening here? You are seeing what you *need* to see. You are watching what you *need* to watch. You are going to where you *need* to go. Well done, a doodle-doo and whoop-a-doodle-doo, because you are going to where the magical mysticism of the unconscious mind is, so you are.

"Now listen, listen carefully; this is imperative: listen to me. Hear me out now. See what you see. Go now. Feel what you feel. Hear what you hear. Smell what you smell. Touch what you are touching. You, at your optimally most powerful, I can make you successful. I can make you think rich, so I can. Grow rich, I tell you. Now listen to these intensely powerful, life-changing suggestions I am now making.

"You are going with me on this path of change—positive, affluent change—where wealth will come your way. It is like what those gods of Self-Help say, which you need to make your mantra: 'I can make you more intelligent. I can make you more positive. I can make you wiser.'

"But *you* need to do more. You need to put that into yourself, into your system, into your locus of self beliefs, and trust me on that one. Too many fuckers think poor, and they don't see how rich they are living their life today, in the power of the now. I was once mega-fuckin' rich, a somebody. I oozed fashion and social status. I am going to be again, and, let me assure you, you are coming with me. Aye, you surely are. Success, success, oh yes, repeat with me: SUCCESS!

"I am telling you, this festival highlights the world of the great author of *Dracula*, the king novel of the vampires. I *made* this festival. I helped UNESCO get involved. I got all these great writers of our time to come over to Dublin to talk to people. It was my idea to get them going down all the laneways at night."

"At night?" Diabolis asked.

"Ah, surely, it will be then. I'll get you a ticket. You'll see how all that hard work came into being, once the festival starts. Do you get me?"

"Why certainly, my good man."

"So you do, surely, get me. I just want you to picture our future shared success. We will both earn promotions at work. And we'll be drinking many Carlsbergs together after work. This self-help stuff has me sane to this very day."

"You know, doing those meditations has got me thinking about where I want to go."

"Really?" Nigel shouted over the blasting dance music. I love to hear an enthusiastic man, an operator like you, getting the excitement going about my self-philosophies. It is like I always have said when I started getting interested in becoming a Celtic Guru, and realized self-help and meditation is the truth and the light. It brings you to your true higher power and brings out your inner creator. Just see all the money pouring down from the skies into your pockets, gushing forth into your hands, and just lick your hands and imagine that this money is like juicy steaks on your plate."

"Exactly," agreed Lucis Diabolis. "I'd like to put on a play for this Bram Stoker Festival."

"Really?" Nigel said. "But I think the advertising has all been done."

"I think you can fit it into your busy festival schedule, if you know what I mean."

"Do you have a theatre company?"

"I most certainly do; just provide me with a stage and I'll look after the rest."

"Okay, but please give me your details. I have to okay this with my bosses."

"My details are on this card. By the way, is it true that there'll be members of the aristocracy at this festival?"

"There surely will—lords and so on are mad into the gothic and the macabre, so they are."

"Make sure they go to my play."

"Well, I need to know the name of your company first."

"Oh, I'll tell you that later. Are we going to sit here all night?"

"I was just thinking about showing you how I move with it and shake it. What d'you say, Mr. Diabolis? I will show you my game," said Nigel, gripping his pint with his hands and grooving to an 80's hit. "Aye, I'm going to show you that the life of a single man in Dublin is pure fucking heaven, so it is—with the drink and the occasional line or so, just to get the buzz flowing through you with the old recreational stimulants, to groove you through the night, aye."

Nigel started shaking himself all over Café En Seine like he was properly in charge of the place, like he was the king of the castle. No one was paying any attention to him. He was simply high as hell from the line he'd snorted in the toilet whilst getting his last stock of drinks. After three tunes that were getting him nowhere on the floor and only helped him look as anonymous as the rest of the people, he sat down again with Diabolis.

"Didn't I just rock the floor there with my groove; shaking my hips like a gangster whore, so I was. I was putting down the beats, truly, I was. My God, I should be up there giving it hell again, so I should."

"Most impressive dancing," Diabolis said.

"Aye, that is how positive expression works. I believe in being a positive man with positive expression. That is why I never watch the fucking news. The media just wants us to be depressed and focus on all that is bad with life. Even if I walk down the road and see a man begging or shooting some gear up, I just choose not to see that. I say, 'Ye're not there, so you are; ye do not exist.' I look at the clouds and place all my focus on the clouds, and I see this as the positivity, not the negativity, in the now. We all live in the now, where we have decisions and choices. And I choose to see the good, positive wave flowing over me. This is what I do. All that negativity? I just wash it away and sprinkle myself with pieces of positivity, so I do."

"So you are," said Diaboli, "a very positive man."

"Aye, aye, I am surely a positive man, so I am. You might think *that man lost money, so he is negative.* Aye, that is what ye might think. Don't you? But that is not what I am. I do daily, routine meditations, so I do. I see the money flowing into me. I think about cash rivers flowing to me. I think of all the money in the world, and I see all of its abundance floating my way. And boy, does that particular visualisation put a happy mood into my system, so it does, surely. I love money. Ach, aye, you could say I'm a rare old breed of Celtic Tiger; I like to get fat off profit. I need money, so I do, and I love and think if you want to earn money you have to change your attitude about it—like you, for

163

example, sitting in the reception all day. What has made you that way?"

Diabolis was utterly lost. "Um…nothing."

"Oh, it has. You have to develop a positive attitude towards money. A lot of people have negative attitudes about money. But I don't. You have to see the money coming into you and love the money, feel it, and maybe sometimes, which is what I do, sleep with the money."

"You think I need to change my ideas about how I feel about money?"

"Look, we all do. You need to start loving your money much more than anything else, and see the luxuries, the expensive items it will give you, see how it will change your life for the better, and see a new and improved version of yourself based on the awesome power that is money."

Diabolis felt like his head was about to explode from this man's passionate focus.

"I, Nigel, am the one the council should thank for the creation of this wonderful, classy, Dublin Bram Stoker Festival. Aye, it is true."

"And you feel that you are not monetarily rewarded adequately by the council."

"Do I feel that I have been adequately rewarded monetarily by the council? I mean, *are you for real?* Them guys should be bowing down and saying, 'Well done on the job you did there.'"

"I can help you get the respect and prestige you deserve," Diabolis said, knowing that his limousine had been parked outside Café En Seine and awaiting his arrival for the past twenty minutes. "Look into my eyes."

"What, Lugosi? You *have* been up too late working all these years."

"What are you afraid of—*my eyes?*"

"Aye, the power, the power!" Nigel said sarcastically, laughing at Diabolis.

"If you think it's funny and that I can't possibly help you, what are you waiting for?"

"This will be a laugh, so it will." Nigel looked straight into Diabolis' eyes.

Diabolis laughed hysterically and said, "Now, you really did not think I was into any of that mesmeric nonsense that you have me following all day long. I mean, seriously!"

"Of course not."

"I'm not Lugosi, you know, or looking for money. I am just me, although you seem to think I have an unhealthy interest in the dark and the macabre."

"Ach, it is not that. You spent your nights working reception, so what else was I to think? So I thought: here is a Walter Mitty who's sure he has the power to make a seasoned campaigner such as myself rich. I can turn anything into gold. If there is money to be found, I can harness it even from a stone, so I can. You don't have to tell a seasoned campaigner like myself what to do."

This could have been less exhausting for Diabolis. He could have walked away from Nigel, or could have extended his fangs and left him sitting there less some blood. But Diabolis remained patient, and announced, "I have our own taxi waiting just outside."

"You called for it on your mobile?" Nigel asked.

"No, not at all! I do not approve of those mobile, cell phone things; they impair one's privacy. One must be able to live without these distractions. I simply went to the counter at the start of the night and asked them to have a cab ready for me outside at this time. So do please follow me out."

"Okay, I will follow you. Sure, and what else would I be doing tonight? But I can't guarantee that I'll be able to get the okay for that play of yours to be put on in Dublin Castle."

"Let's talk about that stuff later. It is better when we are socialising simply to socialise."

Diabolis left with Nigel, going down the stairs and out the door of Café En Seine.

Nigel could not help but give a whistle of appreciation when he saw Diabolis' limousine, and another when Diabolis announced, "By the way, I own this car and this is my full time driver, Anthony."

"Yes," said Anthony in a very upper class English accent. "I am the full-time driver of this gentleman."

"Go away with you! Are you for real? How did you get this? How does a man who sits all night watching Lugosi and friends get a limousine?"

"I am not who you think I am." Diabolis almost cringed at having to get it into Nigel's thick skull that he was not a receptionist by trade.

"That was good one! '**I am not who you think I am**' Then *who* are you? And *where* have you been all my life, baby?" Nigel laughed hysterically.

"Get in, and I will begin to enlighten you."

# X

## True Mastery

"You got rich relatives somewhere, so you do." Nigel told Diabolis, once he was comfortably seated. "Somewhere down the blood line there is wealth pouring. What other explanation is there? A South Side Dubliner like you is not a country man like myself, refined because I've been everywhere in the world. Sure, and I am most cosmopolitan. I've been to Dubai, and all over the oil rich countries, including Baku…great place for the old mineral wealth. I've done a number of things. I am not just a Jack of All Trades. I am the *master* of about three of them, so I am. I guess you could say my trumpet blows itself for me."

"Anthony," Diabolis ordered, "if you could just park the car for awhile, I shall have a libation for myself of red wine from the Donor Club, and Nigel shall have one of my own draughts of wine, my own specially homemade one. Do you understand, Anthony?"

"Yes, I certainly do, sir," Anthony said.

"Really? Your own draught of wine—do you have your own vineyard out in your garden?"

"Well, what I am drinking is an import, but what I am giving you to drink is my own draught."

"Go away! Since when were there vineyards in Dublin?"

"Just relax and enjoy this libation. You will find that once you've sampled a draught such as this, your will to fulfil those positive goals you set will be even stronger. It works impeccably, or, as you say, do you get me?"

Anthony poured the gentlemen libations, of which both were most delighted to be in receipt.

Diabolis raised a weird toast. "You will get to where you have to go. Souls shall be fragmented and put into jars along the way. Souls will be subservient subjects of astral projection. You'll get where you need to go."

"Ha-ha, Lugosi is given a run for his money." Nigel was undismayed by the weirdness.

"Just drink up, and you'll see what you want to see."

"Ah goodness," Nigel said quaffing his strange libation, "this tops the old poteen I was getting from Uncle Andy, and I mean that was sixty to ninety percent alcohol—strongest fuckin' brew in the world—but this is something else!"

"Go on, skull it down the way this type of libation should be drunk. Look, follow me. Down it goes!"

"Aye, I can drink it down like a real man. Watch me."

"Well done, down the hatch!"

"Oh, that's some brew, and I am not talking the Iron-Brew of Scotland. This is *real* brew. I am sure it is made from more than just water, potatoes, sugar, and yeast. I hope I don't turn blind from it; it's powerful stuff man, powerful stuff, aye, aye, it is surely. Get me another one of those brews. Sure, you only live once, and I have been spending my life arsing around getting me work done like a damn slave to money. That libation is weird; it could drive me mad tonight, drive me mad forever, and I wouldn't care if it did.

"I might be seeing five of you. I might be seeing you all over or I might just go loop-dee-loop, but, surely you know, life is too short? You have to seize the day. *Carpe Diem*, me ole chum, Lugosi. What is with ye? You *are* beginning to look more vampiric, like you really are not who I thought. Well done, old

168

sharp tooth! You're beginning to appear right for the festival. Have to say that, aye. Now where's my second libation? I've been buyin' all night, so I have."

"Anthony, pour another glass of my own brew for my friend here. And, for me, can I have another? It is nice to be drinking here, isn't it?"

"Ach, aye it is," Nigel heartily agreed.

"But I was thinking we could go to your home and you could show me your plans for that festival so that we can fit my play in?" Diabolis suggested.

"Ach, I don't know. We'll have to ask the lads on the council about it, or else I may lose the old job…or maybe I am just being overdramatic."

"Of course you are! Can you not see the great influence I am?"

"Ach, give me that brew. Thanks, Anthony, and here's me address. I'll hand it to you; it's on my card in this wallet here. So take us there. Look, who are you really?"

"I'll tell you, but if you laugh I will not say another word."

"Go on then, tell me."

"I have learned to accept who I am. I would accept who I was even if I was working the most menial job in the world."

"Positive self-image must be a good thing to have."

"I've decided to realize what I am—no other than the *Son of Satan*." At these words, Nigel gulped his second libation as quickly as a dart landing on the board. "By the way, that is my blood you're drinking, which will make you subservient to me. It will not give you life, but slavery for eternity. Since I am an eternal slave to blood, you are now an eternal slave to my needs." Nigel, for once, was speechless.

"Do you get me…or don't you? Or, as you keep repeating—*surely*—because you always do what you do exceedingly well, and are always the best at it. From here on out you must be the best at serving me."

Before he could deny it, Nigel's body changed. He felt as dizzy as if he had been knocked in the head. His stomach felt like his inner organs were being devoured by flies. He believed fully that his drinking companion was none other than the Son of The Devil. And he had no spirituality to combat the assaults of the Devil.

"Put out your wrists and, trust me, it is for your own good! I denied what I was, lived apart, and fed as much as I needed to. My human nature has been all but gone for centuries.

Diabolis cut Nigel's wrists. "Do not say a word. Just give me your blood." Diabolis put some of the blood into a jar. "Soul fragment, your will shall be mine. I will have part of you with me to insure that."

"I don't mind serving you if you get my money back. Will I get all the money I lost in the Celtic Tiger when the recession kicked in?"

"Hold on for a moment. Let me taste your blood." Diabolis took a sample of blood and placed it on his fingers. He held no desire for it. He had so much control because his two glasses of 'brew' were vintage blood that Anthony held for him when work such as this needed to be done. What he had taken in these two glasses was the equivalent of a light lunch and certainly enough to satiate him.

"Our blood has been mixed quite well."

"So am I a vampire?"

"Most certainly not! You are what I've needed all along. And now that you have the inside track to this festival I shall take what is rightfully mine."

"What is rightly yours?"

"Let me talk abstractly. You see every living creature that walks these streets of Dublin? Their bodies and souls are all under me. I am over them. I do not need to tell them this. This is neither something that has to be appointed, nor overtly stated. Does anyone ever have to stand on pomp and ceremony when they claim a piece of property that is theirs? Get my point? The Son of the Devil is a hunter who seeks his prey without a sense that some things are within their ownership while others are not."

He examined Nigel and smiled. "Every Dracula needs his Renfield; thank you, Stoker, for this invaluable piece of scholarship and observation."

"Was Renfield not mad?"

"That was how he was presented. I thought this amiable character, the perfect servant, was rather sane. Anthony, have we far to go to this man's house?"

"Just about ten minutes, sir."

"Excellent!"

"You will let me into your house."

"I will do whatever you say, but…I miss my money from the boom, and want it back with interest. It was stolen from me."

"You will just run along, and let me in when the time comes."

"Oh, I will always let you in."

"That is for sure! Always let me in and serve my purpose. You will become what I want you to become. You ask, 'Was Renfield mad?' Even mad people can serve their purpose. Do you understand? Yes, creatures such as those not in their right minds can do splendid things driven by the darkest of passions."

Diabolis laughed loudly when he thought of the possibilities, for chaos greatly pleased him.

They reached Nigel's home. Nigel exited the limousine with Anthony and Diabolis, and walked to his house's front door. Diabolis followed and let his new Renfield open the door for him. He thought tenderly of Nigel, just like humans he saw with pet hamsters they indulged…before sensibly feeding them rat poison.

His poor Renfield was no more than putty in his hands. Diabolis sat him down for his induction and indoctrination about the peculiar state he had entered. Instantly, in Nigel's house, away from the prying eyes of the Dublin public, Diabolis took complete control. *Yes master* never had to be said, nor did Nigel have to call Diabolis 'master'. *Lucis Diabolis* sufficed: Lucis for Lucifer, Diabolis for Diabolical.

Nigel was transfixed by what he saw. There was no more denying the truth of this supernatural creature's true identity. This was not the same person Nigel had introduced himself to at the start of the evening.

"It is only midnight. Good heavens, I do work swiftly! Anthony has helped order me a coffin which shall be here before four am. Look at my face and watch it age as I speak; as words I utter pile up, my true age emerges. When I will it to, I show my true age, as I do now. Watch my youthful black hair greying before your eyes. And my hands and nails? Look how they slowly transform so that they become as sharp as any machete. I can make myself as ugly, aged, and decrepit as you can imagine, and yet remain immortal and still powerful. All of me changes, except my mouth. I can control my fangs.

"I've already eaten, have I not?" Diabolis said, showing his fangs to Nigel, "So I will not go near you." His fangs retracted. He flew to the ceiling and perched on Nigel's chandeliers. "Even when I sleep I won't leave you. I shall be like an eye in the sky. And your life shall be lived as if you were in a prison a lot like those that Bedlam devised but never completed. Everywhere you go, my eyes shall follow you, for there is no escaping that you consented and swore allegiance to me.

"Whatever affinity your soul may have had to the Righteous Power which transcends all creation has now abandoned you; you turned your back on it. The money you lost means more to you than God, and this shall make you my toy. Can you not say anything, as I place my foot upon your head? I can

172

trod on you. Some people say that all men are born free and then discuss the immorality of slavery. But I want my toy. You see, the more you talk of Dracula, the more I enjoy it. Turn on your contraption and enter your password. Yes, nod your head in accord. You shall change, and then make sure that my play is performed, and that the people who I want to be there—the aristocrats with their rich blood—shall have the best view of this theatre of my dreams.

"Good, I see now that you're on your computer. Remember, I see everything you do. Who wants to make errors for their master? All your thoughts must go to these things and pay no heed to the work that Anthony must do around you to make this house my home. You'll be an excellent toy. Just as there is a franchise of toys about superheroes, I'll recommend that there should be a franchise for toys just like you.

"Dear Nigel, my private and very own Renfield, I see how your head shakes backwards and forwards, and how your mind, unstable before I met you, is flowing even more abnormally. Is psychosis coming on you now? Imagine the psychosis and you shall be psychotic. You inhabit what the medical establishment might call a world of fears and paranoia. You see all manner of odd things, and your dreams, should you rest, are owned by these things. But, most of all, you are driven by devotion to me and the project of my forthcoming production."

Before Nigel met Diabolis, and was possessed by him, he'd lacked the common sense that would have informed this otherwise ambitious loner. He thought nothing of going out solo at night; his whole focus was skewed. The psycho-pathogens in his system nourished the seeds of greed. His needs never reached satiety, even at the height of the 1990's and early 2000's booms, when he was doing extremely well. He always wanted more.

Diabolis had psychic strings attached to Nigel; if the strings moved, Nigel was sure to follow. Nigel was, for Diabolis, the stepping stones in a violent river that would take his master to the other side, where the blood hunter could claim what was essential for his survival.

"The drama has only just begun." Nigel was transfixed. "Rearrange that festival. I know you can do it." Diabolis knew Nigel would do exactly as bid. It was the fourteenth of the month. Diabolis' play was scheduled for the twenty-eighth. Of course, he would design an excellent one.

Anthony entered and announced, "This house has been prepared for you to your standards."

"Is all in readiness?"

"Yes, I was even able to get the model of coffin you requested. Will there be anything more for tonight?"

"No, not at all."

Nigel printed out the list of Very Important People who were attending the festival.

"You see, Nigel, this woman who writes scary stuff for the kids—no need for her to be given any special seat—nor any lecturer, author of fiction, or horror movie specialist. Let them be seated with the other plebs. They have no special interest in this night of drama. Better still, un-invite them. Ah now, on to our aristocrats—here is the list: German names, Swiss names, British names, French names, lords and ladies—these I want to have preferential seating. Even if they have mixed with nouveau-rich blood, I'll not deny them their seat, like a good whore who should never be exiled from bed."

Nigel spent thirty minutes quietly arranging cancellations for those previously scheduled to perform at this event and rearranging it to fit in Diabolis' offering.

"People are like zombies, and need to be entertained to distract them from their lives and from the fact that morbidity is staring them straight in the face at all times. Describe my play as unique, the best in the genre, spectacular, and previewed by the council, who have approved this as a true homage to the maker of the novel *Dracula*. The cast is a mix of newcomers and very famous names in horror which shall be unveiled on opening night to keep suspense brewing. Well written, Nigel! Now publish this on the website. And Nigel, do you have annual leave?"

"I do, and was going to go to Spain."

"But Dublin is just fine in October, and you shall ring your boss that you want annual leave until the 27th. You need the time to prepare a very special play. I trust they won't ask any awkward questions."

"But, they…they know…" began Nigel, trembling at the thought of having to explain any type of adversity or problems that he might encounter to anyone. "They know I am in charge and will get this festival going."

"So remind them that everything is exactly as it should be. Goodness, I know how agitated councils get—even the most minor glitch can cause them to have a nervous breakdown. Tell them everything is going exactly to plan, save for the Drama Society, which cancelled for the 28th. So you are arranging for an excellent Horror Drama Society to replace them, one you are sure can outperform and become more famous in time than the ones who intended to be there."

"Okay."

"Of course, okay! This is mere trivia. Wait till it all kicks off."

# XI

## Hold that Tiger

Although Lucis Diabolis was indeed clever, Nigel was in no fit state to go to work. Something in him had broken. Diabolis lay in his tomb, resting like a log, while Nigel went hyper. His first action was to strip naked, except for a leopard-skin thong (kept as a token of his first conquest in his top dresser drawer). He gyrated in place, moving his hips as if he was humping the table.

"Thank you, Master!" he kept shouting. "Fuckin' yeah, yeah, yeah, man, you are the master. I am your servant. Lucis, who's the man? You are, bang on. Look at you up there on the ceiling. You are the master of my universe. Yeah you! I will out-monster anyone, and with a kick up the fucking hole, so I will.

"I used to be the money man, the one who went after others' money. I'll make them that took it give me my fucking money back, those motherfuckers. I was weak, but you up there on the ceiling give me strength, all I fucking need, so you do."

Lucis Diabolis opened his eyes and smiled at Nigel when he heard this. For he saw that he still had power over vulnerable human souls who wanted to take more than their rightful bite in life. Even though he was resting securely, he could compel Nigel anytime, anywhere.

"Man, you are here—you are everywhere. I see my master on the ceiling and hear your voice in my ears. And I am telling you, 'Watch out, world, because this is our world—mine and Mr. Diabolis'. We'll make this world ours, so we will, aye, and I'll get back at those robbing bastards who wanted to put me in jail and say I was fucking bankrupt—bankrupt, my fucking arse! They're playing with fire. They thought they took my power and possessions, and left me to rot. I knew luxury and will know it again. People will be serving me on their fucking knees. My command will be law, so it will; it will hit them like a truckload of bricks on their head. Aye, they'll shite themselves, when I say, all paramilitary-looking-thug-IRA style, 'Down on your knees!' and will feel the power I have over them—of life and death. 'Oh, let me serve you,' they'll beg.

"But then what will I say? 'Listen, don't serve me—serve the Vampire of Dublin—for a reward more important than winning the All-Ireland final in Gaelic football. Aye, get down on your knees and serve a *true* master." The wind in Nigel's mental sails suddenly shifted. "Aye, it's great to be on annual leave. A hard worker like me can finally relax then and release all the tension in his system."

Still wearing nothing but the thong, Nigel started shaking like he was doing a voodoo dance. He got his mop handle and knocked the mop head off it. "My master requires a bit of blood," he said, looking directly towards where he perceived Lucis Diabolis. "Who will feed you when you are hungry? I am hungry too. And ye reply, 'Well, if ye know I'm hungry, why don't ye feed me?' Aye, certainly, Master, I'll feed you because you are hungry and need nourishment, so you do. This stick can become a wand to get the quality stuff right to you, so it can. You ask, 'What will you do to feed me?' Don't fret. Old Nigey is here to make sure there will not be a bother. I still have my big machete to cut you the most prime game. Here I go, a wild and brave Ulster man, to show you what I can get you."

Nigel, in his thong, was about to leave his house. In his left hand he held his decapitated mop. His right hand gripped his machete. He saw himself as nothing short of the bravest of hunters bound for the wilds, and meant to return joyfully to the tribe with his kill.

"Woopsie doodle, tripsy daisy! I forgot my flask. Well, Nigey, you'd forget your head was it not tied onto you, so you'd better be careful not to cut it off with your own machete. You'll never be able to serve tea without a flask. Didn't your mommy always tell you that?"

Nigel was as happy as when he used to sit near rusted steel barrels in the farmyard and watch rainwater fill them. "Those were the glory days back there on the farm in Ulster." He got his flask beside the tea bags in his cupboard. "There'll be the finest tea in South Dublin put into this flask here, aye. Now Nigey, you're fully prepared for the world out there, so you are. That's champion, so it is."

Slamming the door behind him, Nigel strutted forth, proud that he had ridden the Celtic Tiger and survived the ride. He'd always thought everything was relative and everyone played off the same team sheet; his higher power was relativism. *If the man in the moon does not give you what you want, and the dude in the sun either, ask the lad downstairs to give you a hand, and you might just get it; that way you will get your money handed to you and everything will be great.*

He swaggered along, the Bee Gees playing in his ear, sure, by goodness, that he was one hell of a ladies' man in his thong. He was going to show Dublin what he was made of and awe them. He'd spent too many years of thankless labour—waking up like a prick at the crack of dawn to go to work—to let a bunch of robbing bastards like the bank and the tax man could come along and wreck his economy, his Celtic Tiger, his Emerald Garden of Prosperity. Workaholics like him deserved to become millionaires and look down their noses at those who could not hack it like real men. It made Nigel mad, proper fucking mad, and no one was going to take this Ulsterman's booty. Did these Long John Silvers think they could go around filling their Leprechaun pots with his gold?

"Lucis, you are the Robin Hood of Ireland. You are getting the blood of those who mercilessly took the life blood of the people. You know how much I want my money; they're not getting another fucking brown cent off me. I want my fucking money, and I want it now. I'll drain the veins of those human bloodsuckers."

Nigel stomped down Rathgar Road in high dudgeon.

Postman Joe was hurtling down Rathgar Road like he had a herd of Southern Italian Mafioso hard on his heels. He was drunk after wagering money at his bookie's (acquired by stealing a couple of hundred euros from mail). Joe was built square and solid, except for the man boobs that, thanks to his drinking habit, had spoiled this hunk. He might well have been succumbing to lactational insanity after overhearing in Slattery's that they were on the verge of arresting the one responsible for taking money from the envelopes meant for charities.

*Ah, that is me they're discussing,* Joe thought, sad he'd never achieve hero status like Postman Pat had locally for toddlers. It was shocking how fast a fat dude could exit Slattery's. *I'll be fuckin' killed in prison for this when the other prisoners find out I stole from the neediest charities in Irish society!* He glanced down when he felt something wet. The white creamy froth of his latest pint saturated his trousers, causing his crotch area to look like he'd been drilling during work hours. *No! Work hours are for sorting the post and making sure charitable donation mail is well looked after. I can't go to prison, surely I can't.* So Joe ran like Linford Christie, though looking more like Ben Johnson on steroids. The effort had him drowning in perspiration.

Nigel, however, did not see a fat dude breaking all records for exceptional feats of running under extreme cardio stress.

He saw what he thought was a robbing, dirty whore—one of *them*, part of the very organisation that bled his country dry and threw it away: a uniformed minion of the Irish State!

Joe was breaking track records, and when he got close to Nigel, his usual common sense (which would have dictated to him to avoid the naked guy in leopard-skin thongs, despite the intolerably cold Irish weather) simply did not kick in. He just kept running. Nigel, waiting until he was in punching range, struck Joe square in the nose and knocked him down.

"Now I'll fill me flask bloody full," Nigel insisted as he held the dazed man's head by the hair with his right hand to expose his throat. "Yum, yum, yum, like chocolate cookies I used to make for my wives before I was estranged from them. Diabolis will be licking his lips over this."

When Joe saw the size of the machete in Nigel's hands he nearly fainted. "I did not…" Postman Joe began, believing that this might be a distressed victim of his theft, "mean to take the money and put it in my pocket."

"That was *my* money. That was my hard-earned fuckin' money that you robbing cunts took from me. I needed that for my fortune. I was left with not a fraction of my money. Let this machete teach you manners."

"No…no, please stop and think! I will do time in jail, so I will."

"Aye, you and the other bunch of lads who stole from the Irish people and put our economy into austerity, you will go to jail, will you? Will you now? You bastard! You might as well be a stealing, raping, murdering bastard for all the trouble your kind did in Ireland, doing a Jack the Ripper on the guts of the economy, so hard- working men could not dress in their boots and hardhats and go off to work drillin' holes. Picture that it was a head they were drilling into. You know what stopped me from drillin' holes in people's heads back when the country was booming? It was the fact I was earning my cash and no one was stealing my money from me."

"Don't kill me. I didn't mean to steal from the needy and disabled."

"You stole from hard-working construction workers…and geniuses in logistics like me. Ye plundered from us like you were some Viking invader of old. You took what was not fucking yours to take."

"I am bleeding sorry."

"Aye, you're sorry for bleeding the worker dry who breaks his back on scaffolding all the live-long day with the cracks of his arse showing because he is so busy struggling to make enough to survive on. You go around stealing from me with your Dub cunt of an accent, with your city voice coming out of your throat, whilst I am a country man. A real country Irishman *works* for his bread. Aye, I worked day and night for mine. You look down on us country men as bog men that shag sheep because there are no women in the country. I always earned my money and loved it, and even used to take it to bed with me before it was stolen by the likes of you robbing bastards in power in Dublin. Well, shit arse, say your prayers to what ever deity you like because Lucis Diabolis wants your blood to drink. And I am my master's servant, who, ever since this recession, wanted a dark angel of vengeance to help me get my pound of flesh. Well, my pounds of flesh are going to be piling up. I'll cut you up and bleed you dry, and follow you with more, done likewise, I'm sure."

"I did not mean to do it," whined Joe.

"All ye fucking *human* vampires are alike—draining ordinary persons dry, then pretending you're sorry."

"I'm an ordinary worker just like you."

"Oh, fucking spare me."

"*Stop that!*" Nigel heard a commanding voice say.

"Says who?" Nigel asked, eyeing fat Joe suspiciously.

"I swear I didn't say anything," said Joe, eyeing Nigel back as if he hoped for a reprieve.

"I do not want this vulgar blood," said Diabolis. "Let him be and do your thing elsewhere."

"What thing?"

"Do not worry. I will guide you this day. But you'd best be running down the laneway. If the Garda see you they will arrest you."

"But he took my money!"

"Do not worry about him, Nigel. The Garda will arrest him shortly."

The scantily–clad Nigel stood up and fled down a laneway, but his blood was racing so strongly that his whole body was warm. He found a cluster of big black bins and decided to hide behind them.

A Garda, walking up from Rathmines onto Rathgar Road, found the postman lying on the ground, and recognized him as the worker CCTV coverage had revealed to be the robber of the charities' mail. She arrested him without even asking him why his nose was bloody.

After she read him his rights, he said, "I did not know robbing from people could cause so much offence that they'd want to cut my head off."

"Well," said the Garda, "you're not only going to be the talk of the Garda Siochana, but all of Ireland."

"But I did not mean to do it. I just needed enough money for drinking and gambling."

Nigel hid behind the garbage bin and talked away to Lucis Diabolis, who could follow him wherever he went. Lucis was able to do so, even while resting in the tomb, because he had, in a jar, a portion of what was meant to be Nigel's soul—traded in for the promise of getting his money back.

"Get your act together," Lucis Diabolis warned. "What happens to men when they go around the streets of Dublin wearing only a thong like they've lost their minds?"

"I didn't *mean* to act insane," Nigel confessed.

"It is not insanity. Get your act together, Nigel, and do not be apologetic; be servile. What makes you think there's an insane fibre in your being? Those who walk around like they aren't just made of flesh and bone are insane in not knowing the limits to their own capabilities."

"Sure, all this is like the song, *Rock Me Baby*. I was just trying to be your number one man. Like a true devotee should, I was getting blood for you.

"What kind of a bog man are you thinking I am that I, Lucis Diabolis, should like the blood of a thief? A thief who robs from the neediest has blood unfit for consumption, would you not agree?"

"Well, I'm doing my best for you. I even spent a few hours asking more aristocrats to come over, at the expense of journalists who may have wished to attend the festival. That is the best way I can follow you."

"Aristocratic blood really turns me on. One must gather a master class and let only their blood fill special vats. I want to be able to send for it like you would for pints of Guinness from the brewery in Saint James Gate."

"I'd bleed every fucker dry for you."

"I don't doubt that. I can see by the blood hunger in your eyes how much you really want it."

"I do, I do. I will bleed every Lord, Dame, Baron, Baroness, Duke, Duchess, Count, and Countess dry for you. I would do it in a heartbeat if I could."

"Such aristocratic blood is rare. I will need an army of your kind to obtain and store it in flasks."

After those words, Nigel prostrated himself as if he had fallen completely head-over-heels for Diabolis. "For ye, O Master Diabolis, I will do anything, but how will I be special if I am but one amongst many?"

"*Special* you ask?" Diabolis smirked and nearly wet himself. "Why did you not consider this? Every army needs a general."

"*General* Nigel! Aye, what about it? General of *what?*"

"General of King Lucis Diabolis' Army."

"Well, how about making me King of the Castle."

"Yes," agreed Diabolis, "Nigel, the King of Dublin Castle."

"What a proud man I am now. I will do what my master says."

"Why yes, Nigel, simply follow me, my lamb."

"I will do just that."

"There's to be no cutting human throats or killing them in other ways until I say so."

"Yes, Master."

"If you fail, you will not see all the riches of Ireland come your way."

A black cat, tail high, sauntered down the lane meowing and purring. Diabolis nodded at Nigel, who nodded back. "Bring that miniature Celtic Tiger near; he is in mood to cooperate."

Nigel did not come from tender-hearted stock; animals were beneath him. But his motto was anything that Diabolis wanted done would be done. "Come here, you furry fucker," Nigel was about to say, but as he looked at Diabolis, he saw him placing his fingers to his mouth.

Diabolis pointed his long finger and indicated with it for the puss to approach.

The cat instantly went to Nigel. "What do you want me to do, pet it?"

"No," Diabolis said. "I think you know what to do."

"Oh, I do, surely."

Nigel's hand closed in a vice-like grip on the cat. The cat bit his hand, but Nigel held on, irrespective of the cat's clawing deep gouges into Nigel's flesh. Nigel continued holding onto the cat, and said, "Hi there, putty tat. Boy, do I have a snip for you." With his machete, he sliced off the cat's head. "I wonder what an animal-rights activist would think of the work I'm doing here."

Finished, Nigel stuck the cat's head onto his stick where the mop used to be. It reminded him of a hobby horse he'd had as a child. He took up the corpse and started gnawing on it. "Ach, who said you can't eat cat before you cook it is dead wrong, to be sure."

Nigel had always wondered how simple beasts saw the world, so he cut out the cat's eyes, popped them into his mouth, chewed, and swallowed with gusto. "Ach, ach, it's surely gourmet fare here, better than the Shelbourne. No need for me to be a posh Ulsterman—I've got it good right in this laneway, so I do. Forget Paris, ach though Paris is uber splendid, aye, tres bon. But fresh cat makes for fine healthy eating, I'm sure."

Nigel felt his tour of South Dublin was only starting. In his mind, he walked over to the Tram off Palmerston Park, illegally boarded the Luas, and travelled on to Dundrum; then it was off to Leapordstown in his leopard-skin thong, where he would fit right in with the locals. He shook his stick with its cat head and shouted, 'Keep on Rockin' Me'. Oh, he was in fine fettle...at least in his mind.

The zoophagous maniac licked cat innards and stuck them on his chest like medals. "Oh yes, this feels real good, ach, real good. I could fry them in a pan like sausages. They taste better than supermarket meat. Last time I checked that contained traces of horse DNA. This is 100% pure, unadulterated cat, so it is. What, Old Nigey, will the locals say about you now with your Cheshire cat grin on your face?" Nigel cut out the claws of the cat and scraped his skin bloody. "Old Nigey surely is the cat's meow now, so he is."

Nigel licked at the mixture of cat's blood and his own, sure he was capturing the life essence of this sacrificed beast. "And if anyone says anything whatsoever to this Ulsterman about his choice of food, I'll tell them, looking straight at them as if I could spoon their eyeballs out of their heads: 'What fucking business do you have disturbing my breakfast?' And that surely should put the shits straight through them."

Nigel whipped off the cat's tail with his machete and said, "I'll put this in me trousers and finally give the girls something to look at. 'What about you?' I will say when passing them, and they will so want me!"

When Nigel had had enough of the cat, he threw what was left in the nearest bin and laughed away to himself as if he was just after viewing a very amusing comedy. Feeling frisky, he skipped off down the lane as hardy as one of *The Hardy Boys*. But, just as he was about to adjust his thong because the furry tail was tickling him, he heard a crack of thunder in the sky.

"What is it, Diabolis?"

"Throw away that machete or it will bring the wrong type of attention to you."

"Aye, Master, I'll do as you say." And, heeding Lucis Diabolis' orders, he threw his knife down.

"What do you want from me, bar the promise that you will get your noble blood supply?"

"All that your master demands is patience and obedience. You will know what to do. Parade down the streets of Dublin with your cat's head stick and dance like you've come to liberate Ireland from the English."

Those words were music to Nigel's ears. He began gyrating. He felt he'd been freed to party forever by his master. He walked right into the middle of Rathgar Road and started to make humping, thrusting movements, unconcerned that this was not going to gain him any fans among those driving there.

"I am the conqueror," he roared, "I am going to show you people how to protest. They took our blood. They took our fucking bleeding blood. And I am going to show you how to get theirs."

A handsome man driving a black Mercedes stopped his car to avoid Nigel and impatiently eyed his watch. Although well-dressed and looking like he'd reached the pinnacle of success, Cathal felt the weight of the world pressing on him. The expensive haircut, fancy watch, fine manners, and refined, cultivated speech hid the mountains of distress that buried his whole life. It was not that he *wanted* to disturb Nigel's fun, but that he had an important meeting with his bank manager. He needed to show him he could handle his personal finances, be orderly, and survive without scraping by. Yes, looks can be very deceiving, especially in an affluent, upper-middle-class neighbourhood like Rathgar, where everyone was expected to be soft-spoken, passive, inoffensive, and live anonymously, while keeping up appearances. Cathal needed to get to that bank in Terenure Road, and his nerves were eating him alive. Exasperated, he rang 11811 on his cell phone, was answered by an operator, and asked to be referred on to the Rathmines Station.

Nigel heard, but ignored, the sirens…until he saw the two police cars. When the police stopped, got out, and approached him, Nigel shouted at them, "What do you want with me?"

"We just need you to put your stick on the ground and come along with us."

"This is my stick, *mine*! And Dublin is my temple; you can't deny me the right to worship my master."

"Look," said one confident Garda, walking over to him, "We'll give you your stick back, and where you are going you can worship whatever it is you are worshipping all the time— no questions."

"I can worship my master all the time, and you won't disturb me?"

"We would not *dream* of disturbing you in that place."

"Okay, lads, let's go there; it sounds just right for me."

# XII

## Sense and Nonsense

The Garda had no problem finding three doctors to certify Nigel insane, in the floridly acute stage of psychosis, and in need of urgent medical attention.

"I hope I'm going to get plenty of drugs," he told the doctors. "I really could use a little dose to take my mind into a brand new universe of colourful images. You tell me I'm mad, so I say, aye, I'm crazy as the glue coming out of the hatter's head, and want drugs to help me enjoy the weirdness. Ha-ha-ha-ha."

Nigel found his own humour delicious and exquisite. He was laughing so hard that tears squeezed out of his eyes and was so excited he felt like banging his head on the table, but hammered his knuckles there instead.

"Aye, *smarties* would help me—doctor one and doctor two and doctor three."

The doctors were serious experts on the mind and the brain's physiology. They had studied mental illness intensely and observed enough that with such a thorough exposure to nervous disorders, suicidal ideations, perverse thinking, obsessional thoughts, illogical and irrational behaviour, psychotic symptoms, personalities devoid of character, anti-social pathologies, and mental disorders of other varieties (running the entire histrionic and narcissistic, to the psychotic, delusional, and schizophrenic spectrum), that, absorbed with all the other manifestations of developmental/maturational disorders, their *own* ability to feel normal was limited.

The psychiatrists had become so neutral within themselves that they sublimated all emotion in order to function successfully in a profession that was once known as 'alienist'. Psychiatry learned to become alien, or the alienists' personalities and characters had been drowned by excessive exposure to the world of clinical and forensic psychiatry, which, in truth, was toxic to them, or any human being.

As Nigel elucidated why and what kind of *smarties* he wanted them to give him, they considered what they would say to the Consultant Psychiatrist to help Nigel climb out of his mental morass. The treatment of the soul had thus become the purview of Western Scientific psychiatric discourse; the concept that Nigel was possessed by an invasive, evil spirit would never fit the discussion and treatment 'box', save via unorthodox practitioner.

"My master keeps in touch by mobile phone." Nigel tapped his head and winked. "He's aware I'll be your 'guest' for a week or two." The doctors eyed their subject as if sure he'd be with them much longer, for months, if not years. "So, could you write down his phone number? He wants to visit me here."

Nigel tilted his head, listening intently to what only he could hear, then addressed them again, "He says you should save his phone number so he can come and take good care of me."

"I will surely do what you say, Master, surely." Nigel shared the number he heard and watched as the doctors wrote it down. "My friend says, 'Thank you, and be sure to give me a buzz.'"

"Have you often seen and talked to this *friend?*"

"No, he's a new one. He is great craic and he'd make you laugh. He's into all kinds of bloody things—bloody crazy, he is... so dog nuts, he's barking. But he is sound too, so he is. Although he is bloody good craic, he is raw-nerve powerful. He really can

189

command, so he can, but those commands help me. I've been under a great stress these past few years that nearly ate me alive and had me staying up all night."

"*Stress* you say?"

"The type of stress to beat the band! Ever since the arse went out of the economy, I've not been normal. It cut my heart open having to work for someone else. On my own, I was raking in the dosh, so I was—felt angry ever since. But this man, who does not wish me to give you his name, is a good master, but private; he can save me from the misery of being an employee and even make me a king."

"Could you ask his permission to tell us his name?"

"Okay, okay….hey, master, could you please tell these others here who you are? He is saying *no*. I will ask him why and see what he says. He says that all will be revealed in its own time. Very vague our man is, aye, and very abstract, prophetic…and weird, which is what I like most about him. And how do I know he is powerful? I can sense dark power just leaping, jumping, and roaring in him, so I can. By goodness, I enjoy it to no end, so I do. Makes me want to say, 'This is my man, aye, my man.'"

There was nothing more to be said to Nigel, the only one present who could perceive him. Lucis Diabolis placed his finger to his mouth and told him, "Be quiet now, for an open mouth catches the most flies."

Although Nigel always acted like he did not know the meaning of quiet, he understood fully this time and did accordingly. But, just as the psychiatrists began to leave so that Nigel could be assigned a room, he could not help but quip, "How do you guys do it?"

"Do what?" they replied.

"Manage to stay sane in insane places. I know I find it mighty hard."

In answer, Nigel was admitted to the intensive care unit of the psychiatric hospital. His brand of psychosis fit the requirements for admission: being a public nuisance, nearly nude on a cold October day in Ireland, body scars indicating that he was a danger to himself, and the cat's head indicating that he was a danger to animals.

"At least give me my stick! Come on," he begged the nurses, who knew they'd have to keep a firm eye on their charge the next few days.

"Where are you, Lucis Diabolis? Why aren't you there for me?" he whined, and got no answer. "I trust you will come back to me, so you will."

During dinner Nigel ate like a ravenous pig. The other inmates just stared at him and did not say a word. This was the quietest they had ever been. One haggard, alcoholic harridan in her late fifties, who was usually verbally and physically abusive, felt that Nigel was, even by her obnoxious standards, one person to tolerate.

"You are not alone," she whispered, winking. "The Dark Master has sent you here, hasn't he?"

"How did you know that?"

"We *all* know that! The only ones who do not know are the people giving us our meds."

"Well, you better tell the patients not to be going around telling the doctors or nurses here. Understand?"

"Oh," she said, her face brutalized from years of alcohol abuse, "we might be considered lunatics, maniacs, mad, insane, but we are not that crazy! We are more sound than the sane. Those psychiatrists don't know a thing about what they are doing, not like I do."

"You've learnt what life is about, so you have. Enough said. Now go on, and if the master asks you for help, make sure you say, 'Aye, Master, anything you say.' He dislikes insubordination."

"Yes, Master, yes!"

"You've done your learning well."

191

"Ah," she said, winking again, as all the patients lined up.

"What's going on?" Nigel asked, eyeing the clock. "Why are you all are getting into line? It's only five."

"Five pm is medication time. Which ones are you having?"

"They never mentioned anything about me having to take medication, but I'll take what you are taking."

"*You* don't decide what medication to take."

"Who does?"

"Your psychiatrist."

"My fuckin' psychiatrist! And sure, what would they know about old Nigey here?"

"I know, Nigel, but take them anyway. It will make life better for you."

"Okay, I will do it, but just this once." Nigel joined them, and thought that he certainly had no business being there. He paid no attention to the drugs handed to him, save for the fact that, some fifteen minutes later, he was not his usual hyperactive self.

"Goodness," he said to the girl he was chatting up, "I got to take a wee nap."

"Doesn't surprise me," she said. "What they gave you would knock even a bull out for days."

Nigel slept and slept and slept. When he opened his eyes he would see a male nurse injecting him, and would go right back to sleep again. Usually being knocked out leaves not a trace of recollection of that time. Nigel, however, kept seeing a perfect image of Diabolis telling him that it was necessary for him to sleep for this long period.

When he woke up, after what must have been days of being drugged, he opened his eyes, but Diabolis was nowhere. He looked under the bed. He looked up at the ceiling. He thought the master might be hidden in the small wardrobe next to the bed. But he was not there either. He called out to Diabolis and got no answer. This was distressful. Nigel left his room and started walking the halls. After exhausting himself looking throughout the ward, he walked into the smokers' room. The patients there looked like they'd never smiled; like him, they were wearing pyjamas.

One patient, Mark, was also paranoid. Nigel extended his hand and said, "I am Nigel. What about you?"

Mark was so depressed, he gave no introduction, but went straight to, "What are you here for?"

"I don't know. I was just having a dance and had very little on, but, hey, it's supposed to be a free country, isn't it?"

"What were you wearing?"

"If I remember correctly, I was a wearing a leopard-skin thong."

"*That* is not a reason to be here."

"It sure is not a reason to deprive a man of his freedom."

"Guys go around wearing leopard-skin thongs in the gay bars all the time."

"They do surely, and not a word is said to them by the police."

"So what *way* were you dancing?"

"I was doing a bit of Mickey Jackson, trying to conjure up some spirits for the latest Vampire Festival."

"In the George?"

"No. No. I was dancing in the middle of Rathgar Road."

"I am here because I feel that my life is worthless," Mark confided.

"Must be because of the recession. Recession fucked up *my* life totally."

"No, it's worse than that. My life has been made worthless. I hear voices in my head that are very cruel. I have constant headaches from those disgusting voices."

"Can you *see* them, or are they just voices?"

193

"Many times they appear to me—foul, angry, demanding, controlling, negative, aggressive—like they're after my blood. That should be enough, but no, they want more. They are vulgar, emaciated creatures with compelling eyes and sharp features. And, boy, do they act menacing. I tried to escape from the horrid things at night by running down dim streets until my heart beat like a heavy-metal drummer in a rock band. I would look behind me and see a shadowy figure following me. Hands would grab my feet or throat, and mouths would press against my skin. I swear I felt fangs! The whole damn experience was unnatural.

"I could sense when I was in for it, especially while living in London. Finally, I called out, 'What is your name?' The shadow did not choose to answer right away. I kept asking and, eventually, he said in a mocking voice, 'Not that it's anything to you, but my name is *Alex Leman*'.

"He admitted to me later, 'Your blood is precious; you are a hidden treasure—deliciously aristocratic'.

When I told my psychiatrist, of course, it was recorded as symptomatic of paranoid schizophrenia, which tricks me into feeling more special than most. They say my illness drives this belief in my own grandeur."

"And are you of aristocratic blood?"

"The psychiatrists say this is a morbid fantasy, but my anaemia says otherwise. I am a blood donor for a vampire! They think I want to be a vampire, a complex that is rare. One psychiatrist said I had Renfield Syndrome and could be dangerous. He should be laughed down for saying this. I've been here in this unit for ages, and have not exhibited the behaviour of a Renfield. You'd be surprised how often the doctors here make strange diagnoses. I know one man who was called schizophrenic four months ago. Last week he was graduated to being bipolar! Only two weeks before this, a clinical psychologist assessed him as having borderline personality disorder. They believe I, too, wear the hats of many insanities.

"As for me and Renfield Syndrome, I don't get erections at the thought of doing something violent to another animal. I do not find insects or raw meat edible. I do not accept that a vampire could be a master or a higher power. I have not a trace of violence in my history. I have an extraordinary IQ, rendered useless by the schizophrenia which destroys my ability to study what I like—physics and chemistry.

"I am stuck working, when not here, for a minimum wage. I've never hurt an animal or lusted over the blood of another, but I do know what it is like to have my blood taken from me. Leman told me he must never totally kill me or make me a vampire, but must keep me alive so he can drink from what he calls a *vital* source. I moved to Ireland and Leman did not follow, but occasionally has visited. Other hideous things followed me, though. They claim to be the slaves of Leman, who will do anything to return me to London."

"Ach," Nigel said, "he must find your blood very enriching."

"Yes he does. Why? Listen to me. I come from a humble family. At eighteen I learned I was adopted. I have since paid money to do research on this. I worked eighty hours a week, every night in security, to save the money for this. It drove me even madder. But I knew I had to find out the truth of my origins."

"Oh, poor man," said Nigel, "that must have made your health worse."

"The closer it came to me being able to discover through DNA tests the root origin of what I am, the more dreams I had involving tiny blood suckers. The blood suckers exited an egg and began searching for prey. Usually, they found a dying human in the middle of a forest. I would see them swarming over the fallen person and start eating them alive, and I would feel what that victim felt! This would cause me to get so weak that I could not move. These dreams bled over into the waking world. I'd come home from my job and the disgusting creatures had fol-

195

lowed me! Weeks progressed. I saw their bodies enlarge. They would sleep during the day beside me in an egg, which actually grew in size.

"Once I slept uncommonly well. I always remember the rare times I sleep well. I woke up and saw before me myriads of tiny blood suckers obscuring everything. I heard the commanding voice of Alex Leman warning them, 'This is not your food, but mine; as sure as night turns to day, he will return to me'.

"I did *not* return. I wanted to feel that Ireland was my refuge. I am not a Renfield…except that when the health and safety officers came to my home, they found cats' and dogs' heads. The bodies had been consumed by those blood suckers, some of whom grew to the size of a small person. The skins looked very grotesque.

"I have not been to my apartment for five months. I was taken from there to here. And here, every time I ask for help, a different type of madness emerges like a demonic presence. No possession can be worse than this, no control more horrible to endure. When I admitted I have tormentors, people in white suits would listen, ask about my mood, and deliver medication. Every time I complained, a different type of medication—likely just a higher dosage—was administered. The medication was a chemical straightjacket. It was like a hand that was extracting parts of my mind, leaving nothing but a space like wind and a body that stores the wind within.

"When you have an oppressor, it is impossible to trust anyone. I certainly do not. But if I were to say this, it would be written down as symptomatic of paranoia. Nothing I do is perceived as a crisis of spirituality. The country is going through perverse changes, and so is the world; were I to say that the cause and the answer to this disease is spiritual, people would label this mere schizophrenic perception."

"Well, you look normal enough to me," Nigel said. "And is the medication they give you still strong?"

196

"I am playing the game."

"You are playing the game?"

"That is what I said."

"And what does that mean?"

"It means I want to get out of here. The only way you get out of the intensive care unit to less restraining units is to operate a system of garbage in, garbage out. They ask me about my mood. I say I am feeling better. They write down 'stable'. They ask me if I still want to cut animals' bodies up? I tell them that seems like some distant nightmare. (Despite what they found, I know I never hurt an animal in my life.) They write down 'Patient is becoming less of a threat to others.' and ask me if I hear voices? I think about this question. I don't say I hear none. They are smart enough to detect bullshit. So I cut the truth in half. The longer I've been taking their meds, the less I seem to see and hear, and the better I feel. This is good because they have lessened my dose. Now, as for you, were you doing anything else to get here?"

"I was just praising a master I met who looked into my eyes and told me I'd get all my money back from the recession."

"When did you meet this master?"

"Met him the day before I came here."

"What a great master!" said Mark sarcastically. "Is he worthy of your unconditional obedience, if *before* you met him, you had your freedom. He has made a great contribution to your life by getting you in here, hasn't he? THINK! How will you get that money back? How could he possibly get it for you?"

"He has the power to do that."

"No, he does not. Believe me, such creatures are like the Devil who tempted Christ. They'll show you every sort of material wealth and promise that, if you bow down to them, they'll give you the whole world. Tell me one practical thing he has said, anything that made sense about what he would do to help you as a human being."

197

"I trust Lucis Diabolis."

"You *know* Lucis Diabolis?"

"Aye, do you?"

"I've done everything in my power *not* to know him."

"So, you know *about* him."

"I know his maker, Leman, who used to talk about him and his deeds constantly. His stories about Diabolis were told when the blood suckers were invading my home. I can never forget the tales of Diabolis. I would watch those blood suckers grow after coming into my house with all the pets from the neighbourhood. Leman would laugh and say what the suckers harvested in my house would never match the quality he bestowed upon Diabolis, who was his favourite. There will never be a vampire more favoured by him again, he assured me."

"Well, you are going to know *all* about him."

"He has possessed you and controls you, Nigel."

"Like a demon?"

"Is that not what they are?"

"I would not be so sure, Mark."

"Be sure."

"Why?"

"Just be damn sure."

"Are you not possessed by them also? You're in the same institution as me, are you not?"

"I am not going to be possessed anymore. When was the last time he spoke to you or appeared to you?"

"I think I've told you far too much."

"I'm not asking you for my sake. Wake up, man! You are being overcome by a force as evil as any known to mankind. You must not let yourself be sacrificed. What *else* has he got you doing?" Mark stood up and walked over to Nigel. "Look into my eyes if you are not his slave, and the whore of the demonic vampire."

"Lucis Diabolis is *not* a demon."

198

"If he's not a demon, what in hell do you fucking think the name *Lucis Diabolis* means, except Lucifer and devil? This is what the creature is, nothing less."

"He inspired me to go around half naked."

"What did you think that was, some dance act you were part of? He had you going around half naked in Ireland, in this cold, damp place. What a *great* inspiration he is!"

"Aye, and with a stick and a machete. I was going to chop off a person's head, put it on the stick, and dance. I found a black cat instead and, with my machete, put an end to its damn meows."

"He has got you wanting to kill people. This fucker won't have you wealthy and rich. He'll have you doing life. He will take whatever the hell he wants from you. And what is it that he wants?"

"Ummm."

"Come on, spit it out? Have you seen him since you came here?"

"Since I opened my eyes after the heavy medication? No."

"Well, you see, in your case you must trust your doctors, even if they do not get the more spiritual aspects of this. Oh, to you they may come across as overly paid quacks. In truth, they are just decent, hard-working people who really understand the brain's physiology and human behaviour.

"Don't get me wrong. They *do not* get me. I am not that thick to think that just because they are decent people it means that they will get me. They are also limited and straightjacketed by the confines of their education, skills, and training, like any person in this world."

"I am beginning to understand you."

"Do not just understand me. Help yourself! Take their medication. Obviously it disagrees with Diabolis, and he is unable to penetrate the inner layer of your mind."

"Aye, that may be so, but he knows where I am and he will visit. I must be prepared for him."

"What did he say he wanted?"

"Noble blood, the blood of the aristocracy."

"Blood such as mine?"

"Now, come on, surely you're just a loser."

"I also cleaned toilets, washed dishes, was a porter in a hotel, and a messenger boy, though I am not brain dead. I have read as many books as the psychiatrists, since the one thing I've always had at my disposal is time."

"Still doesn't make you a noble, does it?"

"Why?"

"Well, you do know it is all in the blood."

"My DNA was tested, and I can confirm you are right: it as all in the blood, my blood."

"Diabolis is surely going to consider you a gourmet banquet."

"Might he now? And how much of this blood does he want—one person's or more?"

"Oh…at least 80."

"And what does a relatively innocent, if not easily-led person like yourself, have to do with him? Is he not going a bit simple in his vampire old age?"

"I am running the Bram Stoker Festival and bringing them all here."

"And what happens after that?"

"I guess it's like driving cattle to the abattoir…which he will do on the 28th of this month in Dublin Castle. I've already invited them."

"So, your job is done. He won't be coming here anymore."

"No, you see, I have to introduce the play before it starts."

"And does he know that?"

"I explained it to him when I was making the changes."

"He is probably arranging something else."

"Surely."

"When he comes here, do not look at me, and ignore him. I will sense him before you will and act so incoherent that he won't know me. Will there be others there?"

"Other vampires?"

"Surely he won't drink 80 nobles dry himself?"

"I would not know that." Nigel shrugged in dismissal.

"That does not matter. If we can go to Dublin Castle that night, I'll sort this problem out myself."

"Fuck," Nigel said, "you're right! That prick is just using me because he knows I'm in a bad mood with the world."

"That's what these fuckers do. Here, come with me."

Nigel joined Mark in his room. "Look," Mark said, "keep taking your medication. That stuff will help you to be to be less susceptible to Diabolis. Goodness man, don't you know how lucky you are? You were going to cut a man's head off with a machete. Be glad you're here and not in jail, for fuck sake."

Mary, the haggard alcoholic, walked by saying, "I'm fuckin' pissed off with the whole fuckin' lot of you. I swear you fuckin' idiots don't know *who* I fuckin' am."

"Nurses are coming soon," Mark said. "Watch her; I know this routine like clockwork. Her main problem is her character."

*Bloody Mary*, as nicknamed by Mark, was scared shitless of saying her name three times in front of dimly-lit mirrors, lest what was said about her was true concerning what would happen next.

"NO!" Mary roared as the male nurses approached to deal with the situation. "Take your hands off me. I need some time to calm down. But then we need to arrange a meeting with the people here. They need to know the proper way to run this institution."

201

"Diabolis will have a true leader in her. He could wrap her around his finger."

"What is up with her?" asked Nigel.

"She's a raging alcoholic, who pisses and craps herself and walks around with it. She curses at you, tells you where you should be, and asks you where you were."

"Nuts," Nigel responded, making a circular motion with his finger next to his right ear.

"Ah, you don't know the half of it. She's narcissistic as hell, and will fight and punch you if you tell her what to do. Only the male nurses can deal with her. The female nurses are told not to go near her because she has attacked them so many times and even disfigured one of them. But the woman is certified insane, so what the fuck can anyone do about her behaviour? She is a ward of the hospital, if you know what I mean. She bites, scratches, tears hair out, and craves power. She *already* thinks she's the boss here."

"Are ye thinking of using her as some kind of decoy when Diabolis comes?"

"I am not," Mark said. "These people around here are too irrational to be used as decoys or anything else; what they do is their concern. I know what *I* will do if Diabolis comes my way. I plan to fight these fucking vampires, and to defeat them. They've taken too much away from me. But never mind what I will do. Just do as I say. Let me plan the rest."

# XIII

## Anticipation

Diabolis had been in high spirits ever since Nigel went to the psychiatric hospital. Picturing the upcoming planned events as he did, what more could a vampire wish for? The question was: how would he bottle the precious blood the event would net him?

He studied the 'who's who' of the world's aristocracy invited to his Dublin Castle offering. For a person craving to be around high society, reading this list was the wildest of wet dreams come true. This elite group consisted neither of diplomats nor politicians nor new rich, but only the oldest aristocratic blood. For Diabolis they were the finest crop of red wine in the world. Just as a farmer must tend to his crops and livestock, Diabolis had a duty of care. Such blood had to be handled well in the harvesting.

Diabolis played around with Nigel's internet—a magnificent invention, channelling all the information that he could ever want. YouTube actually talked and moved, but email was more useful. Nigel had left Diabolis his email account password and user name. Diabolis learned its quirks through trial and error, excited that real people were mailing information to this account. The more time he spent reading Nigel's email, the more he learned about Nigel, from what he ate, to his most mundane preferences.

Diabolis kept having dreams of how the 28th of October would work out for him. Perhaps some aristocrats would get so sick that they would spew forth a delicious Niagara Falls of blood. He pictured them doing so. His minions would be right there with buckets to collect every precious drop, pour all the buckets into kegs aboard 'beer' trucks, which would be driven off to a secret location where he could spend years living on this 'brew'.

His dreams were looking more feasible by the minute. Email responses flowed in from Luxembourg, San Marino, the Netherlands, Sweden, Norway, Germany, Russia, Monaco, and Britain. These positive responses had the makings of a fantastic night in Dublin Castle. And Diabolis knew precisely which elegant words would entice the hesitant into believing they might miss out on excellent festivities.

The riffraff—those of non-aristocratic blood, the idiots who bought their tickets online, the media hacks and journalists, and 'famed authors' of dark fiction—were informed not to attend this night because there had been a change of plan. As for Joe Public, repayments of tickets would be made on the 29th of October; he wrote this laughing, adding that he regretted this inconvenience due to factors beyond his control (the typical lines of any incompetent who screws up and can't fix the problem in a timely manner).

The irony was as delicious as the orgasm of a first heroin rush, oozing pleasure and sensuality. One could become addicted to treating people like lab rats. He was as industrious as the clever squirrels that gather their nuts in a special place so they can nibble away all winter long. To open aristocratic necks and collect their blood meticulously would be divine, like going to an ice cream machine and watching the treat rolling into the cone. The blood would be rushing out so gorgeously and deliciously that no normal vampire could be expected to wait patiently for blood to fill the bucket. Of all the blood—the gothic blood, the blood of junkies, the blood of the new rich, the blood of the middle class, the blood of the educated soul, the blood of the virgin, the blood of the moral anchorite—noble blood was the most delicious.

Diabolis knew he would have to plunge his fangs into those noble throats—a glorious sensation, as if their blood could both pleasure the recipient and bequeath glowing health and vitality. The thought of sharing this blood was detestable. He'd waited so long to taste this feast, so why share with anyone else? His biggest worry was his own capacity; he wondered whether he could acquire his hunted meal in the orthodox fashion—usually one to five victims—when eighty were available.

Diabolis was determined to proceed slowly to graze upon this healthiest and most nutritious of foods. Their flesh would be covered in the most expensive and fashionable clothing imaginable. He would arrive looking so horrible and morbid that stomachs might turn. For Diabolis to look any other way was unlikely. The stomach can only take in so much food; after that, it gets irritable and upset and does not want to consume. To enjoy this food he needed to fast for days because this was a meal of which he would wish to eat every portion. He did not need a mother figure to tell him to make sure he did not leave a scrap of such rare fare on his plate.

The idea that so many fine-blooded people were coming to this town was delightful. He could care less how they spoke or what they wore, accessorized by what jewelry. Blood is not like any other type of food. It is not made better with additives, but is best served plain. Human personality did not matter to Diabolis.

Anxiety over whether his guests' ships and planes would arrive on time troubled Diabolis. Then he thought how stupid he was in an era where things usually ran on time. He looked around. Nigel's home was even more perfect than his tomb in Harold's Cross. The temperature was ideal for vampire comfort.

He found himself watching Nigel's television. At first it was deplorably bland. He could not figure out how to change channels, which made him want to tear out his hair. Then he picked up the thing beside him which looked like a calculator and played around with it—the channels changed. This discovery was excellent indeed. He felt sedated by the strange rectangular thing hanging on the wall, and as transfixed as victims he'd mesmerized.

On one channel he saw a sick dolphin, whose human minders froze and fed fish for it. This modality of preserving food caused Diabolis to salivate. If he could freeze all the people who attended his presentation and put them into a truck for frozen foods, he could have a total of eighty aristocratic bodies to thaw and drink blood from whenever he wished. But no, the idea was stupid; just like processed foods for humans, thawed blood would never taste as good to vampires as that of a fresh kill. What other intelligent idea could he come up with? What drama would he create for the Bram Stoker Festival?

"Yes, I've got it!" He decided to arrange a meeting with some special folk at eight on Effra Road.

When he considered what else might support such a night, certain music kept sweetly nesting in his ears. "Yes, we must supply our aristocrats with the best punk-rock-horror music. It will help their blood brew nicely while I wait for it to settle and pour."

He googled the internet for music that would create the adequate connection he needed to have with his audience. The sinister chords of the guitar should ooze out, giving the listeners the sense that the skipping rope of life was removed from underneath and was being attached to their necks; playing this sick game meant allowing the chords in their necks to be enwrapped with those in the music. Its notes could burst brains and turn bodies into mush. An explosion of sound could make them feel like terror was besieging them and about to surmount the walls of their hearts. It should be loud and vulgar enough to remind them how much propriety had dwindled as modernity, with the onset of social mobility and change, demanded—from the advent of Republics to the rise of the Reds, unappreciative of just who they were annihilating, whether at the guillotine or in the gulags. (If they had, they would have forced them to breed and put their blood into vats!)

Diabolis thought this extermination of noble bloodlines so wasteful. They were such exquisite gourmet, like truffles, impossible to describe adequately in words, those anaemic bastards that only linguists would be foolish enough to feed on.

To his relief, Diabolis finally located his ideal horror music. His friend YouTube played it for him. Dressed today, as he was, in atypical vampire clothing, he felt as if his cape, bow tie, and hair defied the true style of the vampire, to the disappointment of the present age aficionado. The punk rock did justice to his memories of inquisitorial torture, arousing such strong sentiments of empathy in him. "Yes," he said to this work, "*thank you for your understanding!*" And he laughed insanely.

He read the names billed as attending the festival to commemorate the spirit of Dracula, along with those slaves to horror who visited it in their tales, and he raised the volume of the music. He roared defiantly, happily, "THIS IS MINE, MINE, MINE!" He lay back in his chair and stared at the ceiling and smiled. His smile was not cherubic, but that of the voyeur watching demons chop off heads, collect the blood that poured forth, and who salivated until it was served. After being served a sparkling pint glass and draining its crimson contents, with wild eyes and vile tongue, the drinker bangs his knuckles on the table to demand seconds. (Truthfully, there is more grief over trees felled in the Amazon than when heads roll in Hell's Pub.)

The music was so splendid; it sang to the bitterest parts of his alienated heart and transported him to a land he called Erosium. Ladies were scantily clad and surrounded by buff, toga-clad admirers in these palatial surroundings. Orgies were rife. Libations were poured. Lest their olive skin perspire, feathered fans cooled it. The fans were wielded by slaves whose duty was to forget their own discomforts and focus on the comforts of their masters and mistresses. The rock music called up such scenes. As the heat increased, the masters asked the slaves to fan faster. But the temperature did not decrease. What at first felt like a sauna soon became a furnace.

For Satan, as ransom for their indulgence, would consume them, flesh and bone, letting Diabolis drink voraciously of their blood. Erosium's orgasms would be converted into gore-gasms, while demons danced with joy around naked and dead bodies. Because he never did, Lucis would not join the dance, but merely smile as he watched, sated by his fine dining.

When the punk music stopped playing, it ejected the vampire from his Erosium fantasy. He realized he needed to embrace the fantasy of this gore-gasmic Dublin Bram Stoker Festival, the trademark he was creating for future festivals to replicate internationally. When the demons arrived and agreed to partake in his play, what script would he prepare for them, how would they rehearse, and what costumes and presentation would this play need? He put the horror punk rock he'd selected on again and lapsed into another fantasy of how this play would play out for him.

# XIV

## Interaction

Queen Madhorn was the vilest whore-bitch of Middle Abbey Street, sporting (thanks to her surgeon) in the middle of her forehead, two mini horns she called *incubus one* and *two*. She would shake and caress them and say, "It's okay, mini horns, good things come in small parcels," as if she dared not offend the horns by giving the impression that size counts. She was too fond of her twins for that. But when she earned more money from doing various tricks around town she had her surgeon install on the top of her forehead *succubus one* and *two*. She loved to touch these horns more. None of the tricks she performed could satiate her like they could.

"Rasta man," she used to say, and shake her shoulder-length, black dreads. She put studs in her nose, on her stomach, and, when a customer asked, "shaved and visible down there," which both helped his smile to emerge and her to chill out, relax, and enjoy pleasuring, being pleasured, getting paid, and smoking weed.

Then she stopped feeling empowered by doing this, and switched to doing things that motivated Lucis Diabolis to say, "This is an amoral pervert I could ask at any time to follow me, should I need it."

When Anthony the driver knocked on the door of her tattoo parlour and asked her if she'd go to a meeting with the one she knew simply as 'Lucis ' at a certain address, she smiled such a smile that Anthony swore she *wanted* him just for making this suggestion. (At least the dyed-blue, shaven sides of her scalp turned red.)

"And shall I bring the few followers I've recruited to my ranks?"

Anthony smiled. "Your horde of human vampires impresses Diabolis. He has ordered me to inform you that you will get what you want when you want it, should you follow him."

Her eyes, whitened near the center and very dark further away, glowed. Her grin displayed her fangs (acquired from dental work in Hungary, taking full advantage of their much cheaper dental care in comparison to Ireland's). It elated a queen who was more than happy to do the Devil's work.

Her horde of human wannabe vampires would love to meet a real one that she swore on her life she knew. Her idealisation of George Haigh and his habit of dissolving bodies in sulphuric acid was intriguing. The horde left as sludge in canisters the decomposed humans they had bled to enjoy a libation or two from before returning to lives of ordinary, all-consuming boredom. They left bodies around Ireland in piles, unworried about being apprehended. The demand had lately become much greater for Queen Madhorn to make this crew into the supernatural vampires they craved to become.

Queen Madhorn was beside herself with joy. Blasting loud splatter punk, she imagined being invited to fellate Lucis Diabolis. This was unlikely, given her unnatural appearance. The four horns on her head looked as if whenever she got angry they could grow bigger and drill holes through the skull of her enemy. Her face was pale white in contrast to the soot-black area around her eyes. This was essential so that no mortal creature could look her in the eyes she believed were the pathway to the soul. Her hair was an expression of rioting against order and conformity. The sides of her head were shaved; the crown of her head had long, dark, snaky locks hooked together by a silver clasp in the shape of a band of stars.

But, when she danced ecstatically to the beat, it was of her horns that she was proudest. She repeated what she so often told her followers, even though they weren't there to hear it this time. "Behold these horns of mine. Some say I got them by transplant and without any anaesthetic, a legend that exemplifies my strength. Your silence speaks volumes about what cowards you are. My horns," she lied, "aren't fake. I was born this way."

Finished with her mandatory punk dance, she sat down. She looked at pictures of *George Haigh, the Acid Bath Murderer.* She smiled at them like a lover seduced for the very first time. How she adored the Vampiric Acid Murderer and begged her cult to practise exsanguinations just as John Haigh had, bar the use of a gun. A machete would suffice, for a gun made far too much noise. When blood was collected in a chalice for consummation, the cult had learned to treat the corpse like meat—making a mockery of the concept that civilisation follows respect for the dead. She thought it hilarious to defy this respect; her ideal fun was turning the dead into sludge by putting corpses into vats with acid. Her cult learned how to kill in cold blood, to puncture the arteries of victims with no remorse at the thought of stealing their life blood, a rich source of iron.

Madhorn's cult honoured two minor deities, The Acid Bath Killer and The Brooklyn Vampire. The major deity, because he was truly a creature of the supernatural, was Lucis Diabolis. Queen Madhorn's other personal hero, and broader society's enemy, was The Brooklyn Vampire—also known as The Grey Man and The Werewolf of Hysteria—Albert Fish. What was it about this strange fish that gained her admiration for an otherwise abominable stain on the human race? Queen Madhorn loved his bestial nature, confessing to her fellow vampires, Effsgog, Batsville, Ordog, and, especially, Lady Unmentionable—Athagornia

211

Nebsonia, (who was extremely retiring and red-faced at the mention of sexual matters) that she'd dreamt that she was in the prison with him at his electrocution. Madhorn would have nursed any tendency a vulnerable prisoner could have in this situation to express the humiliating utterances of remorse. She would even have organised a sing-along for The Grey Butcher in the Sing-Sing Facility. No one who followed her realized that amongst her malevolent deities was a child rapist and cannibal. She seemed only to focus on The Butcher's brutality to humans and exclude the other offences which oozed with sheer depravity.

As for John George Haigh, the cult carried out his style of homicide—using acid to dissolve bodies. No one dared admit that, just like the odious Albert Fish, George Haigh was not a true vampire. Both were damaged humans from extremely dysfunctional families, who boasted about the evil they'd committed. No one cared to mention that both were caught in the end and brought to justice for their crimes.

In this vampire cult the authoritarian, brutal, and vulgar communications of Queen Madhorn were always greeted with blind obedience. When she mentioned only John George Haigh and The Brooklyn Vampire her cult's expectations were mundane. They expected only to emulate these murderers by invading homes, draining the occupants' bodies of blood, and performing 'occult' rituals.

When Queen Madhorn had encountered Diabolis and realized that the supernatural vampire exists, she was utterly seduced by him. If she had been smart she'd have kept this secret. But she was not and could not. Pride tempted her to tell all and thus empowered Diabolis to demand from her cult anything that he should need. Once the word got out, she had to do something. She went begging to Diabolis' tomb.

Diabolis considered the whole thing symptomatic of the idiocy of mortality, whereby they are subjects of ambition and its wild manifestations. All he ever said to Madhorn to keep her hopes up was, "I will make you a supernatural vampire when the time comes."

"We will obey your every wish," she replied with ecstatic emotion. "Then will you make me a vampire?"

"I certainly will do that, provided you do whatever is asked of you."

"I shall do anything you ask of me," she replied.

Diabolis was not fooled by her lustful voice, for he was turned off by the sight of Madhorn. He did his utmost to stay polite and left her baser instincts unanswered (her typical customer being the type with perverted sexual demands, the list of which was more rare than common). He watched her text her cult members.

"All my followers have texted me to confirm their attendance at your meeting," she soon assured him.

# XV

## A Meeting of the Membership

Madhorn's cult members, who went by the aliases of Athagornia, Batsville the Ugly, Effsgog, and Ordog, stood out from just about any crowd on any street in Dublin.

Ordog was chalk-pale, with dark eyelashes and darker eyes. He had a long nose, pointy ears, and thin, too-red lips. His strange face was topped by straight, soot-black hair tied back in a pony tail reaching down to his waist. He wore a black shirt with a crimson collar and silver buttons. He had fingernails a cat would envy; they were as long and sharp as if he'd been growing them forever. His physique was equally odd, for he was a seven-foot tall collection of bones under a wafer-thin layer of skin. He was like a tree grown upwards minus the support of a well-developed trunk. He reminded Madhorn of the villain in the silent movie *Nosferatu*.

Like a preoccupied child, Ordog was interested only in the DVD in his hands. "I've got to show this vampire short film I made." At twenty past seven, when he was picked up outside the Garden of Remembrance at the top of O' Connell Street in Madhorn's black van he announced this to his fellow cultists who just wanted him to be quiet.

Batsville was pissed off with him. He felt outraged, yet tried to follow the advice of a Serbian general who once told his men: *Don't get emotional; you'll live longer.* Batsville believed he did his utmost to tame his emotions by committing the evil acts Queen Madhorn had taught him. He moved from controlling his emotions to being controlled. The more apathy he felt holding innocent victims captive until they roared in pain as his group bled them dry, the more he ignored the conscience developed at age eight. Batsville *knew* he was more loyal to Queen Madhorn than despicable and selfish Ordog, the creative artist who constantly tested the boundaries of cult thinking. He also felt free to offer Ordog his opinion.

"Your DVD has no business in this meeting with the only real vampire of Dublin, so keep quiet about it!"

Initially, Batsville had tried a variety of street drugs to literally burn out human emotions. He'd smoked tonnes of cannabis from the age of fifteen. Although this had turned his brain to mush and his voice was slow, it gave the appearance that he was impossibly relaxed. His inner mind was extinct and his outer appearance did not match his inner world. This inner world was certainly a paranoid and discontented place to be in. He was too quiet around people. He always suspected girlfriends were unfaithful, which probably willed them to be, since it is a rule of the mind that you get more of what you focus on. He based this suspicion on the most whimsical of evidence. The slow way he talked hid numerous subversive, misanthropic views, such as his desire to join a terrorist organisation and blow up certain buildings which he attributed to belonging to broader enemy organisations. He illogically reasoned that these enemy organisations fully intended to depopulate the world through mass eugenicist policies, unleash Armageddon, and, of course, were working to wipe out him and his kind in the process.

Madhorn, he was certain, would never approve of Ordog's DVD; sitting in the front seat of the van, Batsville was sure of this. Batsville's emotions had not conflagrated, just led to excess consumption. He achieved his bloating from eating birds, vermin and small animals because he wanted to be the Renfield of the crew. The back of the leather jacket on his lap displayed a lifelike image of a flying bat with a highly accurate anatomy. He massaged the bat and thought of how well he managed to stay drug free by following Queen Madhorn's commands—through the joint activities of homicide and drinking the blood of others without disgust, regret, guilt, shame, embarrassment, self restraint, or pity for the human creature he was destroying.

Effsgog did not care about this issue because his mentality matched his short stature. He said nothing, for he lacked a point of view and copied that of others. Effsgog's appearance showed exactly what he was—expressionless, bland, ridiculously pale, and sporting a short, blue Mohawk.

"Effsgog doesn't mind if I show him the DVD," Ordog said.

"Since when has *Effsgog* been known to possess an opinion about anything?" Batsville replied. He had no respect for someone like Effsgog, whose gullible personality rendered him vulnerable to the type of cults developed by Queen Madhorn. Batsville saw himself as being enlightened by a leader who could teach him to control his addictions and the emotions he believed caused them. Having investigated numerous possible solutions, Madhorn's seemed to work well for him.

Ordog was one of those frustrated artists with a deranged sense of expression who has not the ability to independently find a functioning outlet for their creativity. This mercurial artistic temperament, stymied and patently frustrated, had been redirected into hellish fury.

Lady Unmentionable, Athagornia the Vulgar, felt she did not belong in mainstream society. She stayed quiet and content with doing as she was told, despite Madhorn's abusive style. "Do it, you miserable, cursed piece of filth," Madhorn would command on a killing mission. Madhorn had other names for her,

216

each more vulgar than the next. All she was succeeding in doing was bullying and victimizing Athagornia, who simply obeyed out of fear. If Batsville believed his emotions were now a pile of ash, the same could be said of Athagornia's self-esteem.

Ordog went into Diabolis' house on Effra Road looking like he wanted to rip Batsville to shreds. He held his precious DVD like a child would hold an action figure or a doll. Athagornia looked like she was frightened of her own shadow. Effsgog the Mohawk simply looked like his usual self—a spaced-out weirdo.

"It is confusing," said a disembodied voice. Diabolis knew it was a freak show these rejects wanted. "Where am I?" he teased as they looked around, but saw nothing. "If you dress up as vampires you should know everything about the tricks real vampires play. I would not like to think you do not know your own kind."

Queen Madhorn shouted to her subordinates, "Get down on your knees; HE is amongst us!" She always felt like she could maintain control by issuing orders in the style that compelled others to unequivocally obey. But now she was not in charge and dared not admit that her status was rendered unimportant in Diabolis' presence.

From a puddle of water in the back yard of the house on Effra Road the vampire Diabolis emerged, dumbfounding his guests. Even a black cat walking along the yard's wall dropped off it in shock after sensing the dark spirits in her proximity.

Lucis Diabolis laughed at the cat as she shot away into safer darkness, and said, "I hope you don't show fear like that cat just did. Fear always makes me hungry."

Queen Madhorn walked over to him, prostrated herself, and said, "Oh dark Lord, we are here for you."

"You?" Diabolis said, holding her wrist, sniffing, and then pushing her away. "But you do know you are mortal…mere humans, who dress funny. Oh," he added, shuddering, "what can

217

such odious things want with me? How can they possibly serve me?"

"Make me one of you," Batsville demanded.

"What did IT say?" Diabolis asked as he flew up to the roof of the house. "What did this beast down below demand of me? Make *it* like me? Just because you can drain the blood of humans and have learned how to stamp them out like vermin does not mean that you have a chance of doing likewise with me."

"No," Queen Madhorn intervened, "we do not make demands, just requests."

Diabolis felt revulsion at the thought of making humans vampires, especially those who most wished and acted like they were his kind. This type, needy and demanding and desperate, could never be happy or fulfilled.

"I am organising an event of the macabre variety, creating a play so diabolical that even Lucifer would delight in its content. You shall each be assigned certain duties related to that event."

Ordog's warning glare told Batsville to shut his mouth and say not a word more.

"You will be given specific responsibilities. Carry them out properly and you shall all become vampires. Make a mess of these simple tasks and I shall destroy you, one by one, as you have done your own victims."

# XVI

## Nigel's Visitor

It did not take Nigel long to revert back to his allegiance to Diabolis. No way was he going to keep taking his meds, though he was very good at pretending he was. He waited doglike for Diabolis' return.

Yes, he did hear Mark out, but poor Mark was a shadow of what he used to be after being given a round of electroconvulsive therapy. He appeared as enlightened as a goat about to be sacrificed by Druids. The psychiatrists took his attempt to pull the wool over their eyes seriously, and decided that it was time to show him their game plan. He could hide from them, but could not run. They were in charge.

"Of course," Doctor Murphy said, "his psychosis is just lying dormant, but may erupt at any moment and cause all kinds of mayhem. The best remedy is to give his brain a few jolts and up the dosages of his meds.

"Agreed," said Doctor Fitzgerald, "these patients are a cunning breed when they wish to get things their own way. It is all due to their diseased brains, which our intervention must address."

"Yes," said Doctor Murphy, "he must be brought under control."

Nigel decided that Mark had to be lying about his lineage. He looked too ridiculous to be noble. Nigel waited patiently.

219

When Mark was asleep, Nigel walked over to his bed. Mark was so far under from medication that even when Nigel moved his hand, Mark did not react. He got a needle from an elderly female patient who was knitting in the television room and returned to Mark's side. He lifted the sleeper's right hand and inserted the needle into the tip of his middle finger. When a few drops of blood came out, Nigel collected them in an unused plastic transparent tube for drug capsules, and vowed to show this sample to Diabolis as proof of his loyalty. This lowly creature, Mark, was the enemy.

Mark, Nigel thought, was not at all aristocratic. In fact, he looked as common as the blood sample would prove him to be. He had the eyes of an idiot, the hair of a fool, and the facial expression of a dog. The proof was in the jar. Nigel examined his wardrobe, his clothes and shoes and belongings that he brought to the hospital, and was satisfied with his conclusions.

Nigel returned to his own room. He wished to distract his mind from the human zombies and those who treated Nigel as one of them. Nigel refused to talk any further to them. He had learned more than enough about these young or adult, inebriate, dipsomaniacal, paranoid, cocaine-and/or cannabis-addicted brains-turned-to-mush, and their psychotic souls.

If one conversation which questioned the reality of existence was not ridiculous enough, then the utterances from another mad fool that he was God was for Nigel worse, especially since the common-as-dirt claimant paled by comparison to a real vampire; such claimants to divinity would melt at the sight of Diabolis.

Diabolis, as he walked into the institution from Dublin's South Side, could sense every living creature of Dublin, their every breath, sleeping or waking, their words and their works; he could sense all the souls who walked the street he was walking on now. He could imagine blood flowing out of so many Dubliners and onto the street and into his mouth, like convenient fast food. The beast was hungry. Tramco's, Slattery's, The Inn, and Madigan's—all of Rathmines—were frequented by creatures frothing at the mouth for their usual supply of alcohol, and stabilising themselves with pints either in their hands or going to the counter to ensure that they would be granted their refill (because one pint is never enough).

Diabolis walked to the Portobello Bridge. There he stood and watched how the swans swam gracefully, as beneath them rats swarmed the filth and garbage flung into the river, and which always made its way to the muddy river bed and banks. The eyes of Diabolis reddened. He raised his hands and eyes towards the Dublin sky. The rats sensed their master's presence.

A score of rats sleeping in a shopping trolley leapt up and squeaked for all the other rats to come to them. Diabolis walked to the river's side. The nearest swan felt the indecency of his spirit and swam away from him. He laughed at the swan's disapproval. Though the swan travelled fast and then attempted to take flight, knowing that an assault was imminent, score upon score of rats attacked the swan, ripped off her feathers, leaving them on the river's surface, mingling blood with snow-white feathers. Rats sank their teeth into her eyes and spat out her eyeballs, which dropped like stones to the river's bed. Digging their teeth into the bird, they snapped her neck in two; her decapitated head floated awhile on the river's surface. The rats dragged the swan's headless carcass to the river bank, elated that they had offered such a sacrifice to their vampire lord.

Diabolis nodded his head in approval. His obscene desire to perturb natural tranquillity met, he casually moved along. Squeaking rats followed him. He escorted them to one of the pubs beside the Portobello Bridge and laughed when he heard the customers' terrified shrieks. Inside one pub and without saying a word, he eyed the rats with grave intensity, and they looked at him as if they could read his mind.

*Tut…tut…tut! You know these people are not who I wish to bleed. Go back to your ponds, and continue playing there, for you've had enough fun.* With that, Diabolis exited. The pub workers had no idea who really inspired those rats to leave. They thought it was their brooms. As the rats left, so did the remaining trade for the night. There just was no convincing people that their ratty guests were just there on a once off, a fluke, and would not make a return visit.

Diabolis walked from Rathmines to George Street and onto the Liberties. When Diabolis walked past the Liberties, the stench from the Guinness plant revolted him.

"Fancy a tour of Guinness?" a passing travel agent asked.

"I do not drink Guinness," Diabolis replied, disgusted to be asked about anything to do with a beverage which never satisfied him.

"Well, I am sure when we get inside there will also be wine there. You do like wine?"

"No," Diabolis replied, "I *never* drink wine."

"Not even a bit of red wine?" the operator asked, suspecting Diabolis was having him on, for he thought Diabolis looked like the type who was fond of a jar.

"*That* red colour in a glass would never appease someone like me."

When Diabolis reached the grounds of the psychiatric institution an emaciated man of five feet and nine inches walked back and forth outside it in a shabby security officer's uniform. His brown, greying hair was unwashed, as was his pinched face; it was obvious that this was neglected soul was barely surviving. He grinned at a strutting pigeon near where he was stationed; utterly spaced out, he said nothing to Diabolis, who walked on in. The man continued staring into space and spat gluey scum onto the floor of his hut, where a kettle was boiling, awaiting tea to be put into a cup he evidently had not washed in a long time.

Diabolis paced for ten minutes in the car park at the front entrance of the hospital. Everything was most certainly going as planned. He admired the old trees planted nearby, some of which were as old as he. On the tenth minute, Anthony arrived in Diabolis' limousine and parked it. Diabolis walked slowly over to Anthony and said, "Now all you have to do is wait for the both of us to come out."

Diabolis did not even wait for Anthony to reply, for Anthony knew enough to obey orders.

It was just a matter of simple procedure and Diabolis was able to gain entry to the Intensive Care Unit.

When he arrived in the I.C.U. Diabolis was greeted with the sight of a wonderfully insane Nigel. Nigel's madness was hilarious. He'd walked up to a senile psychotic patient and taken her bra and underpants. She'd said nothing until he took her teddy bear Magoo and decapitated it in front of her. When he'd left the ward she cried frantically until the female nurses went into her room and injected her with a strong sedative.

Nigel had not wasted any time. Those undergarments were just right for the job of a costume as he found himself a mop which he could put the teddy bear head onto.

"Die...die-do-da—da-da-da-da-da-da-Diabolis, come, you sweet juice of Lucifer's seed...aye-aye—aye-aye....come to me...wild and wilder. Come, Lucis Diabolis, and fill me with the ambrosia of conquest. Fill my love holes with your seething cauldron, your red-hot inferno of need—Diabolis...Diabolis, diabolical and deadly....desperate, needing, Lucis Diabolis," he sang out, shaking the mop with the teddy bear head on it. Frustrated and fearing that he could not take the isolation anymore, he'd told himself he had to keep his word.

"I just knew, don't tell me how, that if I performed some weird Karma shite, you'd come back to me. The spiritual things all are off the same hymn sheet, so they are."

"Agreed, they most certainly are."

"But I was getting so frustrated here, so I was."

"Look, I need you to act normal."

"Normal?"

"I know, given where you are, this may be a bit challenging."

"I think I've forgotten what normal is."

"Regardless of what you have forgotten, I still need you to behave in a way that approximates normality. It is time you got dressed and out of those ridiculous clothes. Goodness, what would people think if they saw me with you? It's just as well we are where we are."

Nigel walked to his room and put on his clothes as Diabolis sat and watched. "You know I got myself a blood sample".

"A sample of your own blood?"

"No. I got myself a blood sample off of a crazy that claims to be of aristocratic blood. Aristocratic, my arse, says I to him… well no, I went along with him so he'd keep telling me shite."

"Can you give me that sample?" Diabolis asked.

"Certainly," Nigel said as he finished putting on his shoes.

"Do show me where he is as well."

"Oh, I will—it is on our way out."

Nigel pointed at him as Diabolis continued to the secured door and opened it with his unnatural strength. "When I want to, no door can resist me. Now move on. Anthony is outside in the limousine. I'll follow soon."

After starving himself for days, Diabolis looked like hell. But the thought that this sample blood could be the very blood he was after was too arousing. Nigel did not have to know, just serve, ask very little, and do what his station demanded. What was pure blood to Nigel—certainly not life essence?

Slowly Diabolis opened the lid. He was like a four-year-old child being told that he was about to visit a great big chocolate factory, and because he was so well behaved would be given a full basket of chocolate. Diabolis was such a good vampire. He had sampled much blood over his career; his manifesto, if he were a political party, would echo that of the Fianna Fáil in the election slogan of 2002: *a lot done more to do.*

He'd abstained lately from ripping into peoples' throats, to the extent that he would soon resemble an African in a refugee camp or death camp prisoner of World War II. With the tablet container open and his eyes on that drop of blood at the bottom, he would not simply say, "I am on a special diet," or, as a virgin might tell a lusty beau, "I am saving myself for marriage."

Outside in the car park Nigel was tapping his watch, waiting nervously for Lucis Diabolis to come out of the hospital building. "Where is he?" he asked Anthony in a nasty voice.

Diabolis' driver was noted for a trust and loyalty to his master more profound than Nigel could possibly know or understand. He did not reply.

Inside the hospital, Lucis Diabolis' eyes turned wild as his tongue licked his aroused fangs. There simply was not enough blood to drink it straight, just a drop of it. So he placed the sample onto his finger and was nervous that he might get so excited he would bite his own finger off.

Vampire impotency, loss of the masculine beauty which he longed to have, a sense of not being in control of his earthly domain—if this was noble blood, he might never again have to worry about these things. He was sure this blood would be for him like what Freud once wrote, designating cocaine as a boon to humanity, a panacea for many disorders, and a powerful anti depressant. Why, if this could be described as an intemperate advocacy of cocaine, Lucis Diabolis' advocacy of noble blood would prove the opposite.

He held in trembling hands the key. He could not possibly wait any longer, and licked the blood. Was it noble blood? His senses did not answer. How could he taste, and, from just one drop, know if this blood was the blood of his dreams? He had to have his curiosity sated, or go completely mad. He felt so ravaged by the pain of anxious expectation that his mind blurred. He looked to the ceiling and saw a point on it where a small speck of light reflected from a street light outside. He fixed his eyes on that speck and five times said the word, *calm*.

Usually this incantation would trigger the relaxation response. But this time there was not a chance in hell that he would stay relaxed. He meditated deeply, never an easy task. The night he'd attacked the junkies aerially by appointing rats to help him had been special, a state of concentration in order to acquire that grotesque giant rat appearance.

He jogged his memory back to that time and the mood he was in. By thinking about that state, about the exact way his body had moved, what he thought was not possible tonight actually was possible. He became rat-like and his eyes reddened. But he could be seen, so he focused on every miniscule piece of himself to make his body like an average rat's. He crawled so swiftly that no cat could catch him to the exact place where Mark was. But, as he jumped on his bed and peered around, he emitted ratty squeaks, for Mark was not there!

"Where is Mark?" a nurse asked another nurse, walking by the bed.

"Oh, he's in the room next door, the one to the right."

"And what's he doing there?"

"Undergoing electroconvulsive therapy for his clinical depression."

"Oh, very good, then," the nurse replied.

*How could Nigel know—was he merely raving?* Diabolis did not care if a series of electroshocks were battering their way into Mark's head. But, when he crawled into the room, he noticed that there was a nurse beside Mark. He waited patiently for the nurse to finish the electroshock. A few minutes passed. The nurse unhooked the wires and left the room. Mark stared listlessly into space.

The minute the door closed Diabolis leapt onto Mark's bed. He assumed full size, maintaining his rat body. He clawed Mark's chest until his head jerked with the intensity of the pain. Diabolis smashed his head down against the bed and gnawed his neck. This was indeed noble blood! Diabolis gouged and sucked at the pulse points in his neck, his arms, his wrists, and his legs. It was so tasty!

Once Mark was drained, Diabolis' whole rodent body felt as strong as iron. He left Mark's room, went into the day room where the patients congregated to eat, next to the front window and door to the garden. At the end of the garden was an eleven-foot-high wall. Diabolis smashed through the window and, with the glass falling onto the garden grass, departed to the screams of a female patient institutionalised due to symptoms of acute trauma and re-traumatized at the sight of Mark's mangled body...not to mention the sight of a giant rat.

Diabolis escaped over the wall, dashed to the limousine, and, still looking ever so ratty, told Anthony to get a move on. Nigel stared, awed by this supernatural creature who looked stranger to him than ever before.

Diabolis felt like he'd had a draught of the love juices Aphrodite would emit while making love to Adonis; he was now an Adonis, he was sure, irresistible because of the noble blood he had consumed.

# XVII

## Play Day

Like a hyperactive child, 24 hours before Diabolis' presentation, Nigel felt like a true hero under the vampire's leadership. He sat downstairs at the Effra Road digs, following strict instructions not to return home.

Nigey could not deny his elation about where he was headed and what he was achieving. Diabolis would admit him to his inner, occult world. He expected to become more than a vampire assistant once Diabolis taught him all the occult things he knew. Then, Nigel would find followers to exploit, take them to the cleaners for everything they had, and recoup his financial losses. Anticipation made him high—although he knew Lucis Diabolis was upstairs, throughout his fantasy, Nigel kept seeing him as if he was on a flat screen on the ceiling.

"Aye, Lucis," Nigey said, "keep a good eye on your good vampire assistant. I'm not going anywhere, so I am not, just waiting to bring these keys to Dublin Castle, and open her up, so I will, and make whatever preparations you need. You hear me?"

Diabolis took no notice, for he stood entranced. He was as awed as Narcissus by his reflection in the mirror. Could any sexually ripe female resist him? Ingesting Mark's noble blood endowed him with enough potency to give him a godly bearing. His features had transformed into a beauty that would cause such a heart throbbing attraction for him that his lovers were sure to lose their moral bearings. But Diabolis wept because he knew his duties demanded an *empty* stomach in order to perform his work properly. So he decided there was to be no more standing around and admiring this awesome body. He had to get his hands on a reliable supply of enough precious blood to make his renewal permanent.

He went into the bathroom wretched, cursing the idiocy of what he must do. He took time to dwell on the great blood he had just lustily consumed, and how it made his body so studly that vanity was like swarming bees inside of him. As he lowered his head into the bath he felt as if the most exquisite loveliness had been defiled by acid. He vomited up all that good blood, purging himself of his precious, fleeting beauty. He required truck-loads of noble blood. To get it, he needed to be hungry and wild.

When Diabolis looked at what he had done, he was tempted to drink his own vomit (which would act like multivitamins for a vampire). "Get hold of yourself!" he commanded, and, admirably, he did. It was like a heroin addict walking away from a fully prepared hit. But he walked away because it made perfect sense to his long-term plan. The hour had come to give Nigel his instructions.

"Nigel," he called, "Come here and listen carefully."

Nigel ran upstairs to Diabolis and sat down beside him.

"I know your exact measurements," Diabolis said as he held out a multi-coloured jacket and trousers. I worked most methodically while you were away. Put on your uniform and take your keys to Dublin Castle. Anthony is outside with the details of the exact location in the castle where you are to stay. There you shall blow this pipe without pause. Should numerous vermin arrive, you must not harm them; let them stay and continue playing on the pipe. Am I understood? It would be most foolish not to do as I say."

"Aye, Master, I'll blow away on me pipes in the castle, so I will."

Nigel arrived at an empty Dublin Castle, feeling as if the task assigned him was a personal compliment. After getting over his infatuation with the place, he started playing the flute, and for a full thirty minutes played non-stop. Would Diabolis know if he stopped? After all, he was over two miles away. No results had been gotten from playing the flute, thus far; it seemed stupid to be blowing into thin air. He took the flute out of his mouth, put his hands on his hips, and cursed what he considered a stupid order.

A few minutes later, Nigel's ears twitched, his head shook, his legs felt a biting pain, and he screamed loudly. He looked at his leg, but saw nothing there; he laughed at the idea that he was playing the role of Pied Piper. His insane laughter echoed through the castle. Suddenly, though, he jumped up at the sensation of several bites in his anus from what felt like many little mouths. Was his anus bleeding? When he placed his hand against his bottom, what felt like rats started gnawing on his hand and arm. He was about to curse the rats, but before he could, they formed one man-sized rat and threw Nigel to the floor with a force that almost snapped his spine.

"Continue to play!" Lucis Diabolis commanded.

Nigel, shaken by this experience, picked up the flute and continued blowing. Two, then three hours passed, but nothing happened, and his bottom was incredibly sore. He wanted to stop playing the flute and scratch his wounded bum to relieve the itch from the rat bites. His surroundings, originally so inspiring that Nigel could not stop talking about how awesome castles are and how much Yanks love them, were ruined by the pain in his arse. Exactly on the fourth hour of blowing, when

Nigel thought he was going to pass out, rat after rat entered the hall. The hall was so full of rats that their stench nearly suffocated him; their glowing red eyes told Nigel they were dying to eat him alive.

The rats must have been essential to this night of aristocratic passion. Nigel kept playing the flute until he was sure all of the rats of Dublin had likely joined him. Considering he was their master's second in command, Nigel was actually proud of summoning them.

Lucis Diabolis made his appearance just after dark. Every rat's eye centered upon the vampire's ancient face as he told them, "Yes, you will have good fun tonight."

"Nigel," Diabolis called out, "you may quit playing now."

Nigel stopped, and, as if fully zombified, did not say a word. Behind Lucis Diabolis he could see Queen Madhorn and her 'vampire' horde. The crew had come with the appropriate punk-rock paraphernalia needed to perform. The rats watched, entranced, as the punk rockers set up on-stage.

"Until my delicious guests are seated and introduced to the night's proceedings, not one sound from any of you rats! You are to be quieter than mice," Diabolis sternly instructed.

As Diabolis gave that instruction he could hear Queen Madhorn and her crazies rehearsing. Madhorn's bestial voice screamed repetitive words, like a broken record: "When it is done, it is done." Ordog banged with rage on the drums and Batsville played aggressive guitar.

"I guess," said Diabolis to Nigel, "I should get you out of that ridiculous uniform."

Nigel stripped off and handed his clothes to Diabolis, who placed them in a black plastic bag. Anthony arrived with Nigel's costume for the night.

"Our Anthony," Diabolis said, fondly, "is most proficient on Facebook and Twitter. Since tonight is dedicated to hunters, I decided you should dress up as a bunny."

Nigel, humiliated, accepted the rabbit suit from Anthony. But he could not say a word, for he was repulsed by and utterly fearful of the now-hideous Lucis Diabolis.

"A rabbit knows how to run," Diabolis said, cackling as Nigel donned his ill-fitting costume.

"Run, rabbit, run!" Diabolis said, while Queen Madhorn roared expletive after expletive in the style she fantasized was raw, underground, sinister, heavy-metal, punk rock.

Nigel was to be the official greeter, welcoming invited aristocrats. Diabolis parked his sinister self outside in the back seat of his limousine. He was like a spoiled school boy. He kept all his desires to himself, but his driver knew exactly what he needed and handed him a blood-ice pop to sedate him.

When the nobility started to arrive at Dublin Castle, Diabolis demanded another blood-ice pop, which Anthony had kept refrigerated in the driver's compartment.

Diabolis felt as if his fangs had almost extended to his waist. To calm his nerves he licked at the ice pop the way a whore fellates her client.

"Please be seated, ladies and gentlemen, for a great night of entertainment," Nigey said in his best 'posh'.

Diabolis knew, had he been in the same position as Nigey, he would have ripped a few delicious throats open and had some yum-yums. His vampire dreams were coming true. The attendance was remarkably high, not one commoner amongst them. They took their seats, a true mansion of beauteous delight to Diabolis' eyes, as he left the comfort of his limousine to behold what he had created for this night. He spidered silently up the walls and lay on the ceiling as if it was a bed and gravity was not his enemy.

Everything Nigel did was in absolute conformity to his master's instructions. None of the words he said were his own. Like a death camp attendant, he was simply doing his duty, with no trace of  emotion in his voice. He spoke at length about the legacy of the Dublin-born author, Bram Stoker, beginning, *Having spent the festive days preceding this narration, celebrating Stoker's contribution to the genre, tonight we are honoured by showing what new horrors have been created since his day...*

Madhorn and co were waiting behind the stage to rage forth with their music. Nigel paid no heed to their impatience. He knew exactly what he had to do. Any deviation from the script and his neck would pay. Outside in the courtyard a Guinness truck that usually transported beer kegs was now transporting ten burly men with masks. The truck off-loaded these men before a delighted Anthony.

"Excellent," he said. "Dublin Castle shall be woken from her slumber."

Nigel called out Queen Madhorn and her 'vampire' punks.

"Now," Queen Madhorn hissed to them, "is our time."

All they were required to do was perform, hard, loud, aggressively rude, punk, metal sounds—exactly what was in their hearts. The dark curtains parted, revealing Queen Madhorn; all eyes went to her and her kind. She performed as outrageously as she could, making sure there were absolutely no silent breaks between songs. Diabolis could not help but dance on the ceiling—the Devil's son's dance of no forgiveness or mercy.

To Diabolis there was no worse sight than confined rats, his favourite servants; panther-like, he paced the castle's ceiling, upside-down. Sitting on air, victorious, all his lusts ruled him in their gratification; only a true addict could appreciate the intensity, the desire, the drive, and the want.

"Now rats, dance, dance and be merry!" he ordered.

And they were merry, and glad of it. The music drowned their excited squeaks and scrabbling.

The aristocrats looked disgusted. Half way through the second song they stood up from their seats. If they were not so straightjacketed from their upbringing they would have thrown their seats at the stage. Queen Madhorn and her horde were only more encouraged to be loud, to be more noxiously punk.

"**NOW!!!**"

Diabolis opened the door where the rats were waiting patiently backstage and smiled deliciously at them as they ran. They ran like hell fire was behind them. They bit indiscriminately. They first overtook Nigel. Nigel, knowing he was betrayed, surrendered just like Paris and the entire nation of France had at the opening of World War II. The rats devoured his skin and eyeballs first. Their comrades realized there was not enough of Nigel to go around, so they made their way to the vampire band, as Lucis Diabolis brayed hysterically.

The hands that held Queen Madhorn's microphone ran red. Rats bit into her buttocks, and the horns which defined her fountained blood. Lucis Diabolis knew that his rats needed to devour the punks, for they were under strict instructions to be extra tender to the aristocrats.

"Yes," he said to the rats, "the first course, calling themselves vampires, asked for their nature to be changed; they were mere humans pretending to be vampires. Oh, rats, how well you've changed nature!"

Diabolis watched the aristocrats scurrying for the exits. He'd made sure to take care of all 'alternative exits'. He picked up one rat and licked it like a blood-ice pop. "Look, rats, see how, even though my fangs are fully erect, I do not penetrate this skin. I spare your fellow. Go—go to my delicious friends, my food supply, and restrain them, but be good to them."

Every morsel of aristocratic blood was to be left for Diabolis, not a drop wasted. Perish the thought of such delicious blood being spilt on the ground and not into his mouth.

Every aristocrat was pinned to the ground, in such sweet surrender; not one was capable of resisting. The rats had them pinned by their skin, Diabolis was delighted to see. His masked men came in and started extracting blood so meticulously that they soon filled many Guinness kegs with it.

"A toast, a toast!" Diabolis cried, and quaffed a full libation of noble blood. As sure as night follows day the vampire's decrepit ugliness transformed into stunning, healthy, fully youthful vigour.

It took ninety minutes before everybody was drained of blood. Diabolis surveyed the scene, and the way he had left Dublin Castle, and said, "What a sensual sight!"

The vampire applauded loudly as he saw the truck driving off to a secure location, and then transformed into a bat (after he called the emergency services).

The emergency service providers arrived at Dublin Castle, one after the other, along with armed police, to behold the great carnage that Diabolis had left in his wake.

And Diabolis smiled now that his objective was complete. The lowly Nigel and vampire punks lay dead alongside the high-born corpses mutilated by Lucis' army of loyal rats.

# XVIII

## New Destination

Lucis Diabolis was ecstatic after the orgy of death left in his wake at Dublin Castle. He celebrated this annihilation of nobles as if it was his last day on earth.

Anthony, his driver, played punk music as they rode through Dublin in the limousine. To avoid detection by the authorities, upon reaching the cemetery of Mount Jerome, they switched to a top of the line Mercedes Benz. The Benz took a left turn outside of the gates of Mount Jerome and drove to Sundrive in Crumlin. Lucis Diabolis bowed his head and tapped his nose with his right middle finger. The car they'd abandoned outside Mount Jerome exploded, causing a terror and panic in the old neighbourhood.

"A libation, sir, of exquisite noble blood before we reach base is in order, I believe."

"Why certainly," said Diabolis.

"As an aside, Mr. Diabolis, it is my turn."

"Your turn?"

"Yes. Your rat friends got rid of the dregs—Nigel, and what you laughingly described as THE REAL VAMPIRES. All the stooges are dead. My time has come to know and taste eternal life."

"I realize you feel your time has come, but the ritual is

complex. When we arrive at our private destination, I'll show you how this ritual works."

Anthony handed Diabolis the noble blood in a flagon for toasting. Diabolis looked at the glass and its contents. He cupped in hands long unaccustomed to hard work the most precious substance on earth for a vampire. He placed it to his nose and inhaled the perfume of generations from rich blood lines. He closed his eyes. He did not care if he merited eternal damnation as long as the contents of the glass were all his.

A more intelligent mind would have sensed that his soul was being laid out like a piece of meat for barbecuing on a skewer over hellfire because of the damnable things he had done. Uncaring, Lucis Diabolis had strolled along the road of personal damnation taking pleasure in evil at other persons' expenses.

"Delicious," he announced, as he drained the glass. It dawned on him how potent he was, truly a youthful stallion, of a most cunning, truly dark mindset. He knew how to use his mind to find vintage blood and to manipulate people as objects for his pleasure. He set his glass down to address Anthony

"Have the stocks arrived at the host venue?"

"Yes," the driver replied.

"And in the manner which I requested?"

"We stopped off at the Guinness factory, as ordered."

"And?"

Anthony nervously responded, "Yes, we offloaded the produce to a separate truck. The authorities, at the best of times, have sleepy heads."

"It is truly nothing to worry about?"

"No, I think not."

"But I do wish," the vampire sadly confided, "that we'd blown up the castle. The damn place has cheapened itself over the years. The so-called makeovers they gave the place destroyed its splendour."

237

"Was draining the corpses of the rich not enough destruction for you?"

"Never," Diabolis replied, and Anthony laughed.

Helicopters flew throughout the Dublin sky. Diabolis appeared to ignore the sounds, although his hands were trembling somewhat. Finally he ordered, "Stop the car."

"Why?" Anthony replied.

"I will make my own way to this destination."

"What about me, master?" As soon as he said it, Anthony realized he should not have said 'master', fearing he deserved to be smack so badly that he would pass out and have his own throat torn open.

"What *of* you?" Diabolis replied, trying not to laugh at how pathetic and vulnerable Anthony sounded.

Anthony felt offended at Diabolis' dismissive tone, and the vampire could sense it. As detached as Diabolis was from human blood donors, he could not fault Anthony's loyalty. The driver looked as pitiful as a puppy in the front window of a pet shop, with a price tag on its collar.

Their location in the Dublin-Wicklow Mountains, was the haunt of devotees to secretive, Satanic rituals. Diabolis felt like the nobleman on horseback who looses a hare for the greyhounds to chase, while others of his party lick their lips, massage their hunting rifles, and fondle themselves with anticipation.

"First, it would not be smart to abandon this car. Those people in the sky aren't stupid. If they see us leave they will surely know who and what we are."

"Please," Anthony said, turning his face toward his master, "let me assure you it is not us they are after. I would have gotten a call on my cell. This is a very small country and its walls have big ears; mouths run a lot where money is involved."

Diabolis thought about this. *Yes, he is extremely useful and intelligent and not worth being let out for the hunt.*

"I know these mountains like the back of my hand. It's an ideal place to bring a person. I," Diabolis added with mischief, "had splendid picnics here."

"And you have enough vintage blood to last you some while."

"My diet has been well looked after."

They drove deep into County Wicklow territory, passing through Aughrim, Blessington, and Glendalough.

"This car must be destroyed."

"Let me think about it," said Anthony.

"When I drink more of this blood I shall have no more use for cars. Why so downcast, Anthony? I still have use for *you*. This is, as I'm sure you agree, a new and wondrous era for the vampire."

# XIX

## New Digs

Anthony arrived at the country house. As they pulled up, Diabolis clapped his hands and shouted loudly, "Splendid! No one would ever think to bother us in this fine hellhole."

Indeed, the place was rustic, but Diabolis' quarters were adequate. The area beside Diabolis' coffin displayed neatly shelved bottles of the finest blood a vampire could desire, freshly imported from the Guinness truck.

"You don't have to destroy the car," Anthony said.

"Why not?"

"There's a shed beside the house that can store it."

"This outhouse shall serve our non-automotive purposes perfectly from now on."

Diabolis strode like a prince into his new abode. He left Anthony to tend to the Mercedes. The front of the house was a sorry sight. Visible to the vampire's eye, though now in pitch darkness, were the broken front windows. The light blue, wooden entry appeared to be in the last stages of decay.

As for the front yard, some losers were sleeping in the overgrown weeds underneath a tree not two meters from the front door. Diabolis could smell the manure freshly provided the grounds by these evictees, unhappy about being advised of his intention to not just visit, but to take up permanent residence.

Not only was the sewer pipe in the front not fixed, but the perimeter of the house reeked from ripe refuse. All in all, the new digs were a verminous delight, its odorous standards more than adequate.

As Diabolis entered, he saw Sharon of Acheron (as the ageless redhead eccentrically titled herself) waiting for the vampire's expected arrival.

"Oh," she said, throwing plump arms around him, "what a garden of delight! If I may be your lady for just one night, the sweet memories we shall make!"

"No doubt. We go back a long way and have made memories before," said Diabolis.

"But," Sharon replied, "I don't remember you looking this magnificent."

"Yes," he said, "indeed it is not all only in the genes, but in the blood."

"Fascinating," she replied. "You truly learn something new every day."

Lucis Diabolis took Sharon's freckled hand and replied, "Do see to Anthony, my driver. I worry that he exhausts himself in doing everything I ask. I believe that he should relax more often."

"Why certainly," she agreed, her green eyes twinkling. The vampire winked, laughed, pinched her bum, and Sharon laughed like she was eighteen once more.

Diabolis retired to the bachelor quarters designated especially for him. The vampire's domicile was nothing like the uninhabitable standards Sharon kept to. Her philosophy was simple: to lavish grandeur upon herself was wasteful when she could focus attention on Diabolis instead. He was worthy of the finest her home had to offer; he was a guest of quality.

When the vampire Lucis Diabolis entered his quarters, he smiled in delight at so many bottles of the finest blood arrived safely and securely. *How divine*, he thought.

241

Diabolis knew nothing of what could happen to him after his termination on earth. As he lay down in the coffin, he speculated about being sent to the very center of the earth, where hordes of demons would enrapture his soul and consume it whole. Or maybe hell was a set of camps, all lined up, one after the other, and resembling hastily-built Soviet bloc apartments. There would be no paintings; everything would be minimal and basic (the way Sharon and the Goth Girl decorated).

In Diabolis' reading of the afterlife and destiny, he would have had to pursue sainthood in order to avoid hell, with its endless layers, hordes of demons, and punishments for having succumbed to temptation. Unlike a child anticipating presents, Diabolis was nefarious in his expectations. He could not be sure what was on the other side, but, as a supernatural being, he was sure there was another side and that he was doing well by staying healthy and avoiding it as long as possible.

Anthony entered the house and was greeted by the frowsy but seductive Sharon. "Isn't he exquisite looking!" she said, but refrained from adding, "I bet, like the rest of us, you want to be exactly like him."

Sharon realized she should refrain from cruel truths. That those who want to be near the vampire end up being hypnotized into wanting to be like him was normal human weakness.

"Yes," Anthony agreed, "I assume you know *what* he is? I've known for quite awhile."

"Yes," she said, laughing, "I guess we all know…and we all want it," she said, spreading her legs. "We all crave it intensely," she added. The damp filth of her lair was surreal, yet did not hinder her technique. "I mean," she said with a grin, "some crave it so intensely, that to be without it would be like living without breathing." She smiled the smile of someone used to mastering men. "I'd trade the costliest masterpiece in the Louvre to have such an ability to extract life. There's no escaping the control of a devil who knows everything about you. He knows exactly from one moment to the next what you think. How transparent your thoughts are to his bloody, filthy mind! That's why he loves the filth of this house."

She winked at Anthony. "Yes, you would not want to test him. I never have."

"You know," he said, with an air of smug confidence, "he intends to make me one of his kind?"

"Splendid."

"Yes…splendid," he said, eyeing the dripping tap. "And it seems like you could do with some more work being done on your house".

"That's where you're wrong. This place is Lucis Diabolis' paradise."

"*He* is why you have it in this state?"

"Diabolis detests change. He would prefer to see rot and decay than to be a whore in the harem of home improvement and keeping up appearances. No. He likes things the old, *old* way. The master is amongst us. What more could we ask for?"

"What more could we possibly want?" he parroted.

"The world has seen many things, but Diabolis is unique."

"In what way is he special?" Anthony quizzed, desiring to see things from her point of view.

"To some, even in his present perfection, he is monstrous. To me he is a force. But is that enough to capture the heart, or even the appreciation of another person?"

"No," Anthony responded, "it never is."

"Exactly. Now let me change these clothes for something more comfortable."

"I should change too," Anthony replied.

Sharon walked over and put her arms around Anthony. "I'll tell you what to wear, since you're sleeping with me."

Anthony looked shocked.

"I know that stress written all over your face."

"Stress?"

"Yes, it is the stress of repressed sexuality and unrealized gratification."

"What has this to do with wanting, more than anything, to be a vampire?"

"Everything…and I've been given strict instructions to look after you by Diabolis, which I will do."

Anthony looked at the ground. She discerned that he was not the kind of man comfortable with conquest, either through financial means or by command of another person.

"Not so fast," Sharon said.

"Huh?"

"What I'm not so certain about is, do I want you?"

Her body told him otherwise. But all those hours spent alone behind a wheel driving throughout Dublin with a vampire who rarely engaged him in conversation had made him feel estranged from women. "I'm not sure you are what I want either. You only invite me in because Diabolis ordered you to."

"*Please*," she said, walking to the window near a blue table heaped with mouldering papers, "don't assume cheap things are within me, and I will not assume they are within you. I know, from their eyes, men who need it, and those who could do without it."

"It is not you I want, Sharon, but Diabolis. To become like him will resolve all my problems."

"Why do you think he handed you over to me? If he did not value you, he would have left you as a corpse in Dublin Castle, just like the rest of them. Trust me, I know."

In Diabolis' quarters his renewed body's muscles rippled, his figure resembling Superman, Batman, Thor, or one of the Avengers. But internal worlds are different than external ones. He wished that his home could become an orgy of delight to rival Eden's to take his mind off the truth that he had become utterly abominable. His spirit was immersed in an atomic inferno. He felt diabolical, and knew he had no other choice but to be diabolical.

His inner voice wanted to challenge many of those who had been wronged to strike back, strike back in the most vicious way. It dictated that he should teach others to loathe their enemies. *When injured, strike your enemy with a steel chain and pierce his spine so that he can never stand against you again.* Diabolis let this voice continue to spew the creed of vengeance, where like injury should be returned, ad infinitum.

The vengeful whirlwind of Diabolis' thoughts swept him along, until he hovered above the most blissful garden he'd ever experienced. "This place once existed where modern Iraq lies," a dream guide told him. But he was a relatively young vampire and had seen what was left after explosives from the sky and tanks battered the ground in Iraq, and dismissed any notion that this place could possibly be the same.

He saw a group of men sitting and singing in a language he could not understand, but their language did not annoy him. That they were singing joyfully grated at his nerves, and so he cursed them. "Maybe in time," he said, "you people will experience curses worse than mine."

"And this curse," the voice whispered, "will dispatch a thousand ships and a thousand evil eyes to scourge the world with grief and mayhem."

"And you really think it is a vampire you want to become?"

"Yes," Anthony replied with a sincerity that pained Sharon to hear.

"What would be the benefit?"

"You already know the answer." Anthony said, annoyed.

"No, I do not, and I do not think you know either!"

He was silent, then said, "At moments like this I wish I was not so loyal to Lucis Diabolis."

"I do his bidding, even if it is being loyal to a vampire," said Sharon.

"But was it not you who said, 'Isn't Lucis Diabolis a splendid monster?'"

"I recognize my words when they are said to me, as any normal, intelligent person would."

"But nobody truly *loves* a monster, especially when they buried others' lives in ashes."

"Who said anything about love?" said Sharon, feeling very attracted to Anthony. "You confuse being loyal with being in love."

"Why," he said angrily, "are you playing with me?"

"I'll play with you as I wish and you'll be played with as I see fit. Tonight Diabolis will know that I've serviced you thoroughly."

"Serviced me thoroughly? Do you think men are so simple?"

"I do not think *you* are. After all, you've obeyed him this long. You somehow have understood your limitations and have survived what, after all, is a horror."

"But he wants to make me a predator like him, right?"

"Why do you think that? I've been his dominatrix for years, and not once did I expect him to make me a vampire. He adores being the only one of his kind. Now, please let me show you my basement."

"Will the sound of my shoes disturb his rest?"

"Not even the sound of me being wickedly exploited from behind and savagely hammered as I writhe in pleasure and scream will wake that sleepyhead. He is extremely tired; change of blood is like change of climate or jet lag. He will not wake until midnight. This will give me a decent interval to perform sex therapy."

"What is this?" Anthony inquired, eyeing glass jars with human remains in them.

246

"This is how he pays me for my services."

"And do you like this payment?"

"Yes, I do."

"Why?"

"It reminds me of what he is."

"Yes?"

"I respect him more when he brings me tokens of those he's just ripped apart. Do you disapprove? You *do* want to become him. And he survives on the blood of others. He knows trophies are important to me—these ears, hearts, and other parts of dead mortals. He understands that they're vital to our bond. I dominate him," she said, which sent a thrill through Anthony. She pulled her trousers down and placed her hand on his crotch. She turned around, and said over her shoulder, "I tie him up and tie him down. A vampire, you understand, is what I dominate."

"Is this all you want from Diabolis?"

"It's never a question of *my* desire. When he gives me money other than my salary, for the necessary tools of the trade, I buy cages for him, chains, whips, collars that fit his neck, mouthguards, gas masks. I'm just your decent, ordinary, dominatrix, who dominates a vampire of the most exquisite kind. Look around you at his work. It reminds you, does it not, of what he can *truly* do? Make no mistake while enjoying these fetishes."

She teased his erect member as if she truly longed for it. "Do you think I want it the same way I give it to Diabolis—on floor boards with nails, doing all kinds of aggressive things together?"

"Well, what *is* it that you want?"

"I want what these treasures around us should remind you of."

"And what is that?"

"Submission. I can be a cow. You must be a bull and not relent until I tell you that your work is done."

"Really?" Anthony said, surprised that her desire was totally contrary to her role with Diabolis.

"Come to my bed," she said. "I'm sick of being the saddle, the reigns, and the whip. I'll be the horse tonight. But you'd better know where you're going."

"And," Anthony inquired, "when shall I know I've been an adequate horseman?"

"At the time you get off the saddle and pat me, look into my eyes, and say, 'I no longer wish to be the prototype of Diabolis.' Only then will I know what great work I've done."

# XX

## The Effluent of the Affluent

An unholy trinity of dipso-hobo-bohemian druggies from Dublin City had been evicted from Sharon of Acheron's home. But they were not low-class. The stench of sewage in the home's back garden was not from the bowels of inner city Dubs, or the socially disadvantaged, outside-the-pale culchies and townies of Ireland—victims disenfranchised by the beheading of the Celtic Tiger (now adorning a fence post outside of some Central European house of ill repute). Irish intellectuals and the official voices of Ireland's media might prattle on about how to grow a new head, and then revive the body, but done is done.

The stench in Anthony's nose before he was seduced by the wily redhead was from the rich, middle classes of Dublin, their noses in the air, and emotionally indifferent as the day is long.

A hefty sewer rat devoted to Diabolis was near at hand to answer a question a less experienced rat asked about the excremental differences of the upper echelons in comparison to the lower. The smug younger rat said that to him shit smelled and looked the same, not only in the dark but also the light of day.

"But," Cissus, the elder rat, declared, having been up to his neck in shit all his life and all over the four corners of Ire-

249

land, "Sewage in Munster is a rich flow, for the diet and the sounds are most traditional. In Connacht the diet is poor and the climate even more hellish, making the sewage damper and slicker than Munster's. Ulster sewage is so bland one could not put a tricolour or a Union Jack in the middle of it; the most controversial thing I can say is that parts of the shit are divided irreconcilably."

"And," added Cissus, "don't tell me you do not see with your two eyes how the sewage of the affluent is much different than the non-affluent. The upper echelons of Irish society have been bred to cover their own ass with more than enough toilet paper. That's why this class is so self-absorbed and, no matter how badly they do things, always manage to cover their own ass with professionalism."

Although the affluent did use a terribly excessive amount of toilet paper, Sharon of Acheron had an excellent reason for this class staying with her. They paid her very good money because they wanted to live in filth.

Peter from Rathmines, Oisin from Blackrock, and Richard from Dalkey, from the age of sixteen had driven the best cars money could buy. 500 euros at a time fell into their hands without their having to work for it. And, as for plastic, they had to have credit cards "just in case of emergency." Naturally, they accrued debts, and even were occasionally reproached for having done so. It is not that the three boys could not have had decent careers mapped out for them. All three had parents and relatives well positioned in the insular, nepotistic, and psychologically incestuous world of capitalistic Ireland.

Peter often lampooned this societal structure, gyrating his hips backwards and forwards against a mop in Sharon's home and roaring, "in this small plop of an island," as his melon-sized head (devoid of any real business acumen) bobbed for emphasis, "it is never *what* you know…"

"But always *who* you know!" finished his two friends, howling with laughter.

At this point he gestured obscenely, "but if one is unfortunate in life, one must rephrase the saying: in Ireland it is who you know, or WHO YOU BLOW." Then he would hump the mop harder and bow to the two boys who were applauding him wildly. He had connections, but craved to be always the focus of attention.

The three had graduated from Business School with honours and had jobs awaiting them whenever they wished to pick them up, recession or no recession. These home-grown boys had all they needed in this world.

Peter, partly because of his oversized head, had decided to abandon mainstream life for that of a hobo, drinking cider and vodka and taking drugs, in the wilds of Wicklow. Richard knew all about Sharon's house. She didn't see the vampire enough to justify leaving her home empty and was unable to resist what she believed was huge sums of money paid her to simply stay in her no-frills abode.

Peter was always complaining about the hyper-luxurious surroundings he was born into in the Rathmines area—a huge old house on 10 acres with a mews. His grandfather was a retired, pompous doctor, whose son was sold to corporate Ireland as an accountant. Peter was the first to second Richard's rental suggestion. The third stooge, Oisin, studied business because many stupid people had become famous. Why could he not be one? Richard had been told that Business Studies would tide him over until he got offered the acting career he was long overdue. His father helped him get roles in RTE and home-grown movies. His career had not taken off, so he was one frustrated artist. Oisin resisted awhile. He believed he was only a phone call away from being told that he was the next Bob Dylan, and should therefore stay in the city and keep his ear to the ground. He was finally convinced by the two other

251

boys that moving to Sharon's might foster a period of creative growth.

"Who does that bitch think she is?" Peter said, his big head flapping in rage.

"Our dads," Richard said, lighting a huge refer, "could close her down in a day." He banged his fists on the table as if he wished to break it in two.

"What's the matter, Richard?" said Oisin. "Don't get so excited. Take two Valiums and a Xanax, and wash them down with a glass of *Absolut Vodka* on the rocks."

"Look," said Richard, eyes bulging, "you all know I could be making four million dollars a year in acting. Instead, I just stay with her to show the stupid county of Wicklow what talent I have by gigging in their pubs every now and again."

This statement was greeted with silence. He had millions and did not require more.

"Go on, drink that glass of vodka; it will calm you down."

"We must destroy this bitch," said Richard.

"She's not a bitch," Oisin, the wannabe rock star, quipped. Just like Richard he would have sold his soul to create an album, and paid for marketing in order to gain star status on the Celebs and Gos Pages.

"Well, if she is not a bitch, what in hell is she? And where does she think she is from and who does she think she is, throwing us out? We have to teach her a lesson. The dissidents who sell us the narcos would have no trouble selling us a machine gun or two and a few handguns. They have a lot of them floating around and would love to see them put to use, not only in the Republic, but anywhere and on anyone, as long as they get a decent amount of cash in return. We are loaded and can do what we want with the bitch in her country hut. No one will say boo to us; trust me on this."

All of this mouthing from Richard was causing Peter to lose his head. He lit a cigarette and said, "Oisin is right—she's not a bitch, she's a witch."

"A witch?" Richard intervened. "I never heard her mention anything about the occult."

"Well she is and her boyfriend is a fucking vampire," Peter said, putting his cigarette down. "It is going to have to go down like this. I want to kill her just like the rest of you do. And it is me who is going to be the best equipped; you can bring a handgun, but I have better stuff to use for killing her kind."

"Her kind?" Richard said, "come on!"

Oisin said, "Peter is the brains of our outfit and always has his ear to the ground."

"Hanging around this gaff in Dublin's south side, I got to thinking about how to strike this bitch through the heart. We'll cut her heart out and put it into a glass jar. Oh yes, lads, the day before we left, I snuck into her basement." Peter winked. "Fucking *American Horror Story* down there. I know she has a vampire coming to see her."

"A vampire?" Oisin laughed.

"Yes. So, if I am wrong I am wrong. If it is far-fetched, end of story—simple as that."

"I know, Peter, you're the man and everything, but how do you suggest we kill a fucking vampire?"

"It is common knowledge," Richard said, as if the operation could be done in a heartbeat.

"I know what you're saying, Richard. You probably think it is going to be easy. Well, I have the garlic, the stakes, and even a chainsaw."

"A chainsaw?"

"For cutting off the vampire's head."

"The damn saw will make too much fucking noise!"

"I was thinking that, and that it might not *fully* finish off the immortal fucker she has staying with her."

"Yeah, if he looks like any of the dudes we see on telly he probably gets laid more often than us and he never has to pay for it either."

"Look, let's fucking focus for once in our shitty piss-boring lives. We'll shoot the bitch in the head, strike the fucker in the coffin through the heart with a stake, and chuck some garlic on him. Bob is your uncle: job is done."

"That sounds about right, doesn't it? Except, don't be too fucking logical. Myth is one thing. But it pays to have the benefit of a doubt. In a court of law if reasonable doubt is established the accused walks free."

"So what are you talking about, Peter, other than the fact we come from rich families and can get away with killing this bitch?"

"Oh, there will be a vampire there for us to stake. Mark my word on that one. But what do we really know about the mysterious thing that is the vampire?"

"*Dracula, Interview with the Vampire*, and so on."

"Sure, Oisin, but think about it. This is an immortal creature. Who is to say a simple stake hammered into the heart and a dose of garlic will do the trick?"

"Then what else are we to do—burn his coffin?"

"We will open his coffin when he is sleeping and open his mouth."

"So he can bite your head off?"

"No, he won't. By day they sleep like the dead, still as a corpse. At the moment of opening the coffin we drill the stake into his chest and open his mouth."

"With what?"

"I got some cool dental equipment for this off my uncle, who is always giving me stuff for coke. You know how it goes? Dentists and highbrow Irish professionals love their Class A drugs just as much as the inner city junkie does, mark my word."

"Yeah, the place is awash with lovely, delicious drugs."

"I have two litres of blood I'm going to pour down his throat."

"Have you lost your fucking *mind?*" Oisin asked.

"Blood, yes vampires like to drink blood. But this blood is different. An African from the Sub Saharan region entering the Republic of Ireland was found on a plane in the luggage compartment with his heart spewing out a brownish fluid, and his corpse sliding into mush. My father's professor friend, who works at studying viruses, was elated to discover such an extreme virus for his lab.

"Lately he's been so angry at his job with all the hits he's had to endure—pay cuts, being overlooked for promotion—that he hates the E.U. for making us pay back so much money. He's disgusted with our government. I gave him a healthy sum of money—more, boys, than I wish to tell."

They all brayed at this.

"Two days later, without saying a word, he handed me this bottle and said nothing, as if he was giving me a bottle of wine."

"And how do you know that this is the Ebola virus?"

For a moment Peter was angry at Oisin's question. Holding back from saying, "And why not drink it yourself and find out?" he continued, "Look, when he went out the door I said, 'Is that the virus?' 'You'd better believe it,' he replied."

"And you took his word at face value?"

"The neighbours—I don't know their names, since we don't say anything to each other—like so many South Siders renowned for their hospitality and friendly manner, have a pet gerbil. They display more affection to this rodent than to their neglected kids, who are in full-time day-care."

"Day-care in Ireland is the crappiest, most expensive thing in nearly all of Europe."

"Yes, well, Oisin, I also love gerbils. The neighbours let their gerbil run freely…about the only thing that is free around here. The inconsiderate gerbil did not recognize the boundaries we create for private property, so in he goes to my garden. In the front of their house, and on the occasional pole, they had Pipsqueak's picture with their mobile phone number and the tragic declaration that he was missing. How tragic!"

"Oh, I know if a human dies and the locals attend a funeral they surely will never wear black and surely a there will be just one tear and a prolonged half-hearted expression of grief. But if a feline, canine, or rodent should go AWOL, oh, what humanity will be displayed and what lengths they'll go to in order to return the creature to their home.

"I picked this rodent up in my hand and brought him inside and put him into a cardboard box. I gave him some nice cheese, which he devoured. I walked away to get a bowl of water; when I returned, I found his head."

"And?"

"So what?"

"Oh, did I not finish telling you? The rest of his body, detached from his head, was mush. I will return Pipsie's head to them soon. Who knows, maybe they'll display more signs of human emotion when they see their long-lost rodent's remains."

# XXI

## Decisions, Decisions

Sharon of Acheron lay naked and sated on her bed as Anthony withdrew from her. "For sure, it's better to be the horse and not the one holding the whip. He's no lamb, yet wants to be treated like a submissive."

Anthony was silent, although thanks to his recreation the past few hours, he did feel less anxious.

"I love keeping remains of his victims to reinforce a lesson I must never forget."

"And what is the lesson?"

"When I am in the uniform of the dominatrix and I feel the tight leather against my skin and whip in my hands, occasionally I wear a mask and feel powerful. And if Diabolis comes and asks to be dominated I feel such a high. But it is weird… Let me explain. In Judo the referee signals for a release of the competitor who is grounded. Then the men who are grappling with each other disengage.

"How often I tell Diabolis that he must tell me indicate to me "disengage," but he never does. I know he is not pressing the panic button for his sake, but for mine. Vampire submissiveness is foreign to vampire nature. So I control myself and never go too far with Diabolis. Sometimes I have refused his requests, especially blood games. He wanted to see what exactly his own limits were. I do not."

"And do you wish to be a vampire?"

"Well, these are the very things I have been meaning to tell you. Do you know that today you have been in control? I have been submissive as a lamb. I let you screw me whatever way you liked because I think, deep down, this is what you truly miss, what you truly need".

"And what about being a vampire?"

"Diabolis is a lone ranger. He has a phobia about creatures which are like him. He wants to be dominated, but not for pleasure or to give pleasure. Never forget how powerful he is, how immortal he is, how predatory he is, even for a short while. I can never see him tolerating another vampire."

"No?"

"If he created you he'd instantly kill you."

"Does this mean I should leave?"

"It means he's a lone ranger."

"Oh," Anthony said quietly, "he prefers to be on his own." Anthony put on his jacket to leave.

"Wait," a voice said, "wait." It was Lucis Diabolis.

Anthony looked out at the sky and saw that it was dark.

"Something has occurred to me," Diabolis announced. "Get dressed both of you. I wish to discuss some things."

The vampire looked unusually sedate. Anthony believed he looked reflective.

Sharon and Anthony held hands. They waited for Diabolis, who grabbed a bottle in order to feed. More delicious than a Turkish delight was a full glass of this noble blood to him. Once satisfied, he licked his lips with his tongue to get it all, and stripped naked in order to put on the wonderful suit Sharon had gotten for him. When he came down the stairs like a proud master, a true Lugosi, a true prince, a true lord, Sharon walked over to Diabolis and kissed his hand.

"It is so good that my rats enjoy our garden—such precious pets. We must never forget their worth to me. I am closest to them. May I?" he asked ever so politely, walking to the door. "Now is *not* the time to make you a vampire."

"What did I tell you?" Sharon replied, unable to hide her disappointment. "Does he not lead everyone down the garden path?"

"Today there is not a vampire, other than myself, at the end of this path. That is for certain, a certainty I have known all these years. And always, always at the other end of my domination is a snickering prick of a vampire saying, 'How far? How far do I go before I rip you apart?'"

"Please," said Anthony, looking with love and, oddly, pity at Diabolis.

"Is it right to tell Diabolis these things?"

"I will not give you what you want. Both of you are loyal subjects, but, believe me: every day I stare vividly at Sodom and Gomorrah. I see it fully destroyed before my eyes, and I feel this is my lot. And I ask myself when, not if, never if, always *when* will I be turned into a pillar of salt?

"How well I know your crazed mortal nature of always asking for things from each other...until all of you are dead and there is no one around to ask any favour of. I saw and continue to see humans making their own private Tower of Babel. This destroys them. No, you do not deserve to be vampires. If you still wish to be, leave. There's the door. This is my domain. There's no one to stop your going."

Both said nothing, until each approached and whispered into his ear, "Let me think about it."

# XXII

## Little Visitors

Oisin, Peter, and Richard, those angry and affluent misfits, made their way to Wicklow armed with handguns, stakes, hammers, and garlic; Peter brought along a tainted bottle of blood.

They were true city slickers, walking through the country lanes in flip flops, wearing the latest cool shades and designer jeans, casually smoking cigarettes as if on their way to lounge around a fancy, city center cafe.

"Okay, lads, no time for laughter or smoking—we've got serious work ahead of us."

As he said these words, Peter's flip flops slid on a pile of fresh cow dung, and he fell to the ground on his right elbow, where shit splattered his jacket. He tried to wipe himself off. Instead of sympathy, he got, "Stop trying to clean up. We have work to do."

When the three reached Sharon's front garden the rats there could smell the cow shit; it was delicious, and even more so was the flesh that it sat on. Being creatures trained and reared by Diabolis, they were ready.

"Quietly now," Richard warned. Suddenly, though, he could not move; he felt as if many mouths on his legs and feet were pulling him deeper into the smelly morass.

The rats recognized from their sniffs and tastes the stools they played with every day.

Richard tried to move his feet, but fell to the ground. The tiny, toothy creatures were inserting themselves into his trousers. He could not control his screams as one testicle was neatly severed. Then several rats moved from the front of his trousers to the back and gnawed at his anus. The sensations were too much to tolerate. The pain was so severe that he squirmed around to dislodge the biters. There was one moment of relief, and then the teeth gripped more aggressively, attempting to break through into his bowels and intestines. He shook his bum from side to side to find another brief moment of respite. He looked at the faded front door when he heard a gun blast and what he assumed was the thud of Sharon's body falling to the floor.

"Well done, boys," he called, "well done, lads! Let's beat these bastards once and for all."

With blood pouring from his torn buttocks and testicle, the rats left his body alone; he was sure he was victorious over them and no further assaults would take place. Hearing what he swore was the sound of a coffin lid opening, he started shouting, "BURN, MOTHERFUCKER, BURN!"

He staggered through the front door into the house and spotted a crimson trail, indicating what he believed was Sharon's bloody body being dragged along by Peter and Oisin. He took another step, only to trip over scrambling rats. Fearful that they would sample his anus again, he rolled over. A horde of rats started biting into his throat and neck. It felt like a steel wire about to go taut and saw completely through. Blood spurted, and the larger rats began feasting. Richard closed his eyes, for he had seen the last of this earth.

Lucis Diabolis' coffin lid actually was not yet open. It was Peter who left Oisin to discover the vampire's resting place. He walked up to the coffin lid casually, and opened it. Before him

261

was indeed the vampire. In his many mental rehearsals, he had seen himself simply drive the stake straight through the creature's heart, then open and fill his mouth with the contaminated blood. But the actual moment felt too surreal, and he spasmed, breaking the wine bottle of diseased blood he held. The shards embedded themselves in his flesh, but a few drops of his blood, mixed with the tainted blood, fell onto Diabolis' cheek. The vampire stirred, his heart still un-staked, despite all of Peter's meticulous mental visualizations and rehearsals. Peter froze.

Lucis Diabolis was not sleeping as soundly as he appeared to be. He'd been dreaming that he was a twelve-foot giant and, one after another, was throwing humans into a fetid whirlpool that would, like sulphuric acid, dissolve them. But the right side of his giant cheek burned, which shocked the vampire into wakefulness. Before him was a huge head. The vampire could see a hammer and a broken bottle in the intruder's hand...

Having dealt with the intruder, once the vampire sensed the exact moment that the last living pulse left Peter's body, he heard a friendly shout assuring him he was okay. He tossed the limp body away from the coffin, closed it, shut his eyes, and went back to sleep.

"Hello," Anthony said, entering the house. He could not hear a sound and looked around to see everything in a mess.

"Your master is unharmed," Sharon of Acheron reassured him.

"What happened?"

"We had visitors. I was forewarned and ready, thanks to Diabolis' rats. Maybe this is why he wants us not to be vampires. I got my gun and everything is fine, but we must clean up the mess."

When Diabolis woke up, Anthony and Sharon had dealt with the mess.

"You still want to be a vampire?" said Diabolis to his driver.

"YES!"

"A Rat Man Vampire?"

"I would adore that."

"Be a lamb and obey everything I say. I'm doing this because of your service to me. Is the car clean?"

"I cleaned it until it shone today; if I'd known you were having guests I would have been here."

"I know."

"What about me?" Sharon asked.

"No, dear, I want to keep you just as you are—go upstairs and wait for me."

Diabolis tied Anthony's body to a turnspit and let his rats give him friendly nips. The vampire closed his eyes, placed his head against Anthony's, and kissed his cheeks and mouth. Then his immortal blood flooded Anthony's system, nearly knocking out both of them. Anthony, though clinically dead, had never felt more alive.

"I'm transformed," he said as his body grew into that of a man-sized rat. "I am…splendid!"

"Yes, you are. Now take your well-earned rest, my faithful friend." The vampire helped Anthony into his basement coffin, and proceeded upstairs with eager anticipation.

Diabolis never felt the blow that put an end to his immortality. Sharon, having decided that enough was enough, like any red-blooded redhead, had taken matters—in this case her *da's* axe—into her own hands. She then burned down the filthy house, rats and all, but not the shed. She had plans for that nice, clean Mercedes.

*—Finish—*